Kenneth Tindall

The Banks of the Sea

PS
3570
.I47
.B3
1987

Copyright © 1987 by Kenneth Tindall

ISBN: 0-916583-22-8
Library of Congress Catalog Card Number: 86-073235

Partially funded by grants from The National Endowment for the Arts and The Illinois Arts Council

The Dalkey Archive Press
1817 79th Avenue
Elmwood Park, IL 60635 USA

To the memory of Frank Willard, U.S.N.

Also by Kenneth Tindall

Great Heads

Chapters

1 Indian Paintbrush *7*
2 Bannertail *15*
3 Skate Key and Tuning Fork *31*
4 The Barnacle Goose *50*
5 Watercatch *70*
6 God and Famous *106*
7 Pictures of Jerusalem *124*
8 The Hammer of Wednesday *137*
9 Carrion Moon *151*
10 The Blind Clarinettist of St Mark's Place *181*
11 Silky Valentine *191*
12 The Wind in the Elevator Shaft *204*

1 Indian Paintbrush

IT WAS SUMMER AND NOON, a high pollen count and the air rank from the stinking flowers of the ailanthus tree, which the Chinese called the Tree of Heaven. Some hippies were gathered in the mouldering confines of a tenement courtyard, Jesus freaks doing something in the dubious soil there. The remembering girl sang "Who Killed Cock Robin?" as the digger boy dug a hole. The humidity was oppressive and the tenements close around them as the sun happened to illuminate the ceremony as though lodged in the notch of some tribe's calendar stone. The courtyard was dank. It was window gates and fire escapes, forgotten paint jobs and broken trowel handles, and the bags of garbage which the slum dwellers throw out their kitchen windows. The hippies moved a pile of bricks and they rang like chalk.

They were burying a dead puppy. It was lying on a tray along with a pack of Kools: a pink-nosed mongrel pup with curly white hair like an Airedale's. The bridge of its nose was bowed like an Airedale's, too. The paw pads were pink and a little dirty like a pencil eraser or the first few drags on a cigarette filter and the lips were curled in a tough-guy sneer. But do dogs get leukemia that they should be given ice cream?

There were flies in the sunshine and mosquitoes in the shade. When completed, the grave was about a foot-and-a-half deep. A sheet of freezer foil was spread on the ground and the dog placed on it in a non-stylized position with the tail touching the nose. Then it was gingerly raised again so a girl could sprinkle a layer of koshering salt underneath it. The dog was again placed on the foil and the rest of the box of koshering salt emptied over it. Just then somebody up in one of the tenements started playing the snare drum. Flams and paradiddles, ruffles and a tattoo. He played "The Downfall of Paris," and then "The Crippled Shad." A girl remembered to spread a layer of ivy in the bottom of the grave. Then the foil was carefully closed around the body and the package was lowered. A brick with the initials J. W. & L. was placed in the grave too.

The Negro, with humble majesty, prepared two chillums and lighted them for the partakers. The chillums were passed around and everybody got high. There was some kind of almost indiscernible ritual here, with cookies and ice cream as well as the cannabis, and a bottle of Ripple. They smoked cigarettes and drank the cheap, nearly artificial wine and chatted and one of them turned on his transistor, loud as casual, and there was WNEW-FM with Jonathan Schwarz talking about the Boston Braves, and a commercial for Aunt Rhoda's, and a Stone Ponies number, "The Hobo." One of the hippies started to cry and broke his anonymity.

The chillums were broken—clink, clink,—on the brick in the grave and a few speed freak artifacts—an Iron Cross, an old garnet hatpin, a handful of jacks and a rubber ball—were tossed in after the chillums and some more stuff, a rag doll stuffed with organic lavender. Then the girl who does that emptied another box of koshering salt into the grave and the last slosh of Ripple was slung over the gleaming mound like syrup on a snow cone. The snare drummer kept playing "The Crippled Shad."

The lilting rollicking drum tune was in the courtyard and like a lot of lip spilled over the roofs of the tenements. Down in the street people looked at their watches.

A hippie with a sweatband around his head closed the grave. The hippies were awkward with excruciating ghoul decision although one of them was a cop and two of them were into Scientology. They ate some St. John's bread from the nearby health food store, Mother Nature's Cupboard, as the sods were carefully replaced and a handful of marijuana seeds trodden into them by the heels of hippie jackboots. Then they nonchalantly filed into the basement. They are so wan, like old Kodachrome. The last girl was careful not to look back, not even to lock the door. She did it as though her hands were tied behind her.

A few months later a big Icelandic ship touched down at Kennedy Airport and taxied to the terminal. Among the passengers was a young man named Carol. He and the girl in the seat beside him had slept through much of the flight with her head on his shoulder and they petted deliciously under the blankets without moving them. The girl's name was Terry, and Carol was a published poet.

The Banks of the Sea

The cats are necking
With their tails.

Carol had lived abroad for a couple of years and was curious about America. It was a chilly, windy morning in October when he and Terry descended from the aircraft and Carol exuberantly knelt and kissed the runway. It smelled like rubber.

There's Carol Gamewell at 42nd and Lexington waiting for a bus, beneath the limnological friezes of the Chanin Building and the Detroit gargoyles of the Chrysler Building. There's the Commodore Hotel over there and in the Longchamps boss employees are already eating their hats, while a block away the Horn & Hardart is advertising a slice of pumpkin pie free to anybody who can wiggle his ears. An executive with an attaché case gets into a taxi and Carol admires the together way he slides in and closes the door of the already-moving vehicle. A working stiff saunters past smoking a cigar with his hands in his pockets and suddenly Carol has the mad feeling of standing on Manhattan Island a thousand years ago.

America! America! Equipment bums and tool-pouch niggers, peanut-butter guttersnipes at the prosperous crossroads. Wild dogs have been sighted in the subways.

"But it's not like them to drag a whole big piece of meat all that distance."

"The half-eaten remains of an unknown soldier."

"At first I thought it was a large rat."

"Someone must be feeding them."

"Park Avenoo dogs."

A rubber duck was discovered where the RR line emerges in Queens. The sweet boys are playing with their toys and there are cola bears in the eucalypso trees. And the girls! Such a street number, and a low Dutch tune.

As the forest looks forward to the sea
The trees look forward to the ocean,
So I think fondly of thee
And look forward to the full portion.

"You're something I might prescribe for some terminal case: one Linda twice weekly, say."

"You doan want the whaht man to see you eat yo gravy, does you?"

An African woman was doing a dance in the middle of the street.

"Ah'll spend you fastuh'n mah outside dolla."

He saw some kind of official baby with a sort of lanyard around its neck with a whistle analog hanging vaguely on it and a yellow plastic hardhat for its fontanelle. "How would you like to be one of those?" a little voice asked him. Carol thought, Let's get this show on the road, and picked up his luggage. The bus pulled up to the curb. They were all waiting for color TV.

The bus went as far as Cooper Union and Carol crossed the Bowery and started walking down East 6th Street—but there was Sonja's warmly-lighted pottery shop and he went inside on a payoff hunch. The place was full of pretty girls and the phone rang. Sitting at one of the potter's wheels was a beautiful voluptuous Chinese girl and Carol asked her, "Could you tell me where to find the Home Planet Bookstore?"

She looked at him and smiled, then dipped her hands in a bowl of water to get the clay off and dried them. She offered him a Senior Service, which he accepted, and they each had one.

"My name is Carolyn Wong," she said. She smelled good and had a pigtail, a regular queue. "And you may stay with me if you don't find what you're looking for."

Jackpot. Another girl brought them mugs of tea and Carol introduced himself and told them where he had come from and a story about Iceland. He could leave his heavy things in the pottery shop while he looked. A calico cat came and hooked him on the ankle and another girl showed him one of the perfect kittens and he thought, These are the good old days.

He had Miss Wong's address on a piece of paper and a dog followed him as far as the meat-packing place there on East 6th Street. "Dingo, Dingo," Carol said to the animal. There were drums of offal and the sidewalk was dull with suet. The dog stood there inhaling. Carol strode deeper into Manhattan's Lower East Side.

And there was the peculiar and distinctive smell of Second Avenue, imprinted now on his olfactory core. People looked at him with shit-

The Banks of the Sea

eating grins and hippies glowered, and there was Gautama Panhandler winking at him and asking if he could spare some change. "It's payday, isn't it?" said the bum, and Carol laughed and was generous.

He crossed Second Avenue and a sharp-assed dealer asked him if he wanted to buy some acid. He refused, and it seemed as if he had crossed some kind of border. He stood watching the morning traffic for a few minutes, the enormous jouncy trucks, taxis, flashy cars of uptown New Yorkers heading down to work; then he walked on.

The Lower East Side is a collage of rye-bread union labels and human gaits, the saunter and the amble, yang dog and parve cat. Milky-eyed Ukranian girls speaking Ukranian, the scrubbed Slav stoops and the Gorky bends, Thursday's cider and eggs and the rat-seeded weasel, pale as a mole, emerges from the stoplight relay chest. Carol is the Mayor of Love's Park.

There was a fire in a tenement and children were cheering from a schoolyard. Carol picked his way among the pieces of fire equipment—the Number 11 pumper and the Number 9 ladder, the firemen of Aquarius—and after another block or so of some confectionary street he again thought of his errand. Just then the door of a basement storefront opened and a young woman shook an oil mop. Carol looked down and caught a glimpse of the interior and boy was it spick-and-span down there. She smiled sweetly at him and their eyes locked.

"Excuse me," he said. "Could you tell me how to get to the Home Planet Bookstore?"

"Let me think," said the girl in the doorway, "and in the meantime I can give you something to eat if you help me move some stuff."

Her name is Yvetot. She is an anchor with one fluke, teddy-bear ambergris and Tumwater agates, their liquid embroidery. He kissed her neck and she blushed, Carol loaded as he was from necking with Terry all night. Yvetot's stiff-legged cat. She flung her oil mop and flopped down on the mattress and they made love in the afghan, the sound of people passing in the street. Afterwards she served him beer in a Polish stave mug and they sat naked eating apples from a paper bag. To see her is to remember a river, fish darting.

They had lunch at the B & H on Second Avenue, good lentil soup with English muffins and tea. The place was steamy and crowded, and Carol and Yvetot sat at the rear table.

"So what did you see in Europe?" Yvetot asked him.

"Nigger ski troops in the Dolomites."

It was the morning of the battle and the horses were fed rolled oats and some very fine hay from the nearby salt meadows. The grooms moved among them, speaking softly now and then as they curried and brushed, for the officers would soon want them saddled. Some of the horses had lain on the ground during the night, troubled by their great dreams.

"So what did you do?"

"So I whipped out my swohns and pissed on the snow."

Yvetot grasped Carol's hand on the table and turned red, then leaned back in her chair and looked up at the ceiling with her mouth open, and it was some time before he realized she was laughing. She clenched her other little fist weakly and brought her face down—there were tears in her eyes—and started cackling, you know, and wiping the cobwebs away from in front of her. People stared. Carol was laughing too and people wanted to know, what are these fuckers laughing about?

Everybody knows that pigs fly on leaves that blow in the night, and Carol and Yvetot look like the Chichester-Constable chasuble and the Butler-Bowdon cope. They are so beautiful that the envious want to damage them and they know this. They have just connected gratuitously and here they are laughing out loud, Carol and Yvetot, and the hip scowl and the square slurp. Carol has a little boy's donkey head and Yvetot has hair the color of horse chestnuts and a sweet upper lip. Yvetot Bouchardeau from King's Lisp, Anne Arundel County, East Virginia. She works for a phony advertising agency called The Duckrabbit Effect, and this and tomorrow are her days off.

One of the countermen approaches Carol and becomes special with him.

"Was you just in the toilet a little while ago?" he demands. Carol has been traveling and he left a sixteen-inch turd in the bowl and it won't flush away. He shrugs. "It's not my responsibility," he says.

The counterman reddens, angry. "Well what am *I* supposed to do about it?"

"Why don't you ask it?"

"Don't get wise with me, buddy!"

People were staring again. Carol and Yvetot got up to leave. Carol smiles at the counterman.

"Maybe if you got a stick..."

The Puerto Rican boys are masturbating into their baseball mitts and Carol is fucking Yvetot, telling his whoppers to her sea-soft belly. He doesn't really know her except in the sense of the butterfly's carnal knowledge of the flower, but he loves her and tells her so. Yvetot says, "Carol, I . . ." and comes.

The motorman's compartment is arranged so that he can drive the train in his sleep. Carol and Yvetot are asleep on a mattress on the floor of a loft which Yvetot is moving out of. The only light comes from the billowing blue jets of the gas heater along one wall of the loft. Carol wakes up in the middle of the night because he hears somebody moving about in the kitchen. Yvetot wakes up with him and cuddles him to her and explains, "It's Sammy. He has a key. He's a dealer. Go back to sleep."

And Carol does go back to sleep, lulled by the cipher of the sounds from the kitchen. The dealer is out there capping acid all night. The acid is already cut, and it's a kit that he has to put together, putting the LSD into capsules, tapping them on the counter and capping them. He's high from it, getting his raggedy fingers in it, breathing it, and Carol picks up on the high in his sleep. He has unusual dreams, cats playing.

Of the independent life of the soul. Souls are like naughty children scurrying away from the Death Angel who herds them, however helter-skelter, like an implacable guardian home. For souls are delicate as zoo animals who long for death yet hope to rejoin their fellows in the natural habitat. Sometimes a soul manages to make itself scarce and lodges in a tree or something for a while, but it is always retrieved by the Angel, whose rounds are always made and whose tally is always complete. For the sake of the soul, which is never bored and whose only task is to joyride.

The next morning Carol and the dealer met and recognized each other.

"Hey, isn't it Carol Gamewell? Carolus Bolus! I thought you were in Europe."

"Well Bradley you regular old turd of shit you! I didn't think you'd be wearing a soutane. You look like Father Flanagan."

"Aye, it's the uniform of the day. Can I lay some of these units on you?" He proffered a handful of acid caps.

"Thanks, but I don't take that stuff," said Carol. Then, "Say, Yvetot must be a Libra. It just occurred to me. Are you a Libra, Yvetot?"

"You ain't just a woofin'," Yvetot said into the pillow. "How'd you guess?"

"One Libra girl leads to another, like Pete and Repeat."

"Cruit 'n' recruit's more like it," Bradley snorted, going for the door and petting a cat. "I've got to drag ass now. Have a ball, you two," and he sang like a street vendor all the way down the stairs:

> *"Say it loud,*
> *You're an ass fox,*
> *And you're proud..."*

"I didn't know you knew Sammy," said Yvetot, stretching and fragrant.

"His name is Duane. We were in Nam together."

Carol had his fingers in Yvetot's gizmo and it was wet. He crawled on top of her and stroked it with the end of his cock.

"I have to pee," said Yvetot.

"So do I," said Carol. "Makes it last longer."

He put it to her; she sighed and gave herself over to it. It felt like a sunrise in her and they came utterly. Sometimes somebody pulls a blue window shade up on the south face of the Empire State Building, must be close to the 90th floor. You look up and see it there, one patch of blue like a familiar signal from some western mountain range.

2 *Bannertail*

THE STORE HAD ONCE been a Chinese laundry. After they finished moving her stuff out of the loft, Carol and Yvetot threw themselves into the task of cleaning the place up: patching the plaster, scrubbing everything with Mr. Clean, painting, weatherstripping the windows and doors. There was the storefront itself, the largest room in the place, and a windowless room in the middle where they used the shelves for their gear and had a makeshift workshop, and in the rear was a kitchen that had a bathtub in it. Yvetot had great plans for the middle room. They would build an overhead gallery for storage and use the room for whatever creative fun they desired. Yvetot bought a water bed, and Carol built a case for it out of old door jambs with the paint removed and using tools the former tenant left there.

One sunny morning Carol washed the barred kitchen window and the window in the back door, and suddenly they had a whole backyard to look at. There was a rusty tricycle with ivy in its spokes and some canvas furniture that didn't look as if it could take sitting in, some old Christmas trees and his and Yvetot's huge Halloween pumpkin, and an old rabbit hutch that the cat used for some purpose. It wasn't half dismal in the November afternoon and Carol strung a clothesline for the smalls wash Yvetot did in the deep half of the double sink. Yvetot would come home from work with a carton of ice cream and they would enjoy it with a candle burning on the cable-reel table. They were shacking up on the Lower East Side.

The cable-ship cat. There were so many mice in the place at first that after killing them she carried them off to a not-so-secret hiding place to be devoured at her leisure. This practice might have had something to do with the coming kittens, for she couldn't eat them fast enough herself, and one day Carol had to flush them down the toilet which was enclosed in a corner of the kitchen next to the back door. It too had a tiny window that was polished and looked through.

Yvetot's pussy had a head on it, which is to say that the resiliency of the hairs made a nice pussy-shaped topographical feature immediately apparent and nearly olfactory under her briefs. It was a real treat to watch Yvetot step into her flimflams and give her snatch a proprietary pat as though to set it before getting dressed and going off to work. She had just washed. The clock radio was still playing and Carol played with Yvetot's adorable breasts and stuck his fingers in her armpits before she had put on her deodorant and sniffed them. She was sweet delight and the nape of her neck blushed.

"Angel baby," she called Carol, and, "Perfect boy."

"So how's about one for the road?" he queried, luxuriating back among the pillows and quilts.

He watched his mistress put her hand inside her panties and feel around in there; she winced with concentration and pleasure. Carol thought poetry. Yvetot withdrew her hand eloquently from the nookie and let Carol feast on the nectar. He sucked her fingers, thrilled with the goodness of it, licked between them. He licked her palm and her wrist. She got goose pimples and tried to make for the clothes closet when he embraced her and pulled her back to bed.

"Oh, Yvetot."

She writhed under his kisses and because he was taking her pants off.

"Carol. I'll be late for work. Stop it."

"This is a bad subway connection," he laughed.

She was so nice and rosy, and she hadn't put on her deodorant yet either. The pants were off and his caresses were making her spread her legs.

"But you'll make me pregnant, Carol."

"You want to see my Purple Heart?"

He nestled between her thighs and kissed the place where her breast and arm joined. Her thighs needed a shave, and she was so delicious. She kissed his ear with her tongue and called him by his name.

"But Yvetot, I want to *fuck* you. Oh, Yvetot!"

And there it was, home again. All of a sudden he was inside her, filling her sweetly. They held a little dialogue down there. Honey talk. Her breath already smelled like it. They were the first invention. Soon they were moving together, making something. Then they were done and lay together side by side.

"Carol," said Yvetot softly, touching his hand. "I think we should go someplace for Thanksgiving."

"Hmm. Where?"

"I know a place in Pennsylvania. We can rent a car and drive there."

Carol was silent, thinking of the expense.

"I have money," said Yvetot, stroking his arm. "This is something I really want to do."

U.S. 220 from Williamsport to Altoona, Pennsylvania, is like a bent birch sapling, or like the blade of a great scythe whose handle is the Susquehanna River. "South Williamsport is a street in Akron," thought Carol, imagining a city he had never seen. He drove carefully in the rain, eyes on the road, ignoring the rude importuning of the billboards and illuminated signs.

"They all want you to read them," he said, "and if you don't they'll gang up and try to hypnotize you."

Yvetot stirred in sleep and the blanket fell off her. She was in seat belt and shoulder strap and looked like a dead parachutist. She was dreaming:

After a long drive of many hours and that included the mountains, we arrived late at night to where we were going. The girl was asleep, but she woke up and greeted us warmly, and we were put in bed and slept immediately. The next morning we confirmed what we had just glanced at the night before on arriving in the girl's room—that she did indeed have, or still had, the big dollhouse which we had heard about and which had been on our minds for most of the journey.

Yvetot stretched and rubbed her eyes, and Carol turned the heater off.

"It can't be very far," he said.

The rain had stopped, and the country was rough and sparsely settled. Carol pulled off the road and stopped the car, and they got out and stretched their legs and drank chicken bouillon from the thermos. They sat for a while in the car; Yvetot lighted a Marlboro with the dashboard lighter.

"Carol, what's it like to kill somebody?"

"Well, you drop them."

"You mean like hip talk meaning to swallow them?"

"No, you simply drop them. Like an egg, or a piece of bric-a-brac."

Clouds hung over the hilltops like medicine balls and tackling dummies, and pink dawn light shone through them in the thin places like convertibles with spotlights. Yvetot was driving now. Soon they would cross Young Women's Creek and turn to the right and it would be morning.

They rounded a bend and traversed a place where high-tension masts strode across the landscape like pagodas. Carol turned the radio on just to hear the induction throb. He pushed the buttons and watched the dial needle move—one of them moved it a lot—and the ether sounded like a cockroach on the fritz and a cocked hat full of fresh fish. He was turning the tuning knob slowly when he thought he heard a voice like a lil Injun say: *"American girl give good blow job."*

They arrived far from the highway and pulled their Plymouth into the crowded little parking lot. They got out and yawned at the strange house where the lights were burning, the car engine ticking at rest, and lugged their few bags up the flagstone path. The house smelled of spices and cooking. A girl showed them to their room. No tipping. It was eight in the morning and Carol and Yvetot slept until one, birds singing.

Have you ever gone to a museum and seen an old house facade in one of the historical collections? The original Prozl and Dritzer log cabin is like that—visible and useful within the larger, later building. It is possible to imagine the old parents still living in it while the youngsters added on around them: the splitting and adzing, sawing and fashioning, malleting of pegs. The two families got together and settled in this remote valley in northwestern Pennsylvania, farmed the land, and for a span of about four generations expanded their house as their numbers increased. And then they just up and left. The long-abandoned house was discovered in the 1930s by an NRA drummer from Franklin Roosevelt's Washington.

He was as though thunderstruck, like the bedazed Frenchman who happened upon the ruins of Angkor Wat and called out, *"Hallo! Anybody there?"*

He had left his puddle-jumper and walked half the day, it seemed, along an overgrown field road, and by the time he came upon the house it was so late and what he found there so fascinating and endless in the last light that he spent the night. In a few days he had made a report to

Washington, and soon the WPA artists were in on it. Such now-famous names as Bill Morgenshaw and Nadine Trylor had a hand in restoring the house, which is now recognized as embodying some of the finest expression of the American pioneer spirit.

It is possibly difficult to imagine the gone pattern of life in this extended family dwelling, which is now a national historical landmark operated by the National Parks Service as a motel, reservations in advance. Was there a division of labor? Surely everybody, each individual, was self-maintaining, except the very old and the very young, who were looked after like the lilies of the field. Carol and Yvetot woke up in a room where gusty sunlight shone on walls covered with painted scenes of the Peaceable Kingdom, where the deer and the mountain lion reclined beneath round trees and the wild rabbit frolicked with the bear. A man and a woman in archaic costume stood smiling on a lawn among pointed trees, while above them soared cross-legged angels holding trumpets to their lips.

"The Cross-Legged Angel Artist," said Yvetot. "This is what I wanted to show you."

"Have you been here before?" Carol wondered.

Yvetot laughed into her pillow. "I read about it in a government pamphlet."

They nuzzled and played in the patchwork quilts and forgot the road. In a little while they got up and dressed for dinner.

The leaves were still falling, and that folded egg November light glowed on the old walls as Carol and Yvetot stood embracing on one of the balconies. Sparrows and finches flathered in a replica of one of the original bird feeders. A piece of old single-strand galvanized fence wire was stretched the width of the balcony, and at one end of it was knotted a strip of faded blue cloth that blew a little in the breeze. Yvetot asked him what it was. Carol narrowed his eyes for a moment at the cloth.

"Probably something to tell the weather by," he said.

She took his hand in hers and, smiling, asked, "Carol, do you know what a blue peter is?"

The Thanksgiving dinner had been prepared using some of the original kitchen utensils. The long tables groaned with the abundance of food that steamed in the light of candles in pewter candlesticks. Turkey with all the trimmings. The guests took their places and aproned girls bustled as a woodwind quintet played modern American music from the carved gallery, flames from the huge fireplace dancing off their instruments. As soon as everyone was properly seated, they stopped playing and a man—possibly a clergyman—rose and said a prayer of thanks. Then the guests fell to. Most of them appeared to be civil-service executives and their families.

As soon as everybody had food on their plates the quintet began playing again. Yvetot spooned some cranberry sauce alongside her mashed potatoes and giblet gravy and whispered to Carol, "This place'd make a good whorehouse."

"What?" he sputtered after a moment, through a mouthful of breast. "What did you say?"

"My, my," said a man, helping himself to the candied sweet potatoes. "Bring on the dancing girls," and a little girl said "Mommy?" into her dark meat.

Places had been set for the musicians, and as soon as they finished the first movement of Samuel Barber's *Summer Music* they came down from the gallery and sat at the tables.

"How," said Carol.

"Ugh," replied the bassoonist.

Carol felt uncomfortable after the meal and he told Yvetot that he had eaten too much pumpkin pie and nutmeg ice cream. The real reason, however, was that he had nothing to say to these people except that he was a Vietnam veteran. It was as though the only thing he had to tell them was his name, rank, and service number. Yvetot sensed his discomfort and invited him for a walk. They walked out to the edge of a pasture in the scudding evening and made friends with a couple of horses. She thanked him for coming with her to this place, and all he could say was that he loved her.

That night he built a roaring fire in the fireplace in their room and he made love to her in its light. Birch and apple logs. When they were done and drowsy, he asked her,

"What are the girls of Anne Arundel like?"

"Just like me, I s'pose," she replied.

"You mean they're all musical like you?"

"Well," she drawled, "some of 'em must be mechanical."

Yvetot sat naked on the water bed in the front room putting a new string on her dulcimer. She was going to try the ivory noter that Carol told her he stole for her. He was lying in front of her, firing a pellet rifle into a homemade bullet trap out on the kitchen floor. The cat was outside.

"Carol, what's it like in Vietnam?"

Yvetot had suggested the target practice as a remedy for an astigmatic condition he acquired from a shrapnel wound in the head received in action on the Mekong Delta. Yes, it was doing him good. It was good for his 'stigmatism.

"Vietnam," he said, plinking a round, " 's okay, if you like killin' gooks."

She tuned the dulcimer, the rural sound of it mingling oddly with other metallic noises from the street. Carol kept plinking away.

"Really," she insisted. "What's going on over there?"

"Something makes them do it," he said. "They raise their bloody hands to heaven and cry out, 'Who's putting this on us?' "

"You mean like asking the dancing bear," she persisted, " 'Who's teaching you these tricks?' "

She had a plaque with a phony coat of arms hanging on the wall over the bed where a crucifix might have been. Its motto read: *Easy Beauty – Years of Duty.* He may fuck her some more if he wants to. He can fuck her all he wants to.

Carol stood the gun in a corner and padded out to the kitchen door to let the cat in. When he came back he picked up Yvetot's flute and sounded an E and they warmed up with the C major scale. Then they tuned up together, Yvetot sitting there sweet as a mother's dare with the dulcimer in her lap, nipples small and pink and soft. They went through the G major scale.

The cat came in and flaked out on the table like an open Bible. A leaky safety valve hissed somewhere in the rear of the store even though Yvetot had tied an old pair of her panty hose over it. On the floor were a couple of wadded Kleenexes that she had used and they were soaked with Carol's jizz.

It was a good sound: the intimate sonority of the dulcimer and the clear notes Carol had begun producing on the flute. The little Italian pellet rifle had been unopened and new in its Abercrombie & Fitch wrappings when she handed it to him, smiling, one day, and he had wondered ever since if it hadn't been purchased for him to use, long before he returned to the United States. In any case, the target practice wasn't a mere useful pastime, something for his astigmatism. It was part of some strange equipment she was fitting him with like an orthopedic sculptor. They tried the D major scale. One of the cat's ears twitched and Carol, as he played the C sharp, saw a cockroach crawl out of the Kleenexes.

It seemed to Carol that he was enrolled in a very expensive school. Just the other day Yvetot had said, "Sometimes food labels have messages from alien powers," as she unloaded the grocery bag. There was a can of Bulgarian tomato paste called *Acropole Rouge*.

He thought about how he liked to eat Yvetot's pussy. Scarfing up a woman is an art. You've got to clean out that briefcase. And you don't just lick the clitoris. You take it between your teeth and suck on it like a lollipop. And if you have a cold and it's during her menstruation, have her sit on your chest with her ass in your face and you'll get well right away. No more sickness.

He was dizzy from playing the flute and sat catching his breath while she strummed an East Virginia melody. He loved the ground she walked on.

"Thanks for the noter, Carol. It's really darlin."

She drew him to her and gently pulled on his lob. It was sore from fucking and she very warmly ran the tip of it like a clam's foot up and down the little length of her sweet hole. He hastily put it in and sighed. She stroked his waist and lightly played with his nipples.

"Mmmm," she said. "It feels good."

He was aching, wanting to come. She was soaking wet. She ran a hand down there and tickled his balls to make his tummy relax and wiped up the excess juice from around his cock, then put the fingers inside his mouth all the way to the sour taste buds at the rear of his tongue. He came like a flash. When he was finished she wiped her fingers lightly across his mouth and kissed his eyelids. He was becoming her thrall.

"Mission accomplished, enemy captured," she murmured, cuddling him.

Sometimes it gets so quiet you can hear the clouds moving. Stand at La Guardia Place and Washington Square Park and look downtown and there are the twin towers of the World Trade Center sticking up like the tines of a tuning fork. In the creak and slam and creak and slam of iron shutters it's snowing in River City, and the snowflakes are butterfly kisses on the cheeks of derelicts.

"The One Toys."

"They're a Chinese restaurant?"

"If you want, Love Boy. They're Christmas."

Snowflakes are cutting threads in the sky, Screwball, and the wind has a nose for edible cargoes. The personality fish was wearing her Empire bathrobe. It was quilted, and she smelled like breakfasts. Will she go back home, back to her parents, Yvetot Bouchardeau of King's Lisp, Anne Arundel County, East Virginia? For her parents love her very much. He brought his fist down on the table.

"I don't care what or whom you do as long as you don't do it here!"

"Carol, do you remember Steve Cherin, the guy who had this place before me?"

"Uh huh."

"Well, he had to move to New Jersey because he didn't like it that his old lady was a hooker."

"I don't like it either," he said, feeling her up roughly. "I don't want other guys' snot in this."

"But Carol, there never is."

"You damned retread. You use condoms, don't you. That's why you come home all red down there and it smells like rubber."

The Emma Award for achievement in hysterics. The voices of the dead women would be whining if they weren't cloying and they would be cloying if they weren't so sweet. Their fingernails were shiny where snails had just been, and then there was a vision of a bum standing in Yvetot's kitchen where he was granted, or bestowed, a spoonful of porridge, like one of the Dwarves, and Yvetot's oatmeal lacks salt.

"Oh, no," Baby Hotcake said into the back of her hand. "My Mommy said you'd be asleep or not paying attention."

"Oh, yes," replied the Ogre. "I'm awake and you and I are married and now I'm going to fuck you."

Oleander Flower — an American opera. Scene I. The old woman is sitting on a stool in the hen house catching the hens by their legs with a wire coat hanger. Her idiot son helps her catch them and she clips their wings with a shears. The feathers fly, and the son sings an aria wondering where his sister is. The old woman sings a reply full of allusions to the big city. They sing a duet in anticipation of Christmas and the girl's return. During the scene change the old man is heard ranting in the wings, his cane thumping loudly.

Scene II. In the whorehouse the whores talk about their favorite customers and get horny. One of them sings an aria about a man whose corpse was stuffed into an oil pipeline in Tulsa and it came out in Wilmington. They sing of Christmas at home. One of them sings a recitative describing the farm and they all break down in tears as the phone rings and rings. Pretty soon pimps enter with a free customer. He is short and talks tough and is a sharp dresser. The customer has no role per se and no distinguishing traits except for a slightly too small mackintosh. He is reminiscent of Tin Tin in the Belgian comic strip. The same chicken wire is across the stage as in Scene I.

> They are prostitutes and are reputed to prognosticate the weather, etc. They worship the guitar, which they carry with them, and with its tune they go from house to house foretelling events. . . . In Armenia, it is said that the noblest families dedicated their daughters to the service of the goddess Anaities, where damsels acted as prostitutes for a long time before they were given in marriage, and nobody scrupled to marry one of these girls when her period of service was over. (Ráo Bahadur R. C. Artal: *Basawis in Peninsular India.* Journal of the Anthropological Society of Bombay, Vol. IX, No. 2, page 101. Wednesday, July 27th, 1910)

It was almost menacing, how much she seemed to love him. The days passed and Carol felt that Yvetot was becoming more and more solicitous in a sinister way, as though he were nominated to satisfy some sacrificial purpose, something he would be expected to go through with when the time was ripe. He wrote a little, but couldn't make up his mind to go anywhere since she asked him not to phone her where she worked, and spent a lot of time plinking with the pellet gun and practicing the flute. He didn't know why he was doing these things, just as he didn't know that air rifles, like so much else, are illegal in New York City. They were things he didn't really like doing. It was infernal, and yet he continued, and whenever he walked outside it was shamefacedly. He tried to concentrate on writing.

But only because shame is the proper sentiment for a young hangdog, he thought, smirking around in the backyard in the window glow from the kitchen where his old lady was doing something. How cozy. There was that mateless sock still clothespinned to the clothesline. Was that sock supposed to be a homeopathic analog of Carol? He sobbed inwardly and to save himself retrieved it and put it inside his shirt.

Every time she lighted the oven, a few minutes would go by and then the cockroaches come pouring out of the insulation in the stove. One of the burners was lighted, and when Carol came into the kitchen he saw a cockroach walk through fire.

"Gromphadorhina laevigata," he said.

Yvetot was baking bread. She washed her hands in flour and kneaded.

"Carol," she said, without looking at him, "what animal would you be if you had the choice?"

"Let me think," he said, and after a minute cleared his throat and replied:

>"I would be a stallion in a pasture,
>My road apples convenient in one corner,
>Nicker reassuringly to a succession of mares
>And service them, my fore-hooves dangling,
>Knowing that come is money.
>I would be a stallion in a pasture
>With a brook to drink from
>And munch on clover that tastes like butter,
>Friend of bird and bee, and lift my head skyward
>When a storm played with the trees.
>I would gallop through the wind-pintoed grass
>And toss my mane and stand stock still and wait
>For the lightning to strike me for my fornications.
>I would be a stallion. A stud horsey.
>And then I would be a million-year-old yeast

Cherished in a linen napkin
Handed down from mother to daughter.
Eat me, Daddy. I'm a Wonder Bread."

Yvetot patted the loaves on a greased pan and pouted. "But don't they shoot horses?"

"Naw, they drop them," he said, "with a two-injection combination of pentothal sodium and strychnine."

Little Mary Proctor thought her mother'd socked her. Yvetot slid a pan of risen loaves into the oven without saying a word and rinsed the flour off her hands. The kitchen was bright and warm and the kitten was romping with a piece of calf's liver. Carol watched Yvetot.

"Poor Pearl," he thought.

"Really?"

"She believes in you."

"Like a nigger believes in reincarnation."

They were going to East Virginia for Christmas. He wondered what her people were like. He imagined skates and eels, danglefish and other brackwater denizens, cove satans in the form of a mess of cocktail sausages and the bit of selvage which is in all belly buttons.

Why don't you jump in there and see what you can scare up? he mused. It tickles her merrythought, I'll bet, in such a short space to have been booned and gandled.

The little Spanish girl's name was Rosa. She told Carol what they did with his things, that they made a work clothes scarecrow with a hardhat on its head and a pair of old work gloves. He asked her why, and Yvetot squeezed out a standard explanation: the men would put the scarecrow in one of their lodges and trot it out on feast days to scare the women with. The kitten tried to crawl out the neck of her sweater.

"Get back in there, Gromphador," she scolded.

They made their way up a stony unpaved road with rusty pickups parked here and there and it was cold, flurry-dodged hills looming. At length they came to a little old dilapidated mansion in the perfectly natural countryside of East Virginia. They went inside and heard strange noises. The unprecedented was in progress. The Vice-President of the United States was holding a filibuster.

An old man came out and startled Carol. The rooms were full of garbage if they weren't empty. An old woman appeared with a black tumpline around her head and a devil mask painted on her face with lampblack and charcoal.

"My darling," Carol said to Yvetot, "are these your family?"

"Nobody's been working the land," she said. "I think you should take that fork there," she pointed to an implement standing in a corner, "and go out and turn over a few sods."

He did as she asked. Once outside the house the dog started barking like it had never seen him before. It was one of those barrel-bodied fox terriers the Crusaders called "a keg of thumbs."

The sods were heavy and Carol shook the wormed and pebbly earth out of them and soon he was perspiring. He rested on the verandah and found an old newspaper rolled up as though a paper boy had thrown it there from his bicycle. But surely Yvetot, perhaps dressed as a hippie, had gone to a post office and mailed it to these folks, who then used it to swat the dog with. He opened it carefully and scanned. The paper had been published in Sayville, Long Island, a few days after a political assassination. On the front page was a color picture of an American flag. The picture, the caption claimed, had been taken during the assassination victim's visit to Sayville the previous January, while the only thing wrong, of course, was that the trees in the picture were in full leaf. Further on in the paper was a picture of a house which had been struck by lightning. The story explained that the house had been struck by lightning to punish its owner for his spiritual disaffiliation with the community.

Sounds of a devil dance came from inside the house, and screeches of conspiratorial laughter. Yvetot could be heard saying something backwards. Carol decided to rattle some chains and clodhopped boldly into the front room.

"Where's the platinum?" he demanded. "This is the filthiest place I can think of."

The old woman emitted a cowboy yell, shrieking, *"Coaxum, Charpersons!"* and Yvetot looked at Carol with a forked gaze. The old man was just downright hungry and ornery. The woman neither cooked nor ate meals, and he sustained himself by digging up wildgrown rutabagas with that damned fork and eating those.

"Try lookin in the barn," he said. "There's even filthier places there."

Sort of makes you wonder—a girl who's on both brewer's yeast and iron tablets. There's bound to be some fusel oil. The night before New Year's Eve Carol and Yvetot were lying in bed. There was just the candlelight and WNYC on the radio. Yvetot's small sweet bod. It was pink and pretty, like her face. They had made love. She squeezed his hand.

"Carol, I understand why you have trouble sleeping. Why don't you let me give you a back rub? It's better than camomile tea."

Carol stretched out on his stomach with his arms at his sides. "Have you ever gone to a chiropractor?" he said.

Without replying, she straddled him with her soft moist thighs and started rubbing his back.

"Well the chiropractor," Carol went on, "has you cross your ankles, just like the cross-legged angels."

She rubbed very lightly, using the flats of her fingers, in scroll-like whorls up his back and very delicately lingering on his shoulder blades. After a couple of minutes she rose up and reached over to her cosmetics and took a small red cut glass flagon. Carol felt her pour something from it onto his shoulders.

The liquid tingled slightly and felt immediately and deeply warm. She poured some more on and let it remain in a puddle on his back and run down his sides. Almost immediately he was hallucinating colors, and when he closed his eyes he thought he couldn't breathe. She poured some more of the liquid onto his back.

"Quit it," he gasped.

With great effort, like a ship with its decks awash in a hurricane, he rose up and shook Yvetot off his back. He moaned and clawed at the bedding, and fell with his weight on his fists in order to move the air in his lungs. He was in respiratory paralysis and he was higher than a kite. The water bed was having tsunamis.

"What's the matter?" said Yvetot.

"You're poisoning me."

He leaned on one elbow and looked around the dim room, trying to hang on. The candle would burn out soon and the radio station go off the air for the night. There was the sound of a baby crying.

"There's that damned baby crying again. There's no baby living upstairs. It must be a tape recording."

"Carol," said Yvetot, menacingly sweet, "I'm not trying to poison you."

"Then what's that stuff?"

He was still seeing colors. Auras hung on himself and Yvetot and opium phenomena—flickers of red, blue, and purple light—played around the room. It was spectacular and undeniably, even ravishingly, pleasurable. A person could want to die of it.

"Isn't it good?" she said.

"It's diabolical."

He stretched out on the bed again, on his back, and watched Yvetot put the little decanter back on the bureau. Then he closed his eyes and felt her weight settle beside him. She took his hand. He breathed easy now.

Wait a minute. He could almost pin it down. Yes. What had been happening was an attempt to induce a psychosis in him. And because it hadn't worked. . . . What was that gunk she used? It was something he had read about someplace. He lay there remembering, recollection like the shouts of a drowning man echoing in the fog-batted scale of the waves. Yvetot was smoking a cigarette.

"DMSO," he said. "Dimethyl sulfoxide."

"Carol, when you do decide to get a job," said Yvetot, "I think it should be some dirty work."

"Dimethyl sulfoxide," he repeated. "Paranoid and paranee."

"Carol, you wouldn't ever do anything to hurt me, would you?"

"You don't feel threatened, do you?"

"You say some awfully strange things."

"But you *know* what that stuff is," he said, angrily. "DMSO is a byproduct of wood pulp manufacturing. It carries drugs into the organism through the skin. A little LSD and a lot of heroin, huh? And tubocurarin for the respiratory paralysis. It was developed at the University of Oregon in experiments with rats. Or did you get it from the NYU Medical Center? I hear they experiment on people in Bellevue."

"Oh, Carol. Please..."

"That horse liniment can be analyzed. You'll think you've been castled and cooked."

The telephone rang and Yvetot answered, laughed and chattered. Carol got up and padded across the shiny floor, accompanied by the cat, to the kitchen. He needed a bottle to take a sample with. He took a quick shower in the tub, then rummaged in one of the bottom cupboards and found, way back there, a case of ten Pro-Tex-Mor shroud kits. Three of them were missing. He roared so the cat ran.

"G.I. shroud kits. Well God *damn!*"

3 Skate Key and Tuning Fork

CHILDREN WERE PLAYING in the lobby of the old industrial building. Once upon a time it must have been an imposing room. Now there was water on the floor and the kids were playing a kind of handball against one of the walls where there was a phony fireplace and some pier-glasses.

"Why's the floor wet?" Carol asked them.

"The janitor hosed it down," replied one of the girls. She was Chinese, and she was wearing a skirt. Carol thought she sounded rather cultivated, and she had used the word janitor instead of super. She and Carol gave each other the eye.

The elevator door was open and there was water on the floor there, too, and almost all the paint was gone from the walls. The kids followed him into the elevator.

"What floor ya going to, Mister?"

"Eight. You know where that is?"

They closed the doors expertly and prompted him to start the mechanism, which he did, and they rose. There was a political campaign sticker on one wall of the car.

> Save the runts, orphans
> and oversize litters with
> PIGSAVER

It was like an old department store elevator with wireglass sides and a sunny shaft. The cables rattled and the children let out a cheer when the counterweight passed like the blade of a guillotine. Clock is to telephone dial what elevator is to subway and in no time at all they were at the eighth floor. The car stopped slightly above the sill and Carol had to adjust it with a nautical-looking old hand cable which ran through socketed holes in ceiling and floor. The children were like BBs in an oatmeal box or buckshot in a balloon.

"See you on the roof," they said, as he stepped out into the hall, and they could be heard making thunder in the car as it went up the rest of the way.

The hall was painted white as eights, even the floor, and it's a wonder the windows weren't frosted. Carol walked right for the sake of dawdling and came to a place where a stair of three steps went down to a sunken landing and then up again. There was a door on the landing, and another beyond it where the hall ended with a window, and if the building were sectioned at this point the view across it would resemble a square-root sign seen from behind. The inhabitants must have been aware of this because all of their names—and there were many—were written on cards pasted under the doorbells in a kind of spidery, chancery italic like Leonardo da Vinci's mirror writing: names like Stanley Pazzolla and Dodd Kern, Ruth Gershorn and Benjamin Cooke. The loft to the right of the landing must surely have been L-shaped, or else very long and narrow like a wooden organ pipe or a very low-frequency waveguide. Indeed, the door to the loft rattled now and then with loud subsonic music probably from columnar speakers like slit gongs. Lying on the windowsill was a frondlike potato chip. Carol thought of Imogen and resolutely walked back to where he knew her loft must be: off to the left somewhere, way off, everything white as though it had been Tom Sawyer who stuck his finger in the dike.

A bathtub is not a Mikvah and an eight is not, by any stretch of the imagination, an infinity sign. He found Imogen's door. It sounded like somebody was polishing a speech in there.

"Valiant souldiers, are under God, the supreme refuge and defence, the security and safety of a people. Upon such does very much the earthly security, peace & happiness of a people depend: as they are an awe and guard against the encroaching enemies; or a defense against those that invade and spoil them..."

He rang the doorbell. The oration ceased and in a minute the door opened and Imogen blinked at Carol. She was holding a microphone.

"Oh, Carol. Come in and say something." She was wearing plus fours, and Carol was a little nonplussed as she handed him the mike and said, "Come on. Make a speech. Deliver a diatribe."

So he stood there in her areaway with the street still on him and said things he didn't know he had in him, and the voice was not his own.

"But 'tis lamentable how much a true martial spirit is laid aside; and men are not only careless and unconcerned about it; — as if they had no business, — as if they had no lives, worth fighting for, — no country worth a saving. But speak of it and too often treat it with contempt."

"That's a little bit disconcerting," he said to Imogen. "What happened to my voice?"

"It takes your voice," she explained, "just like in 'Tom Thumb's Blues.' Now, sing a song like you were howling at the moon. It's fun."

Carol hit on "I Got A Gal in Kalamazoo" and crooned into the instrument. But what came out of the speakers, wherever they were, sounded like Rod McKuen singing medieval French.

"Au noble pais de Caux
Ya quatre abbayes royaux,
Six prieurez conventeaux,
Et six barons de grand arroy,
Quatre comptes, trois ducs, un roy . . ."

Imogen was practically stepdancing with enthusiasm. "Isn't it great?" she said.

"Yeah. But what is it?"

"Well, it goes through a computer in Cambridge that reads voices. It belongs to the Rand Corporation."

"You mean you're plugged into a computer in Cambridge, Massachusetts?"

"Yep. We're all poor as churchmice but it's on a grant, you dig, so it doesn't matter and we have, as the Whole Earth Catalog puts it, access to tools. Now, you wanted a job."

He followed her through the decor and props of her photographic studio. A big white German shepherd lay sprawled asleep beneath a skylight whose shaft passed like a milk carton through the two upper stories of the building.

"Don't mind Hollister," she said, negotiating the dog, who should have been cold-nosing the stranger. "He's just playing old."

She likes my poetry, Carol was thinking. She likes me. A poetry magazine had arrived with the mail on New Year's Eve morning and there were two of his poems in it. He showed them around at the party that night and some of the girls really liked them, and while they were dancing Imogen asked him if he'd like to do the captions for her book. He had had the pleasure of seeing Yvetot turn green as a pickled fig. Imogen smiled and chattered.

"I'm still collating these," she said, "but I think I've finally got them together."

She giggled a little with modesty, her voice like silver. She showed him her map table, everything neat as a pin, with two stacks of 8 x 10 prints on it. He assumed that one of them would be his to work with.

"Do you want captions for all of these?" he asked, flipping through the prints.

"Not necessarily," she replied. "They run in themes, and they'll be different sizes. What do you think of them?"

Imogen had arranged the collection with an eye for symbolic coherence. One group was a study of men functioning with hawserlike objects: sailors hauling on a line, telephone company workers pulling on a cable, a schoolboy climbing the rope in gym class, twelve zoo employees holding a giant python.

"You don't think they're phallic, do you?" she asked.

"Is a rolling pin phallic?" he replied. "How about this for a caption? 'Rough necking.' Or, 'Wiggleworm Victory.'"

"Piquant, piquant," she crowed, and put an arm around his waist. She turned to another group of pictures. "Now, these men are working, but what are they working on? Do you mind if I take your picture?"

It was a group of photographs—nearly portraits—of men in various walks of life, though nearly all in attitudes of leisure. One was washing his car. Another mowing his penthouse lawn. A man painting a window frame. Yet there was the equivalent of an astrological similarity about them. Imogen was clacking away with a Nikon. Were they advertising pictures?

"Handsome Charlies," he said. "What are they?"

"A mailman, a short-order cook, an editor, a broker," Imogen giggled. "But all of them have a function in common. They're cherry pickers."

"Cherry pickers?"

Among the portraits were a few object pictures for thematic reference.

The Banks of the Sea 35

One of them was a subway pillar on which was inscribed:

>If you want
>Some sweet hole
>Call Evylyn at
>CY 3-1314
>Btw. 1:00 & 7:00
>Do it fast
>I'm in need
>Of some sweet
>Dick

"Sure. They're always laying virgins."

"Sure," Carol guffawed. "You want a caption like: Sensitive issue."

"Right on. That's why I want you to do the captions. If a chick did them she'd be associating from her standard reactions. It'd be sleazy instead of high-tone porn."

"You mean like instead of a sensitive issue it would be an itchy subject."

"You're a riot," she said, taking his arm affectionately. "You'll want something to eat and some money. Can you be finished in a week?"

She poured wine and they drank to love and art. While she was making lunch Carol looked through the collection of photographs. The book was to be called *Men Working,* and it was intended as pornography for women. It was also a celebration of the city, for the dynamic and creative things the men did—ordinary men, pipe fitters, men nimbly jockeying rolls of newsprint—were captured lovingly against the lineaments of New York.

She made them a cheese-and-onion omelette, and as they ate they talked about themselves. Afterwards, to the rest of the wine, they played in the studio. Imogen had an old bentwood hatrack ablossom with sensible headgear.

>You look like Mary
>With her hat on
>You look like Mary
>With her hat off

> Hat off
> Hat on
> One girl
> Two Marys

Meanwhile the sky outside the windows of the loft was becoming dark as during an eclipse. They stood looking with their arms around each other's waist.

"Let's take the dog on the roof," said Imogen, setting her cap. "Come on, Hollister."

Hollister shuffled to the door and sat down. He looked like a big laundry bag at Imogen's feet. When they got to the roof, she and Carol saw something they wouldn't have spotted had the dog not been with them.

"Look at that!" exclaimed Imogen, and took pictures of it.

"The elevator children must have made it," said Carol, and told her about them.

"It's *tremendous!*"

Using the available materials of junk furniture, discarded household appliances and bejeezomed TV sets, the children had built a sculpture on the roof and topped it with a plastic rocking horse. The steed reared up against the sky and the towers of Downtown.

"It's an equestrian statue, Carol. Get up there in the saddle!"

"It's Pegasus!"

Meanwhile the dog was gyrating like a figure skater around and around, until some inner orienter told him that this was it and he crouched and trembled. A thwacking wind palmed ripples in the thaw puddles. What was obscuring the sun was the smoke from a nearby tenement fire.

"This way to the Egress!" cried Imogen.

"What's that?"

"Come on. It's a model of going to sleep."

Imogen's ex-husband and his lover looked like Mechanics' Hall and Symphony Hall. They were two sculptors who signed their works together and who occupied two floors of the same building. Nyesmith and Blankenship's disgusting vinyl tesseract. Eights have no idea what Nine is doing. Large buildings inhabited by many artists are like pet ant

The Banks of the Sea   37

colonies. Once in a while the kid takes the wraps off it and the ants are seen to scurry about in their suddenly-illuminated tunnels trying to hide the eggs. When that happens to such a building, sometimes people jump out the windows. That's why Blankenship and Nyesmith built their "Egress." Utilizing parts of both floors, it was the ultimate in eights topology, and those who found their way through it successfully found themselves on the street again. Otherwise . . .

"*Without* the dog," stipulated Blankenship. The two faggots were playing with a kitten. It was full of bells that rang when they shook her.

The most constricted parts of the tesseract (a tesseract is a four-dimensional cube) were permanently lubricated. Carol and Imogen had to disrobe and tie their clothes in bundles which they dragged after them by the belts. They tickled each other outrageously and made love in one of the antechambers. There was a telephone and afterwards Carol phoned Yvetot.

Yvetot: You woke me up. It's the middle of the night.
Carol: But it's broad daylight.
Yvetot: Are you phoning from Tokyo?
Carol: It must be another computer trick.
Yvetot: What is?
Carol: There's a computer in Cambridge that's doing all this.
Yvetot: Doing all what?
Carol: Imogen's here.
Yvetot: Hmph.
Carol: Don't worry about it.
Yvetot: (silence)
Carol: (in French) *Adieu, chagrin.* (hangs up)

Sure enough, they found themselves on the street. Garbage cans. And Imogen thought she had forgotten her keys. A junky was having trouble getting across the street.

Carol had money and a job and he had just made it with Imogen. He walked whistling to the storefront and knocked like a stranger on the window, reaching for his key like a husband. Yvetot wasn't home.

"She's doing her pasteups and mechanicals," he said to the cat, who had a greasy cowlick on her back. She wanted to rub herself on his ankles but he sidestepped her.

"Oh, Puss," he said, stroking her cheeks and ears, "I know where you've been. You've been under a parked car, that's where."

He washed her bowls and fed her and changed her box. Imogen was bold enough, he mused, to have asked Yvetot to do the layout for *Men Working*. But girls aren't that good to each other. He packed his grip and left.

As he walked through the streets of the East Village he thought of the Duckrabbit Effect and of what America in her extremity was perpetrating. The streets were full of abandoned cars, and people were looking at him with that cockeyed knowing look. Was he really giving them the slip, or was his move just part of the plan? A bum smiled at him.

There were bums sprawled in their own urine. And there was one lying passed out silhouetted in the glint of a Milky Way of broken bottles. The bums were metaphysical, like Hindu fakirs. Carol thought of Imogen's book. He was getting a lot of impulses from it. He put his grip down on the sidewalk and whipped out his ballpoint and notebook and wrote:

They are pondering the difference between self-indulgence and self-denial.

He was crossing Astor Place when another after-high from Yvetot's back rub hit him. It was only a conditioned reflex, he told himself. He had to catch his breath. He put the grip down and took his mittens and knitted cap off. When he rubbed his sweaty palm sideways on his corduroys it made a zig-zaggy feeling like an electric shock all up his arm. The sensation, he recognized, was a synesthetic hallucination associated with the gigantic red, green and yellow blitz design painted on the wall of a building adjoining the parking lot. He didn't want to hallucinate.

Young girls they come into the canyon. Imogen was on Fifth Avenue navigating by window reflection. She looked along a window and saw a couple cross the street, lovers so beautiful they stopped traffic. It was the evening rush hour and all the cars started honking together. A driver rolled his window down and shook his fist, and there was a column of steam from a manhole cover. Imogen gracefully photographed it. She had selected her fugue for the day and was engrossed in it.

Imogen wore her Honeywell Pentax the way a man "wears" his pipe. She was competent and confident and she smiled now and then at passers-by, reassuring them that instead of stealing their souls she was affirming their existence with the camera. She read the street, and recognized the people by the concept each individual embodied, and if she had a preoccupied look it was because today she had something very special on her mind. She felt that something was missing in *Men Working* and needed an idea. Perhaps she was watching for it in the faces of the passers-by, something so obvious it might have been unknowable.

The realization that the book needed something had to do with her very reason for making *Men Working*. For the fact was that, like many Taurus women, her father was a ne'er-do-well—all things considered. The thought frightened her. The book would be analyzed, picked to pieces, and she needed an idea that would make the whole point of the thing and that would serve the purpose of excusing her. She needed a disguise, for the crisis was not of identity but of anonymity. Then something resolved itself in her mind.

It was at the sudden spaciousness in front of the General Motors building—the sunken garden in the plaza there, like a pause in the counterpoint as when all the machines in a factory pound synchronously—that the thought occurred to her. She had made love with a man on a whim today and it had been like the fulfillment of a desire she had never been aware of. From wherever he was and whatever he was doing in the city at that moment, Imogen was certain that Carol supplied her with the idea.

> *Bedknob and candlestick,*
> *Pistol and taxi,*
> *Where is thy bailiwick,*
> *Girl in maxi?*

She turned and walked down 59th Street to Sixth Avenue and took the subway to Times Square. She would photograph the pimps at work.

People were pouring from the gavel-stroke shuttle. The trainman over at Grand Central pulls a huge lever, yellow-fever steam shovels and a frayed cable's length, people whooshing like corn out the discharge sleeve of a grain elevator. Imogen fought her way to the surface, and the sordidness of Times Square almost made her dive for the subway again. She let her mind fill with the abjectness of prostitution. Cool as a watched pot, she shot pictures of pimps playing pinball machines in the penny arcades.

She assigned them a mock biological function: they are like the tall, watchful rooster whose paranoia compels him to hope that the hens don't think he created chicken hawks. They were simulacrons powered by anger, shaking the amusement machines, all vying to be the toughest flower, and their languor filled Imogen with an almost biblical revulsion like her father exposing himself.

They wanted her camera. They were attracted by its lens and the exposed parts of its mechanism. One of them approached her, grimacing menacingly, and she noticed his hands as he raised them against her; they were puffy and stiff-clawed from heroin addiction. Something awful was happening. The junkies were narrowing their eyes and the speed freaks were wigging. "Yuk!" said Imogen, and punched him in the diaphragm.

He oofed and doubled over and his buddies lunged at her. There must be some police. Where were the plainclothes? She scrammed, skinny as a grab iron, sideways out of the penny arcade, tranvestites grappling after her.

Department store chimes. *"Paging, Orma Lu Smithers."*

The madame sashayed down the hall of the whorehouse checking parkometers. She had a ruby quartz chronometer and one of those lapel hourglasses nurses use to take pulses with. Her quarters were like those of an ordinary concierge. On one wall of the comptoire was a circuit board where a tiny light bulb and a fuse of very low wattage were set up for each room in the house. She could tell at a glance which of the girls had the lights on in her room and who therefore had a customer who wanted to see what he was doing. Girls who had a regular turnaround of eyeballers were more expensive and had proportionally more taken off their cuts. Lula was a regular pot o' gold.

"It's all the same to her," said Madame, pouring herself a Marie Brizard and one for the pimp across the street.

In a parking garage on a side street Imogen found a pay phone that worked and phoned her loft. The dog would hear it ring three times and know it was her. The dial of the phone was Mylar silver, like Andy Warhol's period and the Mylar scotch tape they use in the War Room of the Pentagon. She wanted a picture of a pimp beating on a girl.

Over on West 45th between Eighth and Ninth there were hustlers in just about every doorway. Those girls. Ever see a horse on water skis? And their faces were like the Magic-Markered cardboard facial expressions used in psychological experiments with infants. She could never be such a girl. She had the wrong looks, the wrong body, and the wrong color. Still, some like it thin, and Imogen was as skinny as dog whistle. She could be a Sweetheart Flexi-Straw.

Hollister was on the job, sending his hairy relay out over the dog band. She found what she was looking for on Ninth Avenue someplace in the 40s: a loud slick dude with a Great Dane on a chrome chain and a girl crying. The pimp's car, a suede brogham Continental, was double-parked and the dog was restless. It was starting to rain.

Imogen took a lot of pictures, allowing a few misty droplets on the lens to bring out the graininess of the thing. The girl was bawling and she and the pimp exchanged a few words in Spade, then he hauled off and clipped her on the jaw. Imogen and the girl exchanged an understanding, the white woman and the black woman eyeing each other, neon reflections on the asphalt like hot licks on a licorice stick. Imogen slipped away. A little further up Ninth and she encountered a spade dude pimp dragging a woman down the sidewalk with his hand clamped around her wrist. She was tiny, childlike, and he was huge and he shook her like a rag doll, she squalling, kicking and barefooted. When she caught sight of Imogen she hurled both her shoes at her. Imogen ducked and ran.

The photographer in trenchcoat grabbed a taxi belonging to the Osmiroid Cab Co. and told the driver to take her to the Plaza Hotel. On the way she thought about the pictures she had just gotten away with. Why, she could be a svelte call girl with a Siamese cat named Palomino. Then a strange thing happened. She remembered an old girlfriend, her first roommate in New York, and was nearly overcome with nostalgia.

Imogen told the driver to take her to a certain bar on Madison

Avenue instead. She hadn't been there for a long time and the place had a special significance for her. And so she sat for hours at the bar, drinking Bloody Marys and remembering.

One day years ago, when she lived at the YWCA on Lexington Avenue, Imogen was poking around down in the East Village. She had just bought a *Times* at Gem's Spa and was walking down Second Avenue, when she noticed another white girl who had drawn alongside and was keeping step with her. All at once a panhandler, a bum, emerged from a doorway and accosted the girl, who didn't break stride but kept walking in the businesslike way girls who wear skirts in that part of Manhattan affect. She turned to Imogen and smiled.

"See what happens?" she said. "He started out as a baby and now here he is an old man."

Imogen dug it and suggested they go into Rapoport's for coffee and a piece of apple pie à la mode.

Fredegonde, her name was. A well-built young woman, a little overweight perhaps. She lived at The Barbizon and she was lonely in the city. She had clear features, and a somewhat effervescent air as though she had a lot of irons in the fire. Imogen remembered thinking, The fragile dynamics of her smile.

Oh Second Avenue is not the tassels, braids, puggarees and down to a whole Albuquerque of rubber stamps that is tree-bent Broadway. I mean

"Uptown girl, with her..."

that stretch of Second between Houston and 14th, especially between East Fifth and St Mark's Place on the west side of the avenue, where hippies eat sidewalk scrapings and the tourists eat Aquarius stools. Fredegonde says she has been in Europe for a few years. She speaks with the careful diction of an old Europe hand.

"The young people of Europe, you know, are Marxists, while the ones of this country are waiting for the man."

There's a grubby little Lion supermarket next door to the Fillmore East. Soon the Lion will be destroyed by fire and the Fillmore will close.

"What the movement is to a watch, the action is to an organ."

A small crowd watches some girls fighting around by the wall of the

supermarket. Two tough schoolgirls give another girl a bloody nose.
"That'll teach you, you little bitch!"
They leave her sprawled in her blood and snivels and a guy carrying an A&P shopping bag asks her where she's from.
"Boston," she replies.

>   Us Dewey girls we stand and sit
>   Us Dewey girls don't take no shit
>   Us Dewey girls are here to stay
>   And if you don't like it
>   Cookie was here but now she's gone
>   She left her name to carry on
>   Those who knew her knew her well
>   And those who didn't

Fredegonde and Imogen got an apartment on 14th Street near Avenue A, on the third floor of the building with Lilly's Small Stores. Now and then they would drink tequila together, ritualizing the salt and slices of lemon snowbanked in an abalone shell they bought in a place on 9th Street. Fredegonde had gone to Pembroke, and Imogen found out she had only been a year in Europe and that she was a little nymphomaniac.

"The humidity is 90% and indeed we are nearly underwater."
"Isn't there anything the Mayor can do about this rain?"
"Well now, he could come in out of it."

The Great South Houston Fault. The quenching butts and vending stelae of deserted subway stations. There is going to be a lightning storm. Saint Elmo's fire flickers in the crazycracker cornices and fire escapes, Aquarius creams and it rains a cloudburst and the hippies fast, critical as an astronomer's emulsion.

Fredegonde and Imogen are a Pisces and a Taurus respectively. Fredegonde put her money in the Grownup Savings Bank of New York, Member FDIC, and she had trouble with men.

"In these *existentialistes* the problem of transcendence has to do with developing the individual's shortcomings in order to become authenticity itself."

"You don't say."

The fellow was making ready to leave and Fredegonde, once again embarrassed by her own intelligence, had to turn the situation to advantage.

"I won't smother you. I'll put the butter away instead."

She put the butter in the refrigerator and he was putting his coat on. Fredegonde grasped his lapels and looked him in the eye.

"Aren't you even going to be a gentleman," she said, "and lay me?"

"Look, Baby," he said, kissing her on the cheek, "with that kind of talk I probably couldn't even get it up."

Later Fredegonde asserted, "The only way a man can come onto you is by telling you what to do," and Imogen thought that might be right. And anyway now, isn't that what pimps do?

One of those every other days when the kitten got fed the half can of Figaro from the refrigerator the two girls went ice skating in Central Park. They were dressed warmly but it was a cold day, and they kept moving with little chitchat on the ice. They saw the sun go down red, and the towers of Midtown sparkled and the boys skated roughly. Afterwards they went to the Village and had hamburgers at the White Horse and drank a good deal of red wine. Fredegonde was always a good one to come with the slick phrase.

"We are prisoners of our context," she said, and Imogen could not but agree.

"Americans are all paranoia addicts," Fredegonde said, with a voice like a torn speaker cone.

"I thought they were hydrogen addicts," said a man sitting next to them.

"How come?" Imogen queried. The girls looked at him as though thunderstruck.

"They're addicted to hydrocarbons," the man affirmed, sipping his gin and tonic, "and carbon monoxide. Products of incomplete combustion."

The girls were intrigued. They were sitting at one of the tables in the front room of the White Horse and the jukebox was a little too loud. Fredegonde thought she would stick her foot in it again.

"You're a cop, aren't you?" she asked the man.

"Are you a Pisces?" he responded.

"Yes," said Fredegonde.

Imogen felt the ground crumble away beneath her. "How did you know?" she demanded.

"Because," the man said, winking, "your friend looks like the kind of girl dogs would chase."

"Do you know many Pisces women?" Fredegonde countered, weakly.

"Yes."

"An Airedale chased her coming out of the subway yesterday," said Imogen, pertly. "Betcha can't guess my sign."

"Hmm. What sign is Grace Slick?"

They didn't even ask him his name.

"I'm Bryna, from Detroit," lied Fredegonde, sounding like tuf Teflon.

"And I'm Dylan Thomas," said the man.

They arrived at the apartment, in which the plants had grown some.

"Are these your plants?" he asked Imogen.

"Yes," she said, still trying to think of a phony name for herself.

"You certainly have a green thumb."

"I have a brown thumb."

"You mean you go around goosing people?"

"No, I mean my plants turn brown. And they need to be dusted."

"Hello you purring, good-smelling, tuckered out little critter," the man said, vehemently nuzzling the kitten. They were laughing like crazy, the three humans, piling their coats in an armchair. Fredegonde came with drinks and they chatted for a while about the art on the walls. There was a framed reproduction of Max Ernst's *The Blind Swimmer,* and a big enlargement of a Rudy Burkhardt photo of people crossing an intersection in Manhattan. Both pictures were Imogen's. The enlargement occupied the man's attention for several minutes.

"Imogen calls it B.P.," Fredegonde said, affecting an accent.

"British Petroleum?" the man wondered, intelligently.

"No. Before Puerto Ricans."

Soon Fredegonde was disrobing in the dim light, the peacock feathers and the night motes. She looked like a plaid elephant. There were no doors in the shotgun apartment, only curtains between the rooms, and from where she lay in the adjoining cubicle Imogen could hear every word they said and all their noises.

She had thought of an alias for herself, and she dozed off wondering what kind of girl would have a name like that. She woke up again when she heard Fredegonde say she always liked it best the second time. The man said he would rather do it with Imogen and Fredegonde said Forget it, she's a virgin.

"I'm not either," Imogen muttered, and fell sound asleep.

Imogen was in one of her old haunts Uptown, remembering. It was an old tavern on Madison Avenue, near the gallery where she had a show once a year. There were a lot of galleries nearby, and the place's clientele and its jukebox and its menu were in keeping with the tastes of gallery-goers and artists who have made it. There were well-to-do eccentrics, couples who weren't ready to have children yet, and culture-compatible army guys. The jukebox was playing an old Geri Southern number, "The Cabin," and an old man approached Imogen and exchanged a few words with her.

"I would like to grow a beard," he said, "but the whiskers don't grow like they used to."

Imogen smiled. "Art is merely kid stuff," she said, "carried to an excusable extreme."

The phrase reminded her of something Fredegonde would say.

Imogen and Fredegonde had little things in common, such as calling blacks "androids," and not spreading butter on rye bread. And they were aware that they were a typical New York set of girl friends. They were familiar with Robert Capa's photographs of the Spanish Civil War, and Fredegonde had remarked on the 1930s ads in the Barcelona subways. She uttered outrageous parodies of Spanish radio commercials, like "I was so hungry I put chili on my turkey and ate it grease and all," and *"El hombre de la ciudad cuidar sa ombra."* They were a blonde and a brunette, Fredegonde and Imogen, just like Goya's cartoons of Majas. They were everywhere in Manhattan, pairs of girl friends and roommates, Majas, one of them with a guy, Majas fighting, their stockings ungartered, always a blonde and a brunette. That's why there were so many of them in clothes ads in *The New York Times*

Magazine and elsewhere. Whether they were depicted wearing Kodel or Celanese Arnel or in some Action Scene by Rose Marie Reid, all of Palo Alto was divided into three parts: S, M, and L.

Fredegonde told Imogen about her astrologer. He was a Belgian named 'Oose and he wore an eyepatch.

"He's the Queen of England's astrologer," she boasted.

"You're sure he isn't Hitler's astrologer?" Imogen retorted.

Mr. 'Oose charged a hundred dollars for the first consultation and twenty-five dollars for each subsequent consultation. He lived near the Chelsea Hotel and his dingy apartment stank of Philippine cigars. Fredegonde had her birth chart done the first time and a five-year forecast the next. That was a hundred and twenty-five dollars. She was disappointed.

"Not very snappy, is it?" she said, looking at the chart which meant absolutely nothing to her.

"Well, there may be love in it," said Mr. 'Oose, a yellowed finger poking around in Venus.

"Really?" said Fredegonde.

"Sure. You know, one of those *adeps lanae* who can shuffle a deck of cards and whet a carving knife, you know, snick-snack?"

Thereafter Fredegonde had birth charts done for every one of the men she went to bed with. That she diplomatically eked their data from them—birthplace, date, time—had little to do with the quality of the horoscopes produced from that information, for Mr. 'Oose eschewed computing with anything except Greenwich Mean Time. Twenty-five dollars a shot. And never the guy's name, just "Trebbidge's ♂," and because of Mr. 'Oose's quaintness in abstaining from employing local time the subject's Moon might show up in Cancer instead of in Leo where it properly belonged. Fredegonde swore by Mr. 'Oose.

"It's all the same to her," the astrologer most likely thought. And indeed it might have been all the same to Fredegonde, who habitually dismissed her roommate's somewhat unsophisticated nature by saying, "You're you 'cas that's who you're best at."

Imogen studied photography at Pratt Institute and had a part-time job in the photo archive of a large publisher. Fredegonde worked in a CPA's office on Nassau Street. Some Saturday afternoons they would meet for drinks at Schrafft's on Fifth Avenue.

"There is no such thing as a female geezer," said Fredegonde. "There may be young men geezers, but though women do a lot of things they do not geeze."

There's the cat stalking Venus, Imogen daydreamt. The Psychiatrist of the Annunciation. Fredegonde was talking about men.

"Geezers, duffers, codgers, coots, and *Altekakers.*"

"Merril, Lynch, Pierce, Fenner, and Wong," said Imogen.

The girls laughed in a masculine way, overheard themselves and became abruptly ladylike. They sipped their Bloody Marys. Fredegonde expanded.

"Noetic mimesis is the technique of using déjà vu. It means 'imitating memory' and you set up a model of something evoked in the state of déjà vu."

Imogen was thinking in a visual clangor; Tenebrific moonset waterhammer moonseed gamelan...

"There are three ingredients for carrying out noetic mimesis: 'then then,' a memory from any time context, such as nostalgia for something which hasn't been; 'now then'..."

"Ha, ha."

"... a memory in immediate time, such as it seems like only yesterday; and 'following the template,' which means imitating the route formed by the coincidence of the two preceeding ingredients. Now, you may think this is Doctor Segré's theory of antipasta, but performing noetic mimesis can get you a job and it can get you a lover."

"Give me an example," said Imogen.

Four young girls entered, accompanied by an older woman who wore a tailored suit and was smoking a filter cigarette. The girls appeared to be in her charge, and they were all cheeks and elbows.

"Ces jeunes filles là," Fredegonde said, impulsively. "Elles sont élèveuses dans le Lycée Toonoose."

Imogen was envisioning; Charisma garuda, camel persiflage, Manunka chunk, milk glass salt cellar...

"All right," said Fredegonde. "Here's an example. A kitten is playing in a bathtub. The drain has whirlpooly ghosts that induce her to chase her tail."

The bartender was quick and sure with the bottles behind the bar, like an old time sailing ship sailor who knows where each rope is even in a

The Banks of the Sea 49

storm in the pitch dark night. Imogen understood the young girls. They were full of graw dew, and one of them used Wry-Away.

"I don't understand," she said.

"It's simply the past before another past," Fredegonde explained. "It's in a Spanish grammar they use at Boston University."

4 The Barnacle Goose

This is WTFM, that's Tee-FM, 103.5 on your FM dial, where the music is, Lake Success...

SOMETIMES SOMEBODY would close a store or a theater, and one after another like bowling pins the businesses would close and a shell, sometimes an entire block was left hollow of commerce, left the signs in the windows and the letters on the marquee. Still the elevated flashes ovoid faces, quick mirrors, Myrtle Avenue. How many places are there a pedestal clock up on the sidewalk like a public punishment? Sorry, says the clock. They're doing something in the old foyers, tickets to the globe from shattered box offices, steerages for derelicts in the immigrant night. Stooped in sleep, steeped in transportation, crowds remember boarded-up V-Days, green mossy planks, the whole city in an old man's woodpile. The ax pauses like a skater, enters old shoe-stores' pier windows carpet and lucite footsy mesas scribbled with night like a sugar rink.

Fredegonde held her head in her hands, elbows resting on the plain yellow oilcloth they'd searched for and found, at last, a whole roll of, in a thrift shop in White Plains. Imogen made a mound of the pumpernickel crumbs and Edam rinds, the loaf face down on the slicing board. It was hot and the two girls had discussed buying an air conditioner. They drank iced tea.

"I have come to the conclusion," Fredegonde said with a portly voice, "that you're you 'cas that's who you're best at."

"You've said that before," Imogen chirped, perhaps unkindly. "You can always change your brands if you're dissatisfied with yourself."

Fredegonde folded her hands in front of her and looked hard at her roommate. "You've never taken me seriously," she said.

"What are you going to do?" Imogen laughed. "Jump out of cakes at sales conventions?"

The two girls had been living together for more than a year and the relationship was starting to come unglued. After all, they weren't man and wife. As Fredegonde put it, they thought they were in clover but it was really artichokes. Imogen sighed.

"I don't know what your crazy smarts are cranking out up there," she said, tapping her forehead, "but I think you ought to concentrate on practical goals, Freddie. I really do."

"You're so damned creative!" Fredegonde shouted. "You're always putting me in the position of having to take a dare."

"Simple pleasures, chum," Imogen said, rinsing her glass. "We've got the aquarium balanced, and that's pretty good. So let's go up to the pet store and buy a fish. Come on. Treat you to a lime rickey at the Longview."

"A balanced Aquarius, eh?" Fredegonde smiled slyly. "Hmm. I think I would like to be a Libra."

One of the first things Fredegonde did was to get pregnant with a guy she picked up at the Riviera and then go to Pennsylvania and get an abortion from Dr. Spencer. It changed her menstrual cycle so she and Imogen stopped having their periods at the same time. Meanwhile she was acquiring a new appearance and mannerisms, and other ID. She called herself Bryna.

She knew a guy at Columbia who had a job at Kopy Kwik. He was studying music and he was also a dealer with five different kinds of grass stashed in the laundry bin in the bathroom of his apartment. Some friends of his were into bogus credit cards and airline tickets and in a few weeks she had a Michigan birth certificate, driver's license, and a social security account which had been current for seven years. All she had to do for this was to make a drug meet in Brooklyn Heights. The faggot in tight pants and white sneakers bounding up to her in the liquor store on Clark Street. He had two Salukis and he gave her a doggy bag from a Lebanese restaurant. It contained Algerian couscous and a pound of cocaine and Bryna was afraid of the police.

The drug thing had turned out because she had bought the right kind of wine. Otherwise it might have been awkward and she might not have been able to drink much of it.

That she said she wanted to be a Libra had merely been a red herring for Imogen, for what Bryna really intended was to become a Scorpio, because that sign was said to have as one of its traits an almost unconquerable desire to win. She made an appointment with Fredegonde's astrologer.

"Hello, Miss Trebbidge," he said, welcoming her in his formal way. "My, how you've changed."

Mr. 'Oose's nifty dachshund acted like it didn't know her. She was a little short with the man.

"I'd like an analysis for somebody," she said, and gave him the birth data she wanted. Mr. 'Oose prepared the graph, his slightly spatulate fingers appraising the surface of the paper.

"A Scorpio. Hmm," he said. "Is the individual male or female?"

"The latter," said Bryna.

Mr. 'Oose wrote: Trebbidge's ♀.

She was going to be lithe, presque eel. But meanwhile she was wearing her new white sneakers and there was already egg yolk on them. She quit her job in the CPA's office on Nassau Street and rented a room in the apartment of a Jewish couple in Brooklyn whose children had left home. One day she bought an air conditioner at Kaminstein's and had it installed in the apartment on 14th Street. Then she removed her belongings, left a note and a bottle of tequila on the kitchen table, and walked out of Imogen's life.

Ms. found in a bottle. That's me. I'm your friend. All you have to do is rub the bottle and Ms. Boss comes out of it. Bryna.

The handwriting was different. It was now round with fat uncial characters and the smug, careful cerifs of a well-fed daughter, one who was dutiful, and knew what felt best and what worst.

Fredegonde lived off her savings for a while and didn't spend much time in her room. She took to frequenting gallery openings and artists' loft parties Downtown, where she was already rather well-known, and then scooting Uptown to frolic in the German and Irish nightspots there, and sing along and drink beers that men bought for her, and the worlds never met except in her. A painter would ball her, and then a broker, and the only thing they inkled of each other were marketable inspiration for one and portfolio tips for the other. And so commerce flourished, all because of a pudgy bird who flitted, with the speed of paper, between two societies.

The Banks of the Sea 53

Bryna DeVoto took the civil service exam for postal clerk, and when her cash started getting low she got a job in a chewing gum factory in Long Island City. They started her off cleaning the blending vats with a wire brush and a palette knife, to get the old gum that the solvents missed. Once she went to a union meeting.

On days when she skipped her lunch, sometimes she would use the half-hour break for strolls in the neighborhood. Adjoining a vacant lot between hulking factory buildings was a frame house with a tarpaper shingle roof, broken asbestos siding and a sagging porch. Once it had been a family dwelling, but now it was a brothel. For some reason she looked forward to walking past the house. Perhaps it was for the thrill she got at the shrieks and laughter which sometimes came from the windows where the blinds were always pulled down. Once the screen door opened and out reeled one of her foremen and they recognized each other. Then she got a job at Perfectly Good Food Products, Inc.

One day she walked under the Queensborough Bridge where there was a parking lot and auto wreckers. A dog started barking at her and she stood for a while looking at it through the rusty steel mesh fence. An elevated train keened weirdly somewhere overhead, and a Pontiac with broken shocks whumped over the curb and cut a corner. A skinny German shepherd bitch was barking and lunging at her on the end of a chain. Her doghouse wasn't much more than a packing crate, and there was a spill of scummed water in the bottom of an upturned hubcap for the animal to drink.

"Mrs. Banderacoot spoke before Parliament today."

She's Jessica Flashbush, our Bryna, this tweaknipple Chubette. The black *robota* were aware of her. One of them smiled to her and made an obscene noise with his lips on his open fist. Two Puerto Rican girls, sisters, brawled loudly in the women's locker room. One of the married foremen became overly friendly with her in the cafeteria and Bryna was afraid he knew her real name. She ate with the Greek girls and had picked up on their lingo. She said something to him in Greek and he replied, "There's no news in the truth and there's no truth in the news."

One of the things Bryna was pointing up was her stupidity quotient. She bleached her hair and came on out the corner of her mouth. Bryna was a dumb broad. Dumbbells can get away with murder.

"I like fat girls," said the foreman.

The P.O. job came through and she was assigned to the military mail facility at Long Island Terminal. One of her first nights on the job she spoke with a young white man who was writing a thesis on proto-Christian cargo cults in the ancient world.

"I like fat girls," he said, "because they have nice tight pussies."

Bry could certainly feel smug about that. Long ago she had made up her mind never to have children except by ceserean, for the last thing she wanted to happen was for her hole to rupture during parturition, and everybody knows that a woman without a cunt is like a man without a country.

"Yours is nice and conical, too," he said, feeling it appreciatively. "The lips cone up and enclose the cleft. It's like a little volcano, and it can probably take a lot of punishment."

What she liked was a guy who hadn't masturbated for a while. She could always tell. He had a certain pulsing at the temples and an intenseness of gesture that made her almost queasy with the thought of the load he was carrying. When she thought about it she got wet. At times keeping dry was a problem for her and she wore panty inserts.

"A nice gluteous tuchis," he said, stroking it, "and a nice glutinous little hole."

The cargo cult of Aquarius. The triumph of high-school amateurism and the hick prophet. He who is without sin and the defoliated greenback. This guy was so methodical, and in the heat of August. Cargo of hole.

She was kneeling on the bed and he gently pushed her flat on her tummy and lay on her with his stiff cock bunned between the cheeks of her ass. After a delicious moment he rose and kissed the nape of her neck and at the same time ran his hand down and stroked his finger back and forth in her slit. She spread her legs and hunkered up for him. He wanted her to lie on her back. She rolled over and he played with her clitoris so that she made the bed squeak and caressed his arm.

"You're so pretty," he said, looking at her pussy. Suddenly he was rubbing sideways so that it was like broad-ribbed corduroy.

"Oh, please," she blurted. "You're opening me all up."

He lay on top of her kissing her with his tongue while the tip of his penis found its way into her. She was very wet and it went in easily even though she was so tight.

"This hole," he sighed.

She's the creamy mild one, the gigantic lunar reflecting ovens of the Chattanooga Bakery, Inc., baking their famous Moon Pies and marshmallow sandwiches. He came in her. Some men came at the sight of her. Afterwards, in the homey Queens darkness with the sound of trucks far away, Bryna asked him,

"What's your position on the index of incidence?"

"What's that?"

"I was just wondering," she mused. "Things recur, don't they? And a couple of years ago I met a guy in Greenwich Village who you really remind me of."

"Maybe I'm a replica," he laughed.

"Come on. I mean it."

"Maybe I'm the same guy and it's a coincidence."

"Don't blow my mind," said Bryna. She kissed his shoulder and clutched his hand and thought about that one for a while. Actually, she took it seriously enough to make comparisons. His hand lay gently and appreciatively on her pussy. After a while she cocked one thigh aside, and spoke again.

"Brian, don't you think the post office is a Saggitarian monopoly?"

"Huh?"

"I mean, it's like the flight of an arrow, the miracle of a piece of mail reaching its destination, the complexity of the directness of it . . ."

"Uh huh."

"I mean look what it does to the postal workers. They're Saggitarian thralls. I can just picture some poor stiff setting off drunk and stark naked on snowshoes in the middle of the night."

"Don't blow *my* mind."

He spoke softly into the darkness, idly fondling her.

"You have a lot of unusual, good ideas in your head," he said. "A very remarkable way of looking at things."

His voice was so objective and understanding that Fredegonde wondered—in wondering whether he was going to make love to her a second time—if he were addressing her or some abstraction in the night.

"A great many interesting thoughts. I wonder how you will use them."

Ozone Park, Jamaica, Queens. Laid out about 1880 by Benjamin

W. Hitchcock and named for the invigorating air from the ocean and bay that swept the section. The area had previously been known as South Woodhaven.

Rego Park, Flushing, Queens. Developed about 1923 by the Rego Construction Company, whose name was coined from the first letters of the words "Real Good."

The Gipsy Post Office. Mail bags are called "equipment," and a piece of empty equipment is called a "bum." Bums are manufactured by convict labor in the federal penitentiaries. Postal employees are hired at great expense. They are examined, investigated, fingerprinted, screened, and finally, after they are photographed, an oath is administered to them. Once they are in, postal workers are kept under surveillance by Postal Inspectors who observe them from overhead galleries through peepholes and one-way mirrors. But the post office is only incidental to this story, which is about gum mints.

"Would you do me a favor?"

"Want me to hold it for you?"

"Yeah. It's gettin' kind of heavy."

"But my hands are cold, George."

"The Monster," the sack-sorting machine. Bryna gets to work on this often and is assigned a separation, works hard and loses weight. Hefts bags and bulky parcels and stacks them on wheeled "skids." Trains of loaded skids are hauled away by electric tractors to the Bullpen, the Primaries, Customs.

"Get yer fresh stiffs!"

Labels, seals, flight tags. Army Post Office numbers. APO NY 09777 PARIS. Juiceomat mail for Turkey. Rome gets a lead seal. So does Naples. Mail for the United States military and diplomatic establishment east of the Humboldt Current and west of the Himalayas. The Bullpen foreman rumbles in the alliterative postal jargon: "Now I expect some remarkable results from this heavy-hitting crew."

They sent her to room 13, huge fans thrumming, insouciant Long Island dinner music in the loudspeakers. Limp, involved disc jockey. They were bagging Parcel Airlift mail. Weight in kilos.

Bryna's partner on the unit was a tall slow black who looked like he could have played center forward for the La Brea Tar Pits. The black women on the next unit made wisecracks.

" 'Mazin' what a little vaseline'll do for op'nin' a hole in a fat honkey."

The remark struck Bryna as somehow homosexual. But those android women, if they weren't dykes they certainly were inebriated.

"Ah'd like to put a telephone r'ceiver in that whaht snatch o' hers and lissen to the baby talk."

"What baybuh tock? She ain't never goan have no baybuh."

It felt to Bryna as though she were an owl beleaguered by crows. Sometimes it was so bad she couldn't believe it, like it was supposed to be more convincing than blood. What was his name, the guy on her unit? Curtis? Or Lionel? Some literary or stockbroker name. The spade was mumbling a rebus.

"There is no white man," he said. He was at the scales weighing a bag. "He is cockainian man, originated from the black seed."

Doctor Leakey, huh? Well if there's one thing a monkey likes better 'n bananas it's tobacco. She fished a soft pack of Marlboros out of a tit pocket and tapped a couple of cigarettes out for herself and the black guy.

"Bradstreet," she said. "Bradstreet, did you know that geese come from barnacles?"

Bradstreet got a tar-baby look on his face, rolled those eyes and said, "Momma, she don' lau no 'spersions in heah."

The Android Sisters swore and sucked screwdrivers from a big Wetson's take-out cup with a straw in it. They certainly weren't getting much work done.

"Aint that jus' like a whaht pusson? Know-it-all honkey. Whah, mah chilluns goan tuh go tuh school wid de fahnest whaht yungstuhs. Daze gwine rub up to de lilluh whaht offsprings an git som' dat *excellence.* An daze gon' be inoffensive 'nuf to git dat whaht fokes se-cret."

"Inoffensive mah black bunions! Ah'm gonna git in dere wid de cockroaches and de gobbadge. Ah'm goan slip raht in dere ebry tahm de whaht opens de doah to talk wid oneanother. Day ain't gunna git no real luvvin, kuz ah'm gunna be raht dere wid de stink and de cockroaches and de sickness pissin' on de stairs. Ebbry tahm day smile tuh oneanother daze gwine see de face ob black mizzery."

It made her feel beside herself, like a character in an existentialist novel, a street character, an embodiment of wretchedness as stock-in-trade. Fredegonde. Lovely child. Fredegonde Trebbidge of Smooth Castle Township, New York. Her parents used to call her Silky Valentine.

Bry and Brian. They were rather romantic, made a lot of love and smoked a lot of grass, and didn't have time for much social life. And the sweet domesticity of their relationship made her want to divulge her secret, to blurt it out that she was not what she purported to be. But she didn't have to.

"I'm a king bee," he said, toking up on a joint of grass.

"A king bee? How can that be?"

"The worker bees," he said, gasping, "are all scared of the day the king bee comes and gathers the queens unto him."

Bryna giggled a high giggle and lighted another joint. "So that's your theory, huh?"

"Yeah, the drone dies because it *knows* the queen. According to myth, the women killed Orpheus because he was a mere lyre-player. The king bee, on the other hand, kills all the workers..."

"A mere liar-player!" Bryna squealed. "Why you fatuous lout. What makes you think men can keep on inveighing against women..."

"Inveigh? That's a seventy-five cent word if I ever heard one."

"It's easy to mock, isn't it? Men are hypocrites, screwing women and then blaming them for what they themselves..."

"Women and Negroes have smaller brains."

"Why you swine! You ought to be punished for saying that."

Bryna was so angry she started to cry. She dignifiedly rose from the bed and stalked around. Then she sat down on the bed again and started putting on her stockings.

"You know, you're beautiful when you're angry," said Brian.

"You know, I expected that," she spat.

"C'mon. Make yourself useful," he said, running his fingers under her brassiere and squeezing her nipples so that they, her nipples, became hard as little rosebuds.

"Take it off," he said.

She slapped him and headed for her clothes.

"Freddie," he drawled. "Don't be a cayuse caboose."

It stunned her, his using her real name, so she took off her brassiere and panties without saying a peep. It was hot and they were perspiring. She jutted her jaw out and blew the sweat off her upper lip.

"Whew! Let's turn the light out," she suggested. Her voice had automatically shifted into a kind of Ruby Tuesday practicality. "And turn the fan on. I've got to cool off some."

"And you've got to come, too," he said, brushing a tear-glued lock of hair off her cheek, "and come every time."

"What do you mean?"

"Why, you've got to come to think of it. If you don't come, then you're just a twenty-dollar door-stoop hooker."

This made her cry again and get off the bed. What she ought to do was call the police and tell them that she had found her way into a ring of white slavers and that step by step they were closing a trap on her. But then the trap clicked as she was thinking about it and she realized it was too late, that this was the police. She lifted the telephone receiver and dialed Imogen's number, even though the phone was probably bugged and she didn't want to implicate, or recruit, Imogen yet. The phone rang and rang, and Fredegonde had a vision of her former roommate, lonely and creative, the cat and the house plants, the ignorant genius keeping hearth and high hopes, responsible to the universe. She remembered something Imogen once said to her.

"I think you're afraid to love," she had said.

"What do you mean?"

"Because it attracts androids. You can screw guys but you can't love."

And Fredegonde was one big bawl, standing there in the candlelight in the strange man's room, pink and blubbery and her toes pointing toward each other naturally. Oh, how she did weep. Brian brought her a dishtowel to cry into and put his fingers in her pussy.

"Not so bedraggled," he soothed. "You look like Ypsilanti in November."

She flopped down on the bed and spread her legs completely like a little girl who doesn't know any better. Brian wetted his penis with saliva and slid it into her.

"Little grease cup," he said affectionately. "Fuck flower." He stroked in her like a patented process.

It felt good and she bit her lip enjoying it, looking at the wall. He sensed her reluctance, knew that the enjoyment seemed to her like self-betrayal so that she still shuddered now and then with sobs that made her pussy squeeze deliciously. He wanted her to laugh.

"What's a woom?" he asked her.

"A womb?" she repeated blankly, not looking at him.

"It's a great big elephant in a great big room," he said. "It lets a great big fart and it goes WOOOOM!"

She blinked, closed her eyes and swallowed hard. She lay there passive, her breasts pneumatic and her thighs moist.

"How would you like to be President, Bryna?" he asked, giving her an internal massage. "What about that? You could live in the White House and administer while your husband teaches school in the slums of Washington, D.C."

She looked at him, then looked away. "You're not Jewish enough," she said.

"You know," he said, "you've really slimmed down working at the P.O."

"You're a real medicine ball," she murmured, eyes closed in concentration on her apogee. She was about to come.

"Bryna, what's the difference between an Italian woman and an elephant?"

She panted vocally, the shrillness rising in her throat. It was upon her. He whispered in her ear, "The difference between an Italian woman and an elephant . . . is a hundred pounds and a black dress."

A little while later he asked her, "Did you come to think of it?"

"Oh, yes," she snuggled. "I kept my eyes closed because I was seeing all those beautiful colors and patterns in my head. It was like fireworks, but telling a story. And then I thought, it simply occurred to me, that flowers are always asleep."

She thought for a minute, and then laughed. "It's funny," she said.

"What's funny?"

"Head flowers."

She would work on that for the next few years, her head flowers and the stories they tell, visions like the ones which disturb children when they are falling asleep, something most adults forgot long ago. It would become her job, what was already her vocation: having amour with assigned gentlemen in order to obtain from them the contents of their heads. Women are repositories of culture, like libraries, and relay stations for and unscramblers of information. Where there are diplomacy and military interests there are invariably trollops. And she would be well paid for her work, up until the time when she could no longer come, no longer gather head flowers. For then she was a burntout case, like a coke snorter who can't get off anymore. Fredegonde was a she-gooli, a sanctified prostitute, for the god has condescended to have intercourse with her. Amour and zeal, that is their law. In justifying herself, the girl shrugs and says "Je suis grande dame" (I am the Queen, but it pleases me to remain in the guise of a serving girl), and "Je regne plus bien que le Roi" (sounds like a perfume commercial), and finally "J'assistais à mes actions commisés: elles étaient inévitables" (it was inevitable, so I'll just help it along). And now bedridden old women and girls at their samplers begin to rave.

One day he was gone from the post office. Fall was coming on and she phoned him, but his number was not in service. Once she went by his room and somebody else was living there. Oh, there must be a little dog who laughed at such sport, Bryna cavorting where'er she trod, asking a fellow worker if he had seen Brian.

"He went back to school," was all he said.

She developed a coda of him in her mind: her seducer the talent scout returning to some federal building somewhere to an office full of empty desks and a portrait of the President.

The time clerk's voice rumbled in the loudspeakers: *"Sub Clerk Bryna DeVoto report to the time desk."*

She was sent to the Track One dispatch office and they put her on the ten o'clock Frankfurt dispatch. Space available mail. Military parcel post.

Bryna alone with seven men loading a forty-foot trailer. The bags weighed a maximum of eighty pounds. Three of the men were blacks and it was dark in the trailer. Once in a while one of them would say something or laugh and she could see his teeth. With Brian elsewhere she suddenly had a lot of limbo to think around in and she seized on crumbs of amusement. She took a break and sat for a while on an empty skid and watched the others work. She lighted a Marlboro and inhaled deeply, gratefully. In another ten minutes she would relieve somebody else in the trailer, unloading into it the seemingly endless train of skids piled high with the bulky red airmail bags, fingernails creasing on the ungiving nylon. An express train passed on the nearby Penn Central tracks and she was filled with a sense of longing. She thought of Brian, and of the other guys. There were the old, inured postal workers, called "stiffs," who sat on bales of bums and bums full of bums out of the wind and sight of the foremen, who knew how to unwind a clock without lifting a finger. All of them had broken arches and slouched. The P.O. was a cul-de-sac. And the young guys—stiffs of the future. There was Lacey, who saved rent and lived at the post office, slept on empty skids and carried around a paper bag full of beans cans and crusty milk cartons. And Levy the para-Israeli, who assembled ICBMs in his folks' basement. Sidney the horror fan who wrote Worship Godzilla on subway walls. And Victor the half-mute, who impelled a shock wave of déjà vu ahead of him like the screaming whistle of an express train.

It seemed like so long ago, pioneering it in the big city, enjoying the textures of it, girl-carousing, brisk autumn dawns. It was hard, but sometimes it felt to her that she would be able to clear herself of Brian and remake her life, to return to it, as it were. To using instead of being used, a girl on the make and making it. She was in good shape, now. Supple. She wanted to start going out again. Fredegonde. Rhymes with *La Giaconda.* Lovely child. Fredegonde. Her parents called her Silky Valentine.

Whatever it was responded and this couple, friends of Brian's, phoned and left an invitation to a party. It had begun to snow, and out on the roof terrace partyers were chatting and drinking strong drink with great, almost exaggerated deliberateness, bending their elbows and hoisting stiff ones. The temperature had fallen in two hours, but the people on the terrace were a little pickled and some of the girls rather lightly dressed for the weather. It was snowing small, serious flakes. There was a patch of sky, asymmetrical and schizrhomb, and in the space between two tenements the Empire State Building could be seen poking up into it. The weather would thicken and the tower become less visible, but there were already little drifts in the cornices and by morning some of the stiffness would have gone for it would become mild again.

"Except with the daughters of some of the highest functionaries," the Japanese gentleman was saying, "all girls may from the tenderest age give themselves without any loss of reputation to public prostitution."

The Banks of the Sea

Greenosan licked his lips. He liked Bryna. She was horse piss and sow scum. She finally got the courage to ask the couple about Brian.

"He's home, I guess," said the woman. "How's your 'distribuitor'? Tee hee."

Good food. She ate car brrs with crumbs on them. Amateurish pink chablis. It was a party of decos, shrinks, commercial fellows and junior junctions. Most of the couples were Moody Blues people and there were a lot of faggots.

"Bobby sux."

"Eduardo *sucks!*"

"And very *well,* too! He took all my eight inches without a single gag or tooth."

"Yes, but he took my three inches and got tonsilitis."

"How come he took my dictionary?"

"Because he thinks HEAD is spelled with a *J.*"

"It jizz, jizzn't it?"

"A mother circumcised is a happy motha."

"... gynecocracy. Slave husbands of the sun-clan peoples of the lower Mississippi Valley."

Fredegonde is the one monkey who is unconcerned about the observer, and she also becomes more inappropriate in her responses to the ranks and social signals of the other monkeys. Her physical appearance and personal grooming steadily deteriorate. Similar changes were also noted in a field study of the effects of surgical ablation of the amygdala, including some monkeys being driven into the sea.

"The Icarus lizard flies on its ribs, using its eaves as oars, so to speak, like Aquarius, the Lizard King of a Doors album, rowing a boat. We see the twin comets of his oars here, and in the Jugoslavian fresco ..."

It was only his voice or his subject matter, his speech that attracted her. He had bowed to her, and he had a handshake like a Ford coil. She was so goddamned horny. She assumed a faded smile medieval look and danced with him. Some mailman jokes:

"What did the goddess do to the jerk who saw her in the buff?"

"She turned him into a mailman."

"Ever hear the one about the blind mailman?"

Coruscades of faggot laughter.

There was a pile of coats on a bed in one of the rooms, what old-time innkeeper folk call a "moin." They made it on this moin. They had most of their clothes on and Bryna told him a story that, as she spoke, made his penis uncurl and grow inside of her.

"I was a virgin until my father deflowered me," she said. "It was very beautiful. When I was fourteen I was a rather overweight teenager and some nights he and I used to raid the icebox at about the same time. We would eat together, drumsticks, slices of roast beef and dollops of potato salad, hunks of layer cake with glasses of milk. We feasted and giggled, and once my mother got up and came in, but she never suspected anything.

"We had always been buddies, my sweet daddy and me, and were easy with each other in our looking and touching, and after a while of this raiding the icebox together we got to kissing. Long kisses, shaking with silent laughter. Cake and milk tongue kisses. I hadn't had a boyfriend since I was in grammar school, but now with my father it didn't really matter very much.

"One evening my sister—she's younger than me—had a birthday party. Something upset her and she got angry and cried, and she and my father went into the guest room, where there was a pile of coats on the bed just like right now, and talked something out. Later he and I danced, and he danced close and told me he had something to say to me and that he would do it sometime. Well, one night we met at the refrigerator, almost by agreement, and drank a glass of cold milk each. Then, without a word, we went into the guest room and he layed me. It was very pleasant."

Greenosan was hard and eager. She stroked his sides to calm him and held him to her. She played with his nipples and kissed him.

"What are your plans?" she asked him.

"I'm going to open an office at the World Trade Center," he replied.

"You're *going* to?" she wondered.

"Yes," he said. "It isn't finished yet."

"I'm going to tell you what my father said," she said after a minute and Greenosan was stroking short quick strokes.

"My father said this to me before he creamed in me," she said, softly.

"He said, 'You're so sweet. You're almost sweet enough to have a baby.'"

She put her tongue in his mouth. He moaned and came. She came with him. Mission accomplished, enemy captured.

"And what did you see from the Japanese gentleman?"

"That power towers are like pagodas striding across the landscape."

These were her friends now, this couple, Sloan and Derek. They had taken her into their home, given her baths and fresh clothing, interesting meals and conversation. And she was grateful, for she was spiritually debilitated from solitude and working at night at the post office.

"I am the Pimp of the Forest," said Derek, strutting in his dealer's jackboots and his safari shorts. "How do wild swine differentiate between edible fungi and poisonous finkbenches such as the delicate fly amaryllis?"

" 'S God's flesh," Bryna shrugged, cutely. "You'd think pigs knew enough to pray."

The man postured in his swashbuckle. He was a sunken Spanish supercargo resurrected as cocaine.

"I am the Pimp of the Forest and my woman is the First Procuress."

The woman, Sloan, came in looking like the period when tunics figured largely in books for younger readers. She had an army of monkeys laboring mentally under the desolating blight of an obsession of coconut planting and the effects of overrecruiting.

"This is Owsley's latest," she said, smiling. "It's called 'Trick or Treat.' "

Derek took a handful from the lacquered bowl Sloan was holding and proffered them to Bryna. A small child was crying in another room. Bryna looked at the orange, scored, triangular tablets.

"They're dexedrine," she said, nonchalantly.

The couple had a strange child. Its mother was a girl who was in a state mental hospital, and its favorite toy was an old rubber flashlight that it knew how to push the button on. Once in a while they dropped the kid on its head. This was thought to provoke earthquakes.

After a week had gone by, Bryna had used most of her sick leave at the post office, and she couldn't tell the time desk that she was incapacitated from drugs and insomnia. She told them that she broke her leg in the subway.

She had been given hashish and marijuana, LSD, cocaine, mescalin, and amphetamines. Sloan and Derek were taking turns keeping her entertained and she was utterly exhausted and had been hallucinating for three days. The man was wearing a straw garden hat and sat posing in a floral-festooned swing hanging from the ceiling. He and his woman were dickering.

"What does that have to do with Ferris Booth Hall?" demanded Sloan. "You want a woman you can build a house with."

"We have a groovy kind of love," he said, sleight-of-handing a roll of bills and fanning them at her. "If these dollars could talk they'd tell you which horse to put them on."

"You trying to turn yourself into flypaper?" she responded cooly. "Who's the famous American on traveler's cheques?"

"Your Orbach's handwriting."

"You sure know which side your shingle's been shat on."

He promptly got off the swing, doffed the sunhat and went and sat on the love seat with her. They started billing and cooing.

"Yum of preemies," he said, and after a minute, "Your hands are cold."

"You're a real brick."

"Cold hands, warm heart."

"Soft wax, hard shine."

The apartment was overheated and it was messy from acid trips. Bryna had been given toys. One of them was a stack of dress catalogs from an importer of India printed fabrics and she was lying on the water bed leafing through them. She thought the models looked like Charles Manson girls. The dresses had names and she identified the pinafore she was wearing. It was called "Nooma."

Derek: Waiter, may we have the wine list?

Sloan: Yes, *suh!*

She got up from the love seat and padded out to the kitchen and did some things. In a couple of minutes she came back with a tray clinking and rattling with drinks fixins.

Sloan: Eeeee! Julius Kayser wines.

Derek: Julius Kayser will be fine.

Sloan: Yes, sir. And what kind of dressing would you like on your salad?

Derek: Oil and vinegar, please.

Their mouths were dry and the odor of trip sweat hung in the air. Sloan put ice cubes in three highball glasses, poured in grenadine and

The Banks of the Sea

sparkling water and swirled them around. She brought Derek and Bryna their glasses.

Sloan: I'm sorry Sir, but we don't have much olive oil left and the cook is saving it to abuse himself with.

The phone rang and Sloan took it.

"Sadie Slut isn't here today. She's in Tulsa."

The telephone was on a large Spanish colonial oak table. The only other objects on it—even though they were tripping—were a large book, a linoleum knife, and an unopened economy-size box of Kleenex.

Sloan smiled to Bryna and went out to the kitchen again, and came back carrying a vase of yarrow, or millefoil, commonly called the carpenter's herb, which she placed on the table. Bryna, who had been thoroughly softened by deprivation and the sport of solicitous abuse, was ready to be initiated. They enjoyed their grenadine spritzers.

The Pimp of the Forest and the First Procuress were ostentatiously necking on the love seat when they remembered Bryna and invited her to come and join them. They dandled her on their laps, cooed over her and petted her deliberately. She wasn't wearing anything under her pinafore and both of them fondled her and tickled her. In a little while they moved to the water bed where they continued playing with her.

There was something ceremonial about their sport. Sloan encouraged Bryna to feel her up, kiss and undress her, so that it looked as though the neophyte would succeed in having intercourse with the guru's wife. Meanwhile Derek took the book, which he had stolen (an official theft) from the Newark Public Library, off the table, opened it and began reading aloud:

"The practice of female circumcision by trimming the labia and clitoris is very widespread in every part of Africa. In Ecuador, Jivago girls are deflowered by means of a bone. In Samoa defloration is usually performed digitally, but sometimes a shark's tooth is used. More commonly, however, defloration is carried out in the most thorough manner with a flint knife. It is called by the Arunta 'atna-aritha-kuma,' that is, cutting the vulva. The incision is carried down through most of the 'tain't, and, in the absence of very exact anatomical knowledge, portions of the labia minora and clitoris are cut off as well..."

Bryna lay on the water bed with her legs open. The pinafore was pulled down off one shoulder and one of her round, firm suds was exposed. Sloan licked it and nipped lightly at the nipple with her teeth while masturbating Bryna who helped her do it, tried to squeeze Sloan's whole hand inside her.

"It's nice to be just a hole once in a while," she sighed, squirming.

"The girl," Derek continued reading, *"after she has reached a state of semi-unconsciousness from the liberal potations, is stretched on a stage before the assembled company. The operation is performed by an old and experienced woman with a knife made from the bamboo used for the manufacture of arrows. She cuts all around the introitus vaginae..."*

Derek was warming the linoleum knife in his armpit. Without interrupting his reading, he handed the knife to Sloan who deftly eased it up inside Fredegonde's little nooky.

"... separating the hymen from the labia minora and freeing the clitoris. After the parts have been swabbed with styptic leaves, a phallus fashioned from clay and made to correspond in dimensions with the organ of her intended husband, is moistened and introduced into the vagina. The girl is now ready to be handed over to her husband.

"In southern Persia female circumcision is observed as regularly as male circumcision. Snipping the tip of the clitoris is a sure means of overcoming either complete barrenness or a stubborn perversity in bearing nothing but girls..."

She began to whimper. She knew the knife was inside her and that she was a pink lady. Tears streaming down her temples, she began to rationalize.

"It's a fact," she said, matter-of-factly, "that schizophrenics don't get cancer. It has to do with their body chemistry. So this LSD thing is simply a vaccination against cancer."

"Body chemistry, huh?" said Sloan. "My, weren't you a smarty pants."

"Aren't I still a smarty pants?"

"You sweet thing," Sloan said, stroking the girl's tummy. "You little creamery."

Derek opened the box of Kleenex with a rip and tossed it on the water bed.

The Banks of the Sea

"You're the assassin's cut of grace," he laughed. "You have many husbands."

"Honey pie," said the woman. "You won't be needing any pants for a while. The only thing you'll be needing are a few boxes of these tissues."

"I want to go home," Fredegonde said, her face disintegrating purply.

"You'll do whatever we tell you," said the man. "If she yanks that knife out of your dollager, well, you'll still have a hole, but there won't be any donut."

The phone rang again. It was for her.

5 Watercatch

"You want to buy something?"

Carol stood in the elevator lobby perusing the newsstand's selection of porn. The old newslady was aggravated.

"Don't look at anything unless you want to buy it. You want to buy something?" she repeated.

Fuck. He wasn't even breathing on her goddamn porno magazines. The elevator arrived and he ascended with a contingent of spivs, hustlers, junkies and faggots.

Carol lived in a room on the third floor of the Albert. The hotel was said to be named for Albert Ryder, the American painter, and Thomas Wolfe the novelist had lived there. He unloaded his grocery bags on the bureau: some cans of pork and beans, corned beef hash, chili con carne, Dinty Moore beef stew, artichoke hearts, lima beans, corn, peas and carrots; a jar of peanut butter and a glass of jelly, a box of Ritz crackers, a half pumpernickel and a hunk of New York State cheddar, a carton of milk and a few bottles of Dr. Brown's Cel-Ray. A bottle of Airwick. The radiator could not be turned off and the place smelled like feet. He made himself hot meals by putting a can in the washbasin and letting the scalding water run on it for a few minutes. It was a convenience, and he felt snug and independent in the nitty-gritty little space with a sooty window and a desk no bigger than an apron. It was cold outside, and the geese were going barefoot for they had no shoes.

When he was a kid back in Missouri his father ran a machine pool where the small farmers rented manure spreaders, combines, corn pickers and other implements. One afternoon in the summer of his seventh year one of his casual school chums came strolling down the road and peered in over the gate at him and said, "So this is where you live." Right away they found a toad in the rhubarb, and one on a stone on the shady side of the house, so they built a toad palace. Two little boys in the backyard digging with big tools, panting and sweating like men. By the end of the afternoon they had finished digging the network

The Banks of the Sea　　　　　　　　　　　　　　　　　　　　　　　　71

of passageways and chambers, and covered it over with boards and tarpaper and a layer of earth. Meanwhile the mothers were wondering if the little visitor weren't the lord Krishna on an errand of revelation. The boys had borrowed a dozen or so empty mason jars which they embedded upside down as overhead lighting for the toad passageways. In the light of evening the two collected all the toads they could reasonably find in the front and backyards of the neighborhood and put them all in one of the rooms of the palace. There the amphibians remained, in the soft moist subterrania, the night, and the next morning Carol's friend was over to see if they had roamed. They found one toad sitting in a mason jar, looking out into the daylight. It was sort of forlorn, and it must have been sweating. They must have been hungry toads, because he and Jimmy hadn't put any moths in the tunnels.

He met a guy in the subway who remembered him from a poetry reading in London. Paul, his name was. A sandy-complexioned head who, like a lot of paranoid people, found alleviation in sharing his condition with anybody he could. He slipped like a shiny shadow across the floor of the roaring swaying IRT car and sat down beside him.

"Sam Widge's . . ." He shouted into Carol's ear, then removed his face. Carol turned and looked at him, registered the cocked eyebrow and nodded. It must be a password. He brought his dirty face close to Carol again.

"They'd better not recognize you."

Carol got out his spiral notebook and wrote: *Did you get that way because you know me?*, tore the page out and gave it to him. The train was pulling into the curve at Union Square. It stopped and Paul flitted off, stumbling in disbelief at the words on the paper. Carol waited for the express to continue on its way uptown but the doors of the car remained open. There was a fire in the tunnel up ahead and the station was full of smoke. He got off.

His primary errand on the Lower East Side had been to find the Home Planet Bookstore, and the encounter on the subway train was like a neon sign saying Do It Now. He walked down Avenue A and crossed Tompkins Square Park. A month before, while he was still shacking with Yvetot, he found the address in a tiny ad in the *East Village Other*. Now, as he was about to actually locate the objective, a residual acid rush came on and he started hallucinating a respiratory paralysis right there on the street. He leaned against an abandoned car, folded, and grasped his knees. Somebody tossed a crumpled True pack right in front of him and a dealer—an Ivy-League type, a regular poodle-faker he was—came out of a doorway together with a couple of cats and approached him. Carol felt a friendly arm on his shoulder and a tin of Peak Frean's Pontefract Cakes was held under his nose. Then a gloved hand opened the cake tin and a voice said, "You look like you could use a perker-upper, pal."

The cake tin was full of amyl nitrate ampules. He stood upright and tried to push past the dealer but the two cats—raccoon coats from Grizzly Furs—crowded him in. The dealer chuckled, "Let's see how long you can hold your breath."

Carol gave the cake tin a hard left and amyl nitrate ampules sprayed popping all over the sidewalk. The three creeps reflexively dove for their dope as Carol scrambled through the stripped coachwork and dashed down the other side of the street.

He stood on the corner catching his breath. A wild dog gave him the once-over. Then he crossed Avenue C and went into a grocery store called Lothar's Appetizings. The owner, another white man, glowered at him from behind the meat case.

"I'd like a dill pickle, please," said Carol.

"Anything else?"

"Yes, and a cherry pepper, please."

There was an old book printed in French and English about the exploration of a certain island south of New Zealand. Conway's Island. A peculiar reptile had been discovered living there. The creature was about two-thirds the height of a man, had a back humped like a dromedary's, stout stubby legs like a baby elephant's, and a short neck with a triangular head having a feebly pendulous upper lip resembling a tapir's. The party of explorers were among some aborigines who mockingly described, in their own language, such civilized techniques as Decca navigation and radar. There was neither anchorage nor beach, and the men had to leap up onto the cliffs from the boat which was nearly crushed. In the interior of the island they came upon a landscape in greenish twilight. Rocks. No trees at all. As they looked, the rocks became a closely-nested herd of the reptiles, which moved lethargically, silently. It could be seen that the animals were licking from one another's backs a kind of green fungus that appeared to be their only nourishment. There was another illustration from the book. It showed an aborigine child, a little boy with a large oval wound in his chest in which was growing a brightly colored worm or snake.

The bookstore was on one of those Lower East Side streets that have an air of Old New York in their easy facades. The area had once been a bustling waterfront. It was here, at a shipyard on the East River, that the schooner yacht *America* was built.

"This is a New York poem." Shem looked up from the handwritten sheets and smoothed them with the edge of his palm. "Is it a love poem?"

Carol blushed. "Yes," he said, "but I don't know if it's for anybody in particular. I like the triad effect, where the last word rhymes with the first. It's monumental."

The old poet leafed through the stack. "That's what this city needs. A memorial to Love. Something besides The Cloisters."

The place was so full of déjà vu Carol felt like he was generating the moment out of his head. He assayed the sensation with the others to make sure it wasn't merely one of Yvetot's aftereffects. Shem's old lady Dora smiled.

"It's a plasma," she explained. "It's like an invisible machine performing mathematical functions, deterministic only insofar as you are unaware of it or don't know how it works, how to ride the vector, so to speak, or change the values at will . . ."

Dora was from Montana. People assumed her poetry was a derivative of Shem's, details from the large painting that was his work, while it happened that she regarded poetry as a kind of kinetic sculpture and wrote using an altogether different interface of means. She honored Carol with her expoundings.

"Once you get on it you find yourself engineering coincidences, finding goodies laid aside for you in time. Oh, it isn't invisible like the wind. The parts refract in moving and alter so you see prismatic auras. It takes some getting used to, always remembering to work good instead of evil with it. I don't know whether it's possible to work power with it, though some of the things you read in the papers . . . If you get to the point where you're setting up coincidences in the past you'll be surprised at first at some of the ridiculous tricks of memory. Sometimes there are two sources of time, and the refractions are prismatic in some planes and mirrorlike in others..."

"It isn't a question of working power," Shem pshawed. "It's a question of place. The Indians called it a power spot."

"But Shem, the UFO radiates time. That's why it stalls cars and makes the lights go out."

"I thought it radiated pussy. It does, doesn't it? Doesn't the UFO radiate pussy? I can prove it."

"But Shem, we are creatures of free will. We are astral bodies too, like the Earth and the stars."

"The Earth doesn't exist. Not in our civilization. That's why it isn't anywhere in classical mythology, and anyway I thought it was Jewish girls that make light bulbs go out."

"Classical mythology? You're a pretty heavy poet, ain't you? The kind that deserves a depth job once in a while."

"Whaddya mean a depth job? We're on the Lower East Side, ain't we?"

The two adored each other. Their arguments were an entertainment they put on to astonish new acquaintances, who were expected to weigh in like an old house guest and take up with the one or the other's cause. She was making coffee, Maxwell House Instant in white glass mugs from Woolworth's basement. She paused in her preparations while the water came to a boil. It was one of those electric coils you put in the pot. She lighted a cigarette, rose on tiptoe while jabbing at the air with the glowing end.

"I mean you're like all American men of your generation and origins. Your mothers put braces on your teeth and gave you enemas, and so you keep your mouths shut and your bowels open. It's in your politics like it's in your poetry. It's all a lot of crap."

She unplugged the coil and put it on a plate alongside a pizza crust. The dark foaming in the mugs. "Hawk!" she called. "Coffee!"

"You should read Carol's poetry," Shem said adroitly. "You should hear him read. Feel like a poetry reading in Greenwich Village, Mister Gamewell?"

The store had a corner at the annual comic book convention at the Statler-Hilton. Somebody was in back emptying cardboard boxes and stacking the comic books on shelves. At Dora's call he stopped and came up front. Carol had seen him before. One side of his body was smaller than the other and he limped intricately—like a dance step, Carol thought. He perched on a kitchen stool and grinned lopsidedly at Carol. "Time has ticked a heaven round the stars," he said.

"The Fuckwind Hawk," said Shem, introducing them. "Hawk, this is Carol Gamewell."

"Hi. I know your book," he said, nodding toward the racks of poetry magazines and Home Planet broadsheets. The four sat for a moment looking out the store window at the street which the wind was using for a wind tunnel. A whole Sunday *Times* peeled off somewhere and passed noisily in contraptioning sections. It was starting to snow.

"Vernon Valley is a mountain," said Hawk. He blew on his coffee and looked at Carol. "I never forget a face. Don't you live at the Albert?" Carol nodded. "So do Dora and Shem," said Hawk.

"I've never seen either you or them there," said Carol. "We must keep different hours."

"We never use the elevator," said Dora, laughing. "We use the grand staircase."

"Did you ever get mugged in an elevator?" said Shem.

"I didn't know there was a grand staircase at the Albert," said Carol.

"Sure. Nobody ever uses it except us," said Dora, "and an occasional zombie. Remember the bum on the landing?"

"Christ," said Shem. "I thought it was a stiff." And then he improvised, chuckling,

> "Twice 'neath a twilit hollyhock
> On the Tottenville Rubber Stamp
> Mrs. Fish and old man Brollygock
> Were imposed upon by a tramp . . ."

"Do you remember," he said, putting his arm around Dora's waist, "the kind of stuff you were writing when we first met? The itty-bitty poems?"

"Oh don't," she said in a throaty East Seventies contralto. "It was at Tinker's and it's embarrassing."

"Remember the jug full of dimes behind the bar?"

"It wasn't a jug. It was an ice-cream cone jar."

"We went home to your place. You showed me your typewriter."

"What about it?"

"You bragged about it, said it was a druggist's model. What was it? An Olivetti?"

"It was a Maserati."

"Too bad it got ripped off. Let's hope it's being used for its intended purpose."

"Will you stop belittling me?"

"You? You come from Big Sky country. For instance, you taught me what a shadow rider is. A cowboy who rides along admiring his own shadow..."

"Yes, and a grub-line rider."

"Yeah. A goddamned freeloader. I'm not belittling you, Dora. I'm ratifying you. For instance, what you said about the two sources of time reminds me of something I was thinking the other day. I have sometimes wondered whether there aren't two kinds of time. Really. Is what accounts for the curve of space not like the principle involved when you cause gift-wrap ribbon to form curlicues—that is, by flattening one side in relation to the other? Do you follow me? When I was a kid I earned money by watering people's lawns for them while they were on vacation. There was a water shortage every summer, which meant I had to do it at night. You know, a shadow cast through mist is three dimensional. Imagine a streetlight throwing shadows of the sycamores through mist made by a rapidly rotating lawn sprinkler, and if you've got a porch light and azaleas... remember in *The Divine Comedy*?

> *"Voi potete andare—*
> *e ritrarre a color che vi mandaro,*
> *che 'l corpo di costui è vera carne.*
> *Se per veder la sua ombra restauro..."*

"Hey, my man!"

A figure disengaged itself from the group huddling around the oil drum. They were homeless men, and they had built a bonfire in the drum out of broken packing crates and old furniture. It made a sphere of light in the snowstorm the color of orange sherbet and the figure, silhouetted in the glow, seemed to caper as it approached him.

"Hey, my man! Don't walk away from me like that. You look like you

The Banks of the Sea 77

walkin around wid pure love. Money talks, nobody walks. You get yourself a steed or they won't let you breed. Feedback squeal, automobile, an a kinky deal gets a funky meal. You look like you walkin around wid a love poem. You let your love keep you warm an it'll go in the gobbadge insinuator. Tha's right. Gansevoort Pier gobbadge insinuator. Jump in the river. A good man serves his widowland. Hey, my man! Don't brush me off like that. Johnny Haruka needs you for his money games. He'll give you a love you can carry works for, a star you can take a fix on, an itch a finger can't scratch and a hurt a pill can't reach. Git you a two year hitch walkin round on de edge ob reality. If you don't like the street get it off your feet. Ride a limmazeen to the hotel scene. You dig me? My man, you know what I'm talkin about? Shell shock bed wetter. Hudie Leadbetter. Go your home and write your poem. Go to Bellevue and get warm. The Bellevue gobbadge insinuator. Get warm like Sam. Sam McGee. He he . . . Put your ass away."

Imogen was in love with Carol but he didn't know it. One day he picked up a girl in Washington Square Park. It was a sunny winter Monday morning and she was walking her dog, a part-collie bitch named Scaffy. Suddenly she sat down beside Carol on the curb of the fountain and asked if she could look at the other half of his *Times*.

"Heyday Krengel. What has four legs and eats ants?"

"Two uncles."

She was blonde as the Christmas bawn and her cheery breasts were full of the beestings. What a lucky fellow I am, thought Carol, fondling them in his room. Heyday pulled off her sweaters. It was like sunlight bathing everything.

"Whew!" she said, standing there in her jeans and stocking feet. "Ooof!"

Carol lifted her up and deposited her on the sagging double bed that sounded like a screen door. They laughed and rolled around and soon their pants were off and Carol was playing with her wet milk pod. Scaffy yipped and pranced. Heyday giggled, spread-legged angel, and Carol got on top of her and it went in with almost startling alacrity. In a few minutes they came, like miners finding the vein again.

They are Carol and a blonde girl giving each other head flowers. They close their eyes and see things. The head flowers Heyday gives him include color images reminiscent of American Indian cult objects and pictures of a scientific installation such as a particle accelerator. He wonders about them, but doesn't say anything to her about them. He wonders who she's been balling. They have a good time.

They got around to the sandwiches and beer from the deli on University Place.

"What's a guy like you doing living in a dump like this?" she asked, sitting naked eating her half of the roast beef on rye.

"It's cheap," he said. "The Bowery hotels are cheaper but they don't allow women. And anyway, it's an interesting place. Did you know the desk staff are Haitians?"

Just then the phone rang. He picked up the receiver, listened for a minute and said, "Hey. How'd you like to shit a watermelon?"

"It's those damned kids," he said, hanging up. "They keep ringing me up at odd hours and giggling."

"Why don't you find out where they live?" she suggested. "Take them to Radio City or something."

"Maybe that's where they live."

"Come on. Nobody lives in Radio City."

"Just a buncha tubes."

Scaffy begged decorously and Heyday gave her a corner of her pastrami. She got up and went over to the desk and got a pack of cigarettes out of her jacket pocket. There was a battered typewriter. She touched a key. "Did the room come with this?" she asked.

"I found it on the street," he said. "It was sitting on top of a garbage can on Avenue B."

"Can it write?"

"The Z key sticks. It was snowing and I carried it home on my shoulder and stood it on the radiator. When it was dry I cleaned the type with Clar-O-Type and lubricated the mechanism with a graphite compound called Lock Ease. Sure it can write. It's a Remington Rand. All it needed was a new ribbon."

"Not bad," she said, patting the machine. "What's that?"

He had fished something out of his watch pocket and was showing it to her. It was a tarnished nickel.

"The platen was jammed," he said. "I found this under it."

The room was bright from the snow on the fire escape and the smoke from their cigarettes swirled like fluid marble. She cleared her throat.

"Do you write poetry on it?"

"I've never been able to write poetry on a typewriter. I use it to type them out from notes, and for writing letters."

"Do you write letters on a typewriter?"

"I know you think it's uncouth," Carol laughed, "but I do. Don't you?"

"I don't write letters," she said, shrugging. "When you were in Vietnam, didn't they think it was a little, er, queer that you wrote poetry? I mean the other guys."

"Oh, sure. But I called it doing my fornookies."

"Your fornookies?"

"Sure. I'd say, 'Forgot to do my fornookies today,' whipping out my notebook and ballpoint."

She laughed. But then she narrowed her eyes and said, "You like to live dangerously, don't you?"

"I was wounded in Vietnam," he said. "I got hit in the head by shrapnel. It knocked me literally cockeyed and I can't take drink. Two beers and I'm shellacked." He finished his beer, looked at the bottle a minute, then tossed it into the wastepaper basket. "One time my locker was broken into and my notebooks got stolen. Shit. There's a lot of thievery in the Navy."

She nodded. "Is this a poem?" She craned on the rickety chair and read from the sheet of paper in the typewriter:

> *"The Goslar and the ashlar*
> *And lovage tall with the poplars..."*

He explained. "It's some images from when I was in Europe. Goslar is an old German gingerbread town in the Hartz Mountains. It isn't a poem. I was just playing with words."

Heyday was nodding her head in impatience. "Okay. A small town in Germany. What's an ashlar?"

"Ashlar is hewn stone masonry. An ashlar is a hewn stone."

"Fine, and what's lovage?"

"Guess."

"Come on. You're the poet."

She didn't like his fornookies. She didn't like it that he had found the Remington Rand. It blew her mind. She thought he was a Hartz Mountain canary, that he made a practice of sending poems to friends, alien friends who read secret messages in them. The little couplet, for example, could alert a reader to something or someone—the "lovage" —having to do with the U. S. Strategic Air Command facility at, not Gosport, but Limestone, Maine. Or some such far fetch. Or simply, by inference, the Hartford Locomotive and Steam Boiler Insurance Company. In other words, in other words. If the medium was the message then paranoia was the medium. Writing as art was tolerable only if it were a vehicle—like the carrier wave whose amplitude or frequency is varied in order to transmit a radio or television signal—for the proper communication, and the poet was a functionary. A cipher clerk.

"Lovage is a six-letter word." He grinned. "By the way. I'm saving the nickel for a ride on the Staten Island ferry."

"Oh..."

Her pussy was soft and explosive as cattails and it seemed to fill the dingy room with prismatic gossamer. Objects were beautiful. The dog lay asleep in a pool of light. The dripping faucet was a sculpture. The place where her breast and arm joined was so lovely he could imagine wanting to become it. He told her so, his wrist pressing into her moist sex, and realized his fancy by making love to her. He saw the Norwegian flag. She hadn't thought he would be so nice. For some reason it made her mad. Maybe it was because she thought he had gotten something from her for his poems. More likely it was something she saw. She could have seen the Vale of Tralee.

She lived deep in Little Italy, on Sullivan Street. Carol walked her home. Her dog was obstreperous in the park, ran off with a circus of other dogs, the owners' voices sharp as snapped towels. McDougal. Bleecker. Another block south and all at once she tied the dog to an alternate parking sign and took him inside a building. He was immediately struck by the hen-house smell of it. In the high, dimly-lighted space—it must have been a garage—he could make out tiers of crates of live rabbits and poultry. A human family were there, father, mother, little boy, and they spoke Italian. They told a man wearing a bloody apron what they wanted. They wanted a bunny, there, in that cage, that one. The butcher obliged. He reached an arm into the cage and pulled out the rabbit, took it into an adjoining room with picture window, laid it on a block and brained it with a pick handle. Then he hung it up over a bucket by its hind legs and gutted and skinned it.

Carol drew her away and out into the daylight. The dog was strange and licked at them. He tried to catch her eye. When at length she met his gaze he winked at her and said, "Fussy meat department."

The blue jay liked Ritz crackers. It wasn't as keen on date-nut loaf. At first he was reluctant to open the window because the radiator couldn't be turned off. The astonishing bird looking him in the eye from out on the fire escape with an intensity that made his hackles rise. He registered the situation. It was like a painting of the Annunciation. The bird flew away, returned on the day the chambermaid did the room. Fresh, threadbare towels on the bureau. She told him about a man she had found sitting dead in front of the TV. He wanted to ask her if she knew voodoo. Then it occurred to him that he could keep his milk out on the fire escape. While he was sitting at the typewriter, all at once the saucy hail. He opened the window and the wild bird came and sat on his hand like any Harald Square pigeon. It was so beautiful he could scarcely believe it. He called to it and it came and perched on his thumb and took a cracker from his other hand. Once it came inside the room and sat on his shoulder and they passed the time of day. He called it Chatterjee. It liked to nip at his thumb, and when it was sitting on his hand he was amazed at how much it weighed. Every day for a week it came to the window while he was working, and after a jabber flew away with a Ritz cracker in its beak. Then it flew away and he never saw it again.

Luë opened the window on the mirror-eyed ovoid faces of the clangorous morning.

"I have more to do than twiddle my thumbs," he said, as accurately as language drift would allow. There was the reply; an answering flash came from a train window on the bridge. Buoys and craft, river commerce from the old technique and Best of Earth girls. His heart sank as he closed the window again. Then, turning in the desolate room, he caught sight of Malene and was filled with home.

"Oh, love," he said, overjoyed. Dorrit got up and put her arms around him.

"Who did it, Luë?" she said.

"It's the tall buildings," he replied. "They aren't a monument to the triumph of the human spirit. They are smoking idols of the credit finance system, strutted up by metallurgy and with skins of mud brick, swarming with functionaries who are paid to cut each other's hair. The priests of this bloodthirsty devotion, the brokers, are all puppets of their chauffeurs, whose brothers are hoods. You can see their limousines each lunch time thronging the streets of the financial district like dung beetles, coming to take the brokers to their clubs. The apartments of the middle functionaries have a mock fireplace with a false chimney, like the false door in an Egyptian tomb through which the soul was thought to come and go at its pleasure, and the inhabitants, contemporary and with great shame, apology almost, toss burnt rags and strips of dirty laundry as offerings into these soul holes, sometimes honeycombed with an old gas heater, for the catchall cat. These citizens cultivate the ritual imbibing of dry martinis that they are said to call 'silver bullets,' perhaps aware that a silver bullet is what the Haitian tyrant had to kill himself with."

River City. Tall baby, imbued with straw, awning the buckwheat enemy. Caulked the plimsolled clogs of Gargantua when manna was plentiful and sphagnum scarce as saffron. Tall tugboat, *Erwin L. Bush,* towing a string of heavies on the whitehat Hudson. New York Trap Rock Co. Bucket yard barge of boxcars for Hoboken. Garbage scow from 125th Street for the recycling mills of Yokahama. The aircraft carrier *White Plains,* known to her crew as "the swinging vicar of New Paltz," was the first ship of her class to be launched. She swooped over the waves like a ruptured duck and her unique hull lines made her appear to have been moulded from soya fibre. Indeed, all the ball bearings in her were furnished by the Fafnir factories in an advertising gesture reminiscent of the famous Timken steam locomotive. The crew slept in matrimonial hammocks in the high and airy compartments as General Electric fans sassed them implacably, and the gedunk boasted an expresso machine with an eagle on it. The gunner's mate was

The Banks of the Sea 83

drinking shaving lotion which he had just filtered through a loaf of bread. "Whew!" he said, wiping his chin. "Man! Did I ever tell you about the time we made a platter kill at Painted Post?"

Considered one of the most important and interesting objects of naval memorabilia in America, this figurehead of Andrew Jackson was carved for the U.S. frigate *Constitution* by the noted Boston woodcarver Laban S. Beecher in 1834. During the summer of that year Captain Samuel Dewey, an adventurous anti-Jacksonian, slipped aboard "Old Ironsides" one stormy night and, in spite of heavy guard as the ship lay moored in Boston harbor, sawed off the head and sneaked away with it in a canvas bag. The *Constitution*'s captain, Jesse D. Elliot, sailed to New York with the figurehead flag-draped. There a new head was carved by Dodge & Son. The repaired figure remained on this historic ship for more than forty years. Gift of the Seawanhaka Corinthian Yacht Club.

Ding *dank,* went the bellbuoy. Ding *dank.* All the bottoms anchored in the bay. Wasn't there another Staten Island, down at the bottom of the world? South of South Georgia Island. The spur of Cape Horn. No put-in or anchorage. Unspeakable snaggle crags concealed in icy fog driven by ceaseless antarctic winds. What the incentive? Ships running under clewed tops'ls, crews brought together by the *lackanookievolkerwanderungen.* "American cargoes in American bottoms," says Cap'n Mike, dropping a man-sized mouse turd kerplonk into the flooded mineshaft. What was it Caitlin Thomas called American girls?

He liked Tottenville. Serene, spick-and-span middle-Atlantic idyll. What a pleasant goal for a forenoon's excursion. The postman on his rounds. A calico cat in a window. An old Christmas tree with a spill of tinsel on it in a front yard. The streets bore the names of shipping companies from the days of the Yankee clippers. Aspinwall Street. There was a salty, romantic atmosphere in the little town, a part of New York City, and Carol could imagine himself living there. He went inside the grocery store. There was a stack of home-baked apple turnovers on a sheet of waxed paper on the counter and he bought a couple. Then he walked quickly to the station and made the next train back to St. George.

He sat on the edge of the seat looking out the train window. There was an old ferryboat he had noticed on the way out and he wanted to get a better look. Maybe he would come out here again sometime and go aboard her, though she was likely a place where the local Cannon Fodder Reserve went to use drugs, half-beached as she was on the Perth Amboy Channel. Mary Tierny, said his mind's ear, though the name on the wheelhouse was indiscernible. Sweet ship. Brass and mahogany, smokestack askew. Mary Tierny. She had set her bonnet for somebody.

Henry Brewster. Was in food processing, perhaps one of the companies the Greyhound Corporation had diversified into. Lived in Great Neck, say. Worked in Manahatta. Younger daughter a freshman at Walt Whitman High.

Henry got home and opened the door of his house, opened it on his wife who happened to be out in the hall for some reason. She looked like Ghisela Scapegoat dressed as a Siamese attack pumpkin.

"Hi, Marie."

He dropped his briefcase, which was built to take it, and they embraced. She covered him with kisses and took his hat and coat. Marie was wearing a sleeveless tantrack pants suit, a blue polka-dot scarf in her red hair, an amber choker, and black loafers with silver chains across the instep to ward off werewolves.

"Supper's ready in a minute. Braised tidbits."

"Hmm. What's that on the TV?"

"*The Marylou Show.* I'm not watching it."

Lou: Wanna play lion?
Mary: What's that?
Lou: You get down on the floor and growl and I'll throw the meat to you.
Rival Couple: Him: He wants to be boss.
                    Her: That's not a job. It's a position.

Canned TV laughter. Dog saliva music. A lamp overturning. Henry turned it off and went in to see his daughter.

"Come on in and park your carcass," she said. "My stomach feels as though somebody had opened an umbrella in it."

Frances Brewster sitting there in bed like the potato in the exhaust pipe. She's got porcelain pull and that ain't no bull. She had one of her grandmother's blue china plates with the pig snouts on the tree trunks and was nibbling at a rusk. He kissed her on the forehead.

"Here's your reading matter," he said, handing her the flat paper bag

The Banks of the Sea 85

from the newsdealer. He sat down in her Bikini overstuffed. "How're you doing, girl?"

"Just fine, Daddy. And thank you for the *Seventeen* and the *Grit.*"

The cat rose from the foot of her bed, stretched and showed Henry what the inside of his mouth looked like. Fran was ready with a brewer's yeast tablet and Wiggy begged and received. A cat will stand up for brewer's yeast, which sort of makes you wonder about a girl who is on both brewer's yeast and iron tablets. There's bound to be some fusel oil produced in there somewhere. Fran the hardon-browed unicorn roat. He caught her making eyes at his moustache. The girl's mother came in with her food on a tray. Frances mush mouse.

"As for you," he said to Marie as they sat down opposite each other at the candle-lit table (the cute reminder elephant on the buffet almost made him forget what he was going to say), "we're going to coronoleum the congoleum, Lilly, of cuprinoleum tonight."

Marie was one of those old-fashioned deeply satisfying push-button-type lightswitches. She's as efficient as a gas refrigerator, thought Henry, digging into the Libra boss's pent-up oyster mantle shirts and ties. A slice of kidney vibrated on Wiggy's claw like the safety valve of a pressure cooker. He played with it, ate it, purring through his teeth, and used his box. Then sat on the floor with a straight tail and licked his belly.

"If you're so good why did Hewlett-Packard almost give you the heave ho?"

"Because Artesian Honeywell had the hots for me."

He had a favorite kitchen chair he liked to sharpen his claws on and one leg of it was shredded. They were a popular Mexican import, ladder-backed and with rush bottoms and made of soft, unpainted wood. Henry and Marie were putting the dishes in the dishwasher when Fran barefooted in and stood leaning against the kitchen doorjamb. She was wearing a flannel nightgown and she scratched a calf with a big toe. One of her guppies was going to have babies.

"Go in your room, dear, and Daddy will come and fix your vaporizer."

Afterwards Henry sat in his easy chair in front of the bookcase and read the local paper.

... Many highly efficient machines are built for pastry making, ovens for making "pizza," mixing and blending machines, filling machines for pastries; there are fruit candiers, butter and sugar blenders, nutchoppers, automatic sweet roll makers and machines for marzipan making.

A company in Bologna, for example, is specialized in the fabrication of machines turning out peanut candied bars and in the building of devices for other nut candies, barley candies, almond creams, etc. Another firm makes only blenders for fine powders like flour, potato starch, leavening, milk flour, cocoa, etc.

These blenders have rotating devices for total mixing and automatic electronic devices to invert rotation along with timers. Italian machines in this sector are guaranteed for absolute hygiene in processing operations.

Customers are among Third World countries, as well as among highly industrialized countries like those of the Common Market or the United States.

Another important feature of Italian machines of this type is the ease of maintenance combined with highest possible automation . . .

Marie came in from the kitchen and said, "Henry." A scissors grinder was singing a song outside. People were opening their windows. Pretty soon the scissors grinder came to the back door and Henry let him in. He looked like John Jacob Niles wearing an old pair of women's slacks. The cat was nowhere to be seen.

Scissors Grinder: I'll sharpen anything you have that's smaller than a lawnmower.

Henry: How about a Ronson electric carving knife?

Scissors Grinder: If you like.

Marie had come up with all the blades in their kitchen, including the old knives from the back drawer where she kept such things as a nutmeg grater and a brace of shish-kebab skewers.

Marie: Here. The Ronson'll take care of itself.

Scissors Grinder: Shears? Garden tools?

Henry: Too much trouble to fetch.

Scissors Grinder: Keys you want copied?

Henry: Good thing you said that.

Marie: And here's a pair of nose scissors.

The scissors grinder had his setup in the back of an old panel truck. The all-night children were out there watching him. His fingers were spatulate and knew how to be deft without getting in the way. The sparks flew and he sang.

> "I've got a knife
> As old as me mutter.
> It'll cut anything
> 'cept cookies and butter..."

Henry looked in on Frances. She was asleep in her bed with the vaporizer hissing and aquarium light on. She was his whole world. Her breathing was very apparent, almost animated, under the covers. Fran the pomegranate. Her meaty seeds would be enjoyed by birds when their beaks had evolved to her. She was an apple on an unreachable bough over a stream, the fact of snow and the accident of milk...

Carol was rewarded for these reveries by a covey of high-school girls getting on the train at Great Kills. They rollicked giggling around the car and he flirted with them. One of them, a rosy-cheeked, blue-eyed brunette, sat down beside him and took the wad of chewing gum out of her mouth and let him feed her some of his apple turnover. She was warm and cuddly and smelled like spearmint, and her hair smelled good. She stuck her gum under the seat and skittered off to her girlfriends. Were they playing hookey? Their mothers doing the ironing in front of the TV watching "Daughter of Darkness." She reminded him of Yvetot. The answer came like the clap of revelation. They were witches and this was the homeland which the founding fathers, in their enlightenment and freemasonry, created for them.

Not that he pictured George Washington praying to the Devil, or the Rotarians or the Lions Club going about conjuring Asmodean spirits at their meetings. Fourth of July parades. The drill teams. The lodges, ladies' auxiliaries in white oxfords. His grandfather was not an evil man. Or was he? Once his mother fumed over the old guy's "farting around," whatever that meant. And he didn't wear a fez like Major Hoople, even though one of his First World War buddies had been mustard-gassed and didn't have a chin like Andy Gump. Every Sunday the First World War invalids in the local VA hospital were brought to the ball park in their wheelchairs to watch the double-header. He thought of Germany, where "they had Jews scrubbing the sidewalks with their eyebrows." What Hitler accomplished in ten years using twentieth-century technology. The fact was that by the 1700s, since the invention of polyphonic music at the cathedral of Notre Dame in Paris in the thirteenth century, some nine million people had perished in the holocaust of the witch hunts. America was a land of secret societies, interlocking signals passed like a perfumed handshake, the Three Kings of Orient R and Mickey Mouse as the sorcerer's apprentice. Rigmarole and deadpan tomfoolery in the copes and chasubles of wizards, ceremonial aprons, kilts, satin jellabas and hairdresser's sanbenitos. The opiate of the American people may be the church but their religion was the lodge. Politics was conducted not in smoke-filled rooms but from hermetic chambers and the freedoms of the open society were but the hoopla of a Shriners' circus.

sanbenito *n.* (pl. -s.) Penitential scapular-shaped yellow garment with red St Andrew's cross before & behind worn by confessed & penitent heretic under Spanish Inquisition; similar black garment painted with flames & devils worn by impenitent heretic at auto-da-fé. (Spanish, from *San Benito*—St. Benedict—shaped like scapular introduced by him.)

"Shine, Mister?"

It was one of the shoeshine kids who worked the ferries. Gave Carol's old desert boots a treatment with the brass suede brush. Instead of exterminating witches make them work, like James Bond, who was a thrall witch. The idea must have arisen during the Thirty Years War. Old Cardinal Richelieu. Introduced the use of passports and put a tax on tobacco. Slapped a lien on Maybelline. Carol slipped the shine a frogskin. There were a fair number of passengers. A scratchwork frieze of Americans sitting with their legs crossed fallen from some mud cornice and a whole waiting room full of nigger bodhisattvas. Shit, man. Old Solomon did. Used demons and spirits to build the temple in Jerusalem.

Puerto Ricans. Another people come on the rumor of a chance to

The Banks of the Sea

love. The edge of the world was Ellis Island, all of them sailing over the edge, actually falling in the biblical sense. People who haven't fallen aren't worth a vellum poker chip because you can't get a purchase on them. But the allure of America. The feeling of authenticity. Maybe it was the Katanga copper in the Statue of Liberty.

Odd, how pervasive the order was. The expression *to make a girl* came from the Masonic to "make" someone, to convert him to freemasonry.

How incredibly beautiful the Manhattan skyline was. It seemed somehow alien, like a quirk of geology.

Take the back of a dollar bill. The great seal of the United States was shown with the front on the right hand side as though reading from right to left. The eagle. The name of a deodorant. Right Guard. The word *one*. Then the reverse of the seal. A pyramid capped by an eye. What did it mean? It was Masonic symbolism. But pictorially it could represent every large city in America. The tall buildings topped with television. Or a taxi radio, like the Chanin Building. Or simply a red eye winking its communication.

Steam wisped from a roof into the frosty sky. An outbound ferry blew its whistle and the sound was batted around in the skyscrapers of the witches.

Harry Truman was a Mason and he was from Missouri, and his own grandfather had an elk's tooth on a gold watch chain. They weren't evil men. After all, the Odd Fellows weren't the Malevolent and Fraternal Exploitive Order of Vampires. Be that as it may, Carol too had a dream, unutterably lovely, of beatification in the breezy colonnade of the Masonic Valhalla, where your old man, who was a good guy all his life, is.

Not a Howard Johnson's mansion, thirty-one flavors notwithstanding, but something overlooking the Potomac. Not the Lee place, where they buried the Union dead in the front yard, but a place up the river. In the twilight of the western sun, to sit on the porch and watch the river become a streak of indigo at the bottom of the dark lawn and the eastern star come out. The lamp is lighted. Then you go inside, passing through the double seal, to the Dark Lady of Shakespeare and Mozart who is young and dewy-limbed. You may look back, but don't break the seal, the Egyptian double tutelaries smiling.

(Cream playing "Strange Brew.")

"Cream! Hey, Disc Person, how are you?"

"Awright, Jon."

"I wasn't here yesterday. I was on tape. And here you are. Back from Baton Rouge, Louisiana?"

"No. Uh, where is Baton Rouge anyway? Is that near, uh..."

"Clear out in the woods... Well, you're from New Orleans."

"Louisiana State. Isn't Baton..."

"Where did you spend your vaca..."

"From nine and one..."

"Ha, ha, ha..."

"No bull."

"Where'd you spend your vacation?"

"Actually I went to Atlanta, and then to Nassau, and not Nassau County."

"Why Atlanta?"

"To a radio symposium. To discuss things that are happening in radio."

"I see."

"We discussed the Jonathan Schwarz show."

"I assume..."

"Briefly."

"I assume favorably. Favorably."

"Yes."

"Heh, heh, heh, heh, heh, heh, heh, heh. Welcome back, Mister Disc Person, and I ask you and everyone to be of good cheer. I'll be here tomorrow night. This is Jonathan Schwarz, just playing in the light of the Disc Person, all red faced and alcoholic."

"Kids like kids and mud pies."

"WNEW-FM, New York."

(The news.)

"Thank you. Scot Munie here on WNEW-FM, after Mister Schwarz and I traded a few words. Jonathan now winging his way home on, the wind? Yes."

Carol met Imogen at Grand Central. She had spent the day in Mt. Kisco at a shower for one of her old school friends. She thought he was in a peculiar frame of mind. They took a taxicab at the Vanderbilt

Avenue entrance.

"Did she like the old teapot?"

"She literally hugged it. She had it on her lap like a kitten."

"Did she scratch the bottom of it?"

"What do you mean?"

"Where I come from a teapot like that is called a guitar. You can get a ringing sound in your ear if you scratch it on the bottom. Wasn't there a man?"

"Of course not, silly. Or did you want to be there?"

"I'm no groom's proxy."

"What in the world are you talking about?"

"A shower. It's like a Tupperware party."

"A Tupperware party indeed!"

"You know what Dylan Thomas's wife called them."

"No I don't."

"When she saw the girls at Vassar, she said they looked like intellectual witches."

"Good God, Carol. Have you been drinking?"

In the eyes of the Housing Authority the building in Soho was industrial premises, and so the artists who, like Imogen, lived there in their lofts did so unofficially. Accordingly there was no Department of Sanitation garbage collection at the address.

"You may talk about giving dogs table scraps, but I don't particularly want to experiment on a dog I love."

At night the elevator was locked. Imogen used her little key and they descended. The dog's eagerness, sitting, standing up, sitting again, toenails articulate on the floor of the car. Carol, hoping they weren't leaking, hugged the bags from under the sink.

"Who'd want to experiment on ol' Hollister?" he said. Hollister licked his teeth and sneezed. Out through the dark lobby, the moon in the sky and on the sidewalk a patch of ice the size of the Empire State Building at fifty blocks.

A dog's nose is the tenderest most indispensable part of him, yet there it is right out front and in the way. The way a dog lives you'd think he was trying to get around that nose. According to ancient belief the moon was supposed to send dogs on the earth to obtain food for it, and the Ainus of Hokkaido believe the mother of their race was impregnated by a dog. Hollister, hackles raised and white as milkweed in the mercury arc, ranged on Kenmare Street, the world disappearing in the whirlpools of his nostrils.

"Oh you silly mature dog," laughed Imogen, hauling in on the long leash.

Night moochers. A truck passed jarring the pavement, shifted gears on the incline of the Williamsburg Bridge. A police car turned the corner, looked at them for a minute, and when it was out of sight Carol put the garbage bags in a public trash basket.

New York women speak as though embarrassed by their language, hoping it sounds like an obscure tooth-cavity French once in a while and at a distance and the pigeons wheel and wheel and break flight with a laughter of wings, yuk yuk. Imogen was so slim and tender, like a young girl at the awkward age. He held her face between his hands and marveled at the exquisiteness of her living, her white skin and the odor of her hair. Her fine gray eyes saw so much. Saw only him. She blushed and he kissed her. "You're beautiful," he said, and buried his face in her shoulder.

Oh Chatterjee. His room had been broken into, the lock forced and everything dumped on the floor. He was afraid his notebooks were gone, but they were intact. The poor Remington Rand, however, looked as if it had been broken up with a sledge hammer, like what the police used to do to slot machines they found in speakeasies.

He threw out all the food not in cans—the boysenberry jam, the peanut butter, the crackers, the fruit and the Vermont cheddar he bought at the place on Sixth Avenue—because he was afraid it might be drug contaminated. "Pappa Doc has one policeman for each citizen," Shem explained when Carol told him what had happened. "Which isn't bad. Something like a modest crew-passenger ratio on a cruise ship. You're still going to read on Friday, aren't you?"

The windup. The delivery. He asked Imogen if he could practice his rostrum on her. They were in his room and she thought he was too loud, that it disturbed the other hotel guests. "You needn't roar," she said.

They made love. That was when she asked him to live with her. "Maybe I'm still hung up on Yvetot," he said, feeling ashamed and enthralled. "She's just an old girlfriend of yours, that's all," she said. "Come on, Carol. Jump at the chance."

As realistic as any photographer, Imogen was an effective coaxer and with kissing tongue and knowing fingers she soon had Carol backed into a corner of the bed. "Come on," she said, stroking his hard-on. "You get plenty of these and I like them and what will happen to them if we're not together? Don't you like to be inside me? It's good, easy loving."

Carol just groaned and balled her again. Then they lay side by side on the sagging bed in a hotel room that was as scummed and grimy as if there had been a flood. Up in one corner the plaster had blistered through the layers of wallpaper and paint in a shape like a hardhat with a walkie-talkie. They heard jazz music.

She squeezed his hand and told him about a sculptor she knew. He was a Chinese guy, and he made monumental sculptures in his studio, a former bank building on the corner of Houston and Suffolk Street. One morning he was knifed to death on the sidewalk outside the door of his studio. She told him about the burglar alarm in her loft and the mugger button that set off a klaxon. There was a guy who had a loft on the Bowery and who was into electronic art. He installed burglar alarms in artists' studios and lofts all over Lower Manhattan. They were beautiful things. Exquisite kinetic concepts.

"What about Dora and Shem?"

"Oh Carol, they have their grand staircase."

Somebody was playing jazz on the cornet. Over and over again, the same figure from a riff. A diminished seventh arpeggio. A diminished seventh. A diminished seventh.

"Now?" said Carol.

"Right now."

He scrambled out of the bed and in half an hour had packed and checked out.

The reading was to be held at the Rienzi on McDougal Street. Carol and Imogen came early and had a bite to eat. They looked good together and made an entrance, Imogen bundled up and wearing sheepskin puttees crisscrossed with the thongs of her sandals. When they found a table Carol gallantly took her wrap and it could be seen that she was wearing a transparent chemise the color of lemon ice. She was carrying a promotion copy of *Men Working*. Carol ordered some of the Westphalian ham.

Poetry on a full stomach, after a stint of busking on the Continent. Potluck at Le Mistral in Paris. Munich, a bag of *Paprikaschoten* in the Englischer Garten. The Salvation Army Hostel in Great Peter Street, London. Being shaken awake on a bench in front of St. Paul's Cathedral. It was a bobby. "Good morning, sir. Just wanted to see if you were still warm." Too much poetry. Thought becoming reality. What the hyacinth imparted to the jasmine, admiring the pothandle for its usedness. The waitress must have been a dancer. At any rate she was wearing a black leotard. The Rienzi's cheesecake and a pot of jasmine tea. Dora and Fuckwind. The breathy hares tussling in a field and the plover's hawk lark, and now Shem was introducing Carol as an American poet of love and war. Beethoven raising his hand for silence. Carol stood up and recited.

> "What had I forgotten
> From when I used to sniff my fingers,
> Used to go around smelling old houses?
> Turds and flare stubs between the ties
> And I longed for a hot box
> My red flag ready
> And got lots of oily waste.
> Friends in my early lush
> Kept me from the flanges
> On the source side of the moon's
> Portage across the Pacific
> And I'd waited long enough
> Having never fucked my beloved
> To get it inside you.
> This is no hobby,
> No plaster of paris in a rubber mould
> Nor your ears' open hearth taking
> The coarse pigs of my discourse.
> I mean the fleet thoughts of the drowned,
> Reverberating in space,
> Flashed across your phosphor when this

> Impossible naval architecture let us down,
> You teething my hard reed.
> The instrument bleats,
> Bulkheads blister and buckle
> At the long quench
> Of your diehard stokehold."

There was a to-do in the hall. It was a couple and a friend of theirs, a girl with something on her head. The man was energetically strumming a mandolin and doing a little dance that made his dyed ostrich-feather headdress jiggle and sway. He was also wearing a rubber mask, but Carol knew who he was. It was somebody from Imogen's past who called himself Kier Ingoldsby and was a shrink. He ho-ho-ho'd like Santa.

"The hero with a thousand silly faces! Also," he said, taking off the Mardi Gras outfit, "der Katzenabend des schweizisher Weinachtskindern! Congratulations on the book. We just got back from Mexico. Lorna has a present for you."

He hugged Imogen as his wife—lots of silver and turquoise—unfolded a colorful heavy woolen blanket. Ingoldsby grabbed a corner of it. "We were in Guanajuato. We found a tribe of Indians who weave these."

"Why it's marvelous!" Imogen crowed, fingering it. "It's like a wolfskin. I'll hang it on the wall."

"Put it on the bed and see what happens," said Ingoldsby, winking to his wife as he eyed Carol. "So you're the poet."

"Put it on the floor," said Carol, ignoring him. "It's clean, and people like to sit on the floor at parties, like Indians."

"The floor it is," said Imogen. "And some pillows."

"But Imo," said Lorna in dulcet Bronx, "you didn't tell us he was the dominating type."

"The floor is your most valuable piece of furniture," Carol avowed.

"Not if it's fulla knots," retorted Ingoldsby. "Would you like a drink dear?" As he turned and headed for the liquor table it could be seen that there was a rectangular puff of powdered chalk on his coat as though somebody had thrown an eraser at him.

The buffet at Imogen's party was extraordinarily popular, and not on account of the Greek olives. Perhaps it was the bushels of steamed Nissequogue mussels or the *riistaffel*-like array of dips, the platters of stuffed avocados, fillets of smoked venison on a maple trencher. The trough of cold potato salad made with sour cream and fresh windowsill dill. The Liederkranz from before the factory burned down. A highlight of the evening was when one of Imogen's neighbors—a painter named Coddington—brought in a 16 mm projector and showed a stack of home movies bought at a rummage sale in Hoosick Falls.

"Her husband finally provided her with a home fit for her to receive her paramours in . . ."

"Servel came out with a model that had an electric outlet in the food chest. Very discreet, mind you. It wasn't mentioned in the booklet. Well this baby really started to move. Couldn't keep 'em on the floor . . ."

"A Snow Pup will clear your driveway in half the time and at a fraction of the cost."

"Kissing her is like trying to make toast with a dashboard lighter."

"One to warm up on," he said, tossing back a double bourbon. He peeled a Budweiser. "And one to keep cool on."

Barry Kiggins was, as he put it, a member of the over-forty club of unemployed nuclear physicists. His last job was at the State University of New York at Stony Brook. For the past two years he had been living off his savings. He wrinkled his nose. "An idle mind is the Devil's workshop."

"You're not serious," said Carol.

"See that guy over there? He'll stand on his head to make a deal with you."

"Where did you see that?"

"On channel seven. He stands on his head and swallows his tie."

There was an old Stan Getz number, a blues in waltz time. "News for Blueport." Later Carol danced with Barry's old lady.

Judith Schoolcraft was a painter, but from her efforts to burst through the limitations of the traditional canvas surface she had become involved in working with a form of textile sculpture. One of her pieces hung in Imogen's loft and every now and then Imogen, perhaps to effect a resolution in a train of thought, would walk up to it and turn it inside out.

He danced close with her. She smelled like temperas and new mercerizing. He complimented her on her potato salad.

"Do you know how Imogen got the pictures for *Men Working?*" she asked. Carol said he could imagine. "I don't know anybody like Imogen," she said.

"External effect versus internal structure. External manifestation versus internal process. Call it osmotic stress. He is expected to act on an emotion which is recognizably genuine. When the Aquarius..."

Kier Ingoldsby taught applied psychiatry at Columbia University. He and his wife lived in an apartment on Claremont Avenue, across from Barnard College, and they had a lodger, a young woman, whom they brought with them to Imogen's party.

"... the Aquarius," he said with a slight accent. It evoked in Carol's mind a Mexican cherman, or even a Brazilian cherman. An Albrecht Dürer etching of the Emperor Maximillian on horseback. Ach *so!* He pinned it down. Ingoldsby had studied in Zurich, and on the GI Bill into the bargain.

"... the Royal Hermaphrodite of the *opus alchymicum*..." He noticed Carol looking at his chammy-skin chief's shirt. He grinned. "It's from Abercrombie & Fitch. So far so good—eh, poet?"

As at many artists' parties, the hootch at Imogen's blowout was in half-gallon bottles from the state liquor stores of New Hampshire. Somebody put on a Stan Kenton LP. *Stan Kenton Plays Wagner.* Carol danced. The girls were getting good and juiced up and were fun on the slow numbers and he enjoyed himself. He danced with a woman named Caroline Winnarick who owned the gallery where Imogen had her shows.

"... an alcestuous relationship is abrewing in the big house and Hattie wants to dispel it. So she hustles out to her cabin and rattles some pots and pans, works some kind of ritual disguised as a household task. Something with the soup bone, say. The soup bone in doll's clothing. Maybe that's too overt. Or she takes a handful of cotton seeds and parches them on a dry skillet, turns her damper up so the smoke goes out into the room..."

"I'll say I will," affirmed Nyesmith, backing rump-first out of the kitchen. "Every mud civilization *scant*ling knows the authority of my turd!" Clegg was coming on strong, at last breaking the beer can he had been bending back and forth. "An Alsatian," he said, "the color of ripe bananas. I'm not sure he actually has sex with his mother but I know for a fact that he goes down on her."

She was holding a paper plate containing a plastic fork and part of a peeled half-avocado stuffed with shrimp curry salad. She put it down on the map table and cautiously touched the *objet.*

"What did you do, pound it with a sledge hammer?"

"I must have."

"And then mounted it on a slab of . . ."

"Men's room marble. With epoxy."

"I see. And what do you call it?"

"J2149886."

She picked up the paper plate again and took a bite of the avocado. She pursed her lips while chewing.

"Interesting," she said. "How much do you want for it?"

"A thousand dollars," Carol said.

"I'll give you a hundred."

>Cakes that jiggle and cakes that sway,
>Cakes that make all the jackasses bray.
>A cake as big as a manhole cover
>And one that'll make you a bad-ass lover.
>Cakes to cover the marble floors
>And a cake as big as the great outdoors.
>A cake as soft as American women
>And one you'd swear was water to swim in.
>Cakes with fingers and cookies with toes
>And a creme-filled bride with an edible rose . . .

"I hope she had the presence of mind to ask him his name."

He danced with Imogen again, and then with the Ingoldsbys' lodger. She called herself Thursday's Child.

Her silken hair was loose and she was wearing a crown of pentacles fashioned from mistletoe and apple blossoms. She told him she was at his poetry reading. He took her by the hand, led her into the darkroom and kissed her eyelids and blew on them. The noises outside were indistinct. A conch surf of voices, Soundcrafts jugging: *the hep burn, the hud nut, and the hubbub bub. The hubbub bub.* Carol turned off the red light and asked her where she got the apple blossoms. "From a tree in a parking lot," she replied. Oh, the things you can see when kissing a girl. A man has got to choose his Jerusalem.

". . . These systems have to be constituted in such a way that they offer the libido a kind of natural gradient. For the libido does not incline to anything, otherwise it would be possible to turn it in any direction one chose. But that is the case only with voluntary processes, and then only to a limited degree. The libido has, as it were, a natural penchant: it is like water, which must have a gradient if it is to flow. The nature of the analogies is therefore a serious problem because they must be ideas which attract the libido. Their special character is to be discerned in the fact that they are archetypes, that is, universal and inherited patterns which, taken together, constitute the structure of the unconscious . . ."

"Aw, for Christ's sake . . ."

"Come on, Barry . . ."

Judy Schoolcraft getting her old man home.

". . . If you aren't nice then all the nice things will disappear and there'll be nothing but meece and rubbish all over everything . . ."

U.S. Bureau of Standards . . . United States Government master specification for rubber ice bags . . . specification for helmet-shaped ice bags . . . One of the good things in life is waking up with a beaut and getting a little off the little woman.

And modern art advanced, but without the pitter-patter of little feet. Kiggins and Schoolcraft, Kier and Lorna; ask any of Imogen's couples friends and they would probably reply that they weren't ready to have children yet. Carol thought it was remarkable, like a folkway. West Village couples had kids and they put them in the Perry Street Kindergarten. But those people could levitate. One evening he saw a couple coming toward him on Bank Street and they were walking six inches above the ground. Funny. Somehow his sense of orientation was partially canceled whenever he sniffed around that neighborhood of Greenwich Village, went around smelling old houses. He would always wind up back on Abingdon Square as though impelled by a force field. The terminus of the Eighth Avenue bus line there. Lumbering vehicles looming out of the night. Once he almost got on one of them. Even in the daytime. One afternoon he must have spent an hour sitting in an empty church on West 11th Street. The children of the artists had to be someplace or other, maybe in another dimension; on a different time plane, and Nyesmith and Blankenship were charging admission.

It may be true that dogs dream in color-blind, but one night Carol had a particularly vivid dream which had a compelling effect as of a decision having been made for him. He dreamed he was walking out of a town in the early morning. The grass was green and dewy and birds were singing in the trees and he came upon a camp for psychically-gifted children. He walked inside and took a look around. There was the usual playground equipment—swings, seesaws and slides—and there were things too which resembled a miniature golf course with runways and mazes, and clatter-lath constructions that moved and could have been sculptures but obviously were appliances the children trained their psychic abilities on. They were familiar to Carol as models of his own street-wanderings. So that's how it worked: a kind of time plasma navigation. The children were all white or Asiatic and it was in America so the training camp, he reasoned in the dream, must be a private institution. Then the children, the lovely ESP progeny, woke up and found him and he was one of them, and it was all irresistible and erotic. He woke up with Imogen playing with his hard-on.

He told her about the dream. "It sounds like science fiction," he said, apologetically enthusiastic.

Imogen chewed on it. At length she said, "Don't be conned by your dreams."

"What do you mean?"

"That there's always a reason for joining the army, and a dream is as good as any. It's a recruiting pitch. An army marches on its stomach and a dream is usually something you ate."

"I think that's about right," he said.

She giggled and planted herself on top of him. She was wet, she was clean, she was his. "Do you know the old Chinese proverb?" she said.

"I guess so."

"Confucius say, Eat pussy and speak the truth."

"Why you sly she-weasel."

Imogen was delightful and Carol was happy living with her, but it was the One Toys that got him. They sound like a Chinese restaurant. He remembered what Yvetot told him about the people who give their children one toy on a certain Christmas and that toy lasts them the rest of their lives. They must be awfully ecology-minded. In fact, they are perfect. Such together little families and so anonymous you'd think the real Pope is a Hutterite in North Dakota. Carol, with nostalgia for something that hasn't been, wondered what that toy could be, for he was certain he had one coming, so long as he completed the course. Was it a seamless garment? Or a puzzle with a moral? A gold-plated Zippo? Or something as simple and forthright as a good wife? Imogen was addicted to her art. She would never be a little homemaker for, as the old Ipana toothpaste ad put it, "Can a model mother be a model mother?" So Carol, wanting the whole cookie, gave himself over to mooning around the city and following his warp.

His head felt like a half-rotten rutabaga held to some metaphysical grindstone in a mug shot photographer's brace. His ability to make sensible decisions was confined to finding survival choices in the situations the pinball slope of his yearning to have children with Yvetot seemed to empty him into. His intellectual functions were characterized by over-inclusive thinking and he had difficulty concentrating. In order to hold onto a feeling of being master of the situation he had recourse to personal habits learned in childhood: he was "tying his change up in his handkerchief," often with a herculean effort. (A cat's paw: Carol Gamewell's real mission is unknown to him. In buying, while thinking on Yvetot's cues, a combination of certain packaged groceries, he supplies an observer with the location of the Soviet Union's liquid helium factory.) He was sitting in a booth in a shoe repair place on Seventh Avenue while new soles and heels were being put on his boots. It was good to get off the street for a few minutes and sit in the warm locale. An old colored woman was in the next booth and she wanted to talk. All at once she balanced back on her buttocks and showed Carol her yam feet.

His beard smelled like the subway and he usually washed when he got back to the loft. One night he crawled into bed with Imogen and she woke up and said he smelled like the river.

The snow clouds looked like people's shadows that the witch had laundered and hung out to dry. It was a bitter cold March afternoon when Carol went in McSorley's and sat at a table beside the hot roaring stove. The old pub was redolent and muzzy, and lively for the early hour and uncrowded. There were old-timers reading the paper and having a pipe with their beer. There were many Irish. The sweet Irish, with names like birdcalls. Would they sing a song? Not now, for how shall we sing the Lord's song in a strange land? Let's drink awhile.

The obligatory two small mugs of draft. Carol drank the dark. The bartender deftly trimming the suds. King Twofer, he thought. At dusk another young man came in and stood at the bar, then sat down at the same table. He was drinking light. He opened a notebook and wrote in it and Carol, legitimately, wondered if he were an undergraduate.

"Are you a writer?" he asked after a minute.

The other fellow took a swallow of beer and licked the suds off his lip. "I was at the public library," he said, "trying to find out why Connecticut is called the Nutmeg State."

"Did you find out?"

"I found out that in a pageant for the tri-centenary of the state a wooden nutmeg says, 'Oh, the little wooden nutmeg will never desert her Yankee Peddler.'"

The personnel were alert. The waiter came over and poured more coke in the stove. The door clanked and it was cozy and good-smelling.

The guy was leafing through his notes. "This is Hooker at Hartford," he explained, and then he read aloud like reading a script.

"'Us?...' 'Our servant—a Negro—was with me.' 'Could he not have brought the dispatches?' 'A slave? Oh no, Sir!' She suddenly smiled up at him. 'And he's afraid of the dark.' 'I care not a snap of my finger for Boston Common.' 'Don't be angry. Be brave. White girls must be brave...'"

"Would you mind repeating that last?" said Carol.

"Sure. 'Don't be angry. Be brave. White girls must be brave.'"

He shut the notebook and smiled, then drank some beer. Carol eyed him narrowly. "Who are you?" he asked.

"Aquarius."

"Gee. I've seen you before. I thought you were a bum."

"Okay. I've only panhandled once. You want to walk a mile in my moccasins?"

"Those are vain words."

"The song is about me."

Why not? Carol got up and bought a round. He plunked the full mugs down on the smeary table with the empty ones and the two men drank.

"Know any more songs?" Carol asked.

"Love the One You're With," replied Aquarius.

He nodded in the direction of the rear room. The place was filling up and a bunch of guys were back there getting two girls drunk and feeling them up and it looked like the both of them were going to get gang-layed that night. So what? It's fun to screw a drunk woman. At the next table a guy was lacing a football.

"Shouldn't you be at The Paradox with the dealers and freaks?" Carol asked, raising an eyebrow.

Aquarius shrugged. "I like beer," he said, "and anyway I'm not into Scientology."

"You better be careful. Janis Ian might make a meal out of you."

"If this be treason, then let us make the most of it."

There were a lot of faggots standing at the bar and they took a deep interest. One of them took a flash photo and Carol and Aquarius were in it. Now out of the midst of the jabbering crowd a bunch of guys stood up from the table where the two girls were being handled and trooped out through the front room. They were pissed off about something and as they passed Carol's table they all—all five of them—looked at him with looks that said Overdoses Afterwards. He felt a passing threat.

Aquarius went up to the bar and bought a round. A collection of ancient wishbones was arrayed on a disused gas lamp over the bar and they were thick with dust like old books waiting for somebody to crack them. Carol looked around the locale. Among the cherished relics—from Peter Cooper's chair to a piece of the Blarney Stone, the pebbled phone booth and the political souvenirs—he thought he saw, perhaps hanging beside a faded memento of local history, a cloven sneaker. He thought to himself, If this guy is Aquarius then I'm King Clootie.

They drank. "What other research are you doing?" Carol asked.

"Do you know anything about cargo cults?" Aquarius replied. "I'm looking for material on the Earth as a figure in mythology."

"Have you found any?"

"Surprisingly little. In the Vedic literature of the Hindu Aryans the Earth is indeed personified as Prithivi, 'The Broad One,' but there is no worship and hardly any significance attached to her..."

To his astonishment, Carol discovered that a kitten had crawled up his pants leg. He held the little purring thing in one hand and picked the sawdust out of its fur.

". . . that at one time women were executioners. In the Sudan the Amazonian queens are pictured in the traditional attitude, spearing their defeated enemies or slaughtering them with their swords."

Carol looked at him skeptically, with one eyebrow. The other fellow looked long into his beer, then quickly drank a swallow and wiped his mouth.

"No, really," said Aquarius. "Dogs shit when they see me."

"Come come," said Carol, arch. "Where in the Bible does it prophesy Aquarius?"

"You cannot prophesy something which exists simultaneously in all time, but I know what you're getting at and I'll mention two passages."

The fellow cleared his throat and creased his forehead. He certainly looked earnest enough.

"One place," he said, "is where Jesus says, 'Let him who is without sin cast the first stone.' Another is in the Gospel of Saint Mark where Jesus declares that it is not His to decide who is to sit with Him in Paradise on His right hand and on His left hand."

"I see," said Carol, handing him the kitten. "You're the one who can cast the first stone and you're the one who can decide."

"Right. You know that Jimi Hendrix number called 'Third Stone From the Sun'?"

"Man, you talk like a disc jockey."

"That's part of the cargo cult."

"Can I ask you something? Would you ever lie?"

"Of course I'd lie."

"What do you mean?"

"I'd lie to save my own skin. That's the only reason for beating the draft, isn't it? To save your skin?"

An old man started singing and Aquarius put the kitten on the floor and got up to leave.

"Every bush, ev'ry bower,
Every rose and wild flower
Reminds me of my Mary
On the banks of the Lee . . ."

Carol looked at the guy as though accusing him of being a fake as well as a liar.

"Of course I'd lie," he repeated. He was putting on his perfectly ordinary overcoat. "Shit, man. Galileo did."

He looked around the locale, smiled and said, "Remember, now. Strictly heterosexual."

6 God and Famous

> *"And the souldiers likewise demanded of him, saying, and what shall we do?..."*
>
> The Rev. Thomas Ruggles
> *On the Usefulness and Expediency of Souldiers*

CAROL WALKED THE BLOCK from McSorley's to Sylvja's Pottery Shoppe and looked in the window to see if he could discern a message for him. There were pots and mugs and bowls and ashtrays, and a cluster of bells on thongs such as Yvetot had hanging with some plants over the sink. A girl was working in the pottery, bending over to get something in one of the kilns. She had a nice ass, and her thighs were so well apart that he would be able to put the whole palm of his hand over her crotch without spreading them. Her name was Pauline, he remembered.

Carol pissed in a doorway like any bum, then walked to 4th and Bowery and looked in on Phebe's. The place was full of gay vaqueros and perfumed stevedores and Mrs. Astor's pet horse. He walked out again and stood on the street looking at the clock on Cooper Union. Then he remembered a place uptown called Dorrian's Red Hand. He took the IRT.

Let me take you back to a land where strawberries grow in the salt sea and ships sail in the forest, back before pottery shops and marijuana, when we fell in love and drank tea and a glass of wine for the knotty pine. Remember Pandora's Box? There used to be a lot of brick-paved streets in Manhattan, great ruddy avenues, and the intersection of Bond Street and Lafayette is still all stone ballast cobbles. The old paving is still visible when dig Con Edison must and layers of asphalt are jackhammered away. And archeology is in the making at the World Trade Center where torched-off I-beams of the old Hudson Terminal building

The Banks of the Sea

are being used to pier one of the new buildings, while through a gap in the mosaic tile floor of the old Hudson Tubes station a bulldozer can be seen at work in the new subbasement. But this is fleeting, like a Rockette named Rochelle.

Meanwhile Carol has found his way to Dorrian's, sits with a hamburger and a beer in the heated sidewalk terrace and falls into conversation with two couples. It is interesting to watch a woman "troll" for offensive behavior from her man while he is drinking so she can shake her finger at him the next morning.

"New York is only beautiful. How would you like to live in a place that's only beautiful? New York is half a dollar bill Scotch-taped to a pocket mirror."

"I didn't come here looking for somebody to love."

"You know what's wrong with her? She can't doubletalk."

"I don't know what to say, darling."

"Your politics is like an unwanted pregnancy."

The man laughs loudly and the other couple chuckle. Harmless entertainment put on for them by their companions. Remember the couple in the Silva Thin cigarette ad? Arthur continues.

"Her incomplete gestures like a cuckoo's couk in late June..."

"Unlike Arthur's mother who looked like a whipped dog and had a floating kidney," said Diane. "Sometimes you'd think men are a different species in disguise."

This is where Carol begged their pardon and asked them for a light. Oh the Indies are a cushion of broken timbers for ships to wear themselves out on, and taxis creep through Uptown streets where little girls whose coats are too big for them are sleeping. Arthur and Diane are well and good, but Carol recognized the other guy immediately. His name was Gordon Breckenridge and he had killed a woman two years ago in Denmark. They introduced themselves.

"Where does your name come from?" the other girl, Gordon's girl, asked. "I thought it was a girl's name."

"They're daughters of Charlemagne," said Carol.

"Ah. *Karl den Store*." She smiled and rolled her eyes skyward like a Frenchwoman saying Ooo la la. Her name was Astrid and she was Norwegian and blonde. That must be why Arthur was needling his brunette wife, who cut her eyes at Astrid.

"The only time she has a shadow is at night," said Arthur.

"I have enemies," Diane pouted theatrically, "who would kill me for my sexual advantage."

"Yeah, like they murdered the Jews," said Carol. "Jewish women can tell when they're ovulating."

So he put his oar in and they were silent and looked at him. Then the Norwegian girl blew the lid off it.

"All women know that," she said. "They learn it from their mothers. Anything else is myth," she sipped for effectiveness, "and politics."

Her voice lilted like water and her eyes were almost oriental.

"Ah, so the chickens were inculcated," said Arthur, "and their mothers told them to keep it under the tea cozy. You don't have power unless you've got a good secret."

"The moon is made of gray matter..." said Gordon.

"New York was made for lovers," said Carol, cheerfully.

"It's as clear as new piss," said Arthur, ungallantly, "that the Willendorf Venus is a sterility symbol."

"But Arty," said Diane, "how can the Willendorf Venus be a sterility symbol?"

"For the same reason," he raised his voice a little, "that for every woman like you there are fifteen faggots."

"Ow. That hurt. I want to go home."

"I found her in Paterson. On Cult Street."

"Do you remember Don Zimmer?" Carol asked Gordon. "Used to be first baseman for the Dodgers?"

"Sure," said Gordon with the enthusiasm of the recent expatriate. "Now he's manager of the San Diego Padres."

"Remember how he used to get beaned by pitched balls?"

"Yeah. Sometimes he'd be in a coma. Out for days."

"It's a wonder it never did anything to his brain," said Arthur.

"I dunno," said Carol.

"Wha?" said Arthur.

"I don't know whether it did anything to his brain."

"Why," said Gordon, "with that buncha bananas he has in the bullpen..."

"Naw, man," said Carol, "he saves rubber bands. He's got two garages and one of them's full of rubber bands. Every once in a while he

The Banks of the Sea 109

drives his car into it."

The waiter appeared and they paid and left. Diane and Arthur—friends of Gordon's sister in San Francisco—drove off in their Mustang, and Carol and Gordon looked at each other.

"Now I know where I've seen you before," said Gordon.

"Sweden," said Carol, softly.

They took a cab down Second Avenue and went to a place near NYU called Crewe's Head. The waitresses were pretty and there was a fire in the fireplace, and Carol and Gordon and Astrid drank and Carol got drunk. The place was full of carousing draft dodgers and all that cannon fodder on the hoof had an air of the Resurrection about it.

"Good to see you still alive," said Carol.

"You too," said Gordon.

"I'll join you on that," said Astrid, and smiled distantly like sunshine through a windowpane. They drank to the beaver whose felling a tree made the Mississippi and the St. Lawrence separate but equal.

The draft dodgers were noisily overcompensating for the frustration, in the American civilization, of men who have not known military service. Carol observed some people at a neighboring table. They were mannishly talking about their drug experiences, and the waitress brought them their brandy Alexanders and the wooden bowl full of chocolate chip cookies which the place provided instead of pretzels. One of them looked like a faggot on account of his effeminate mannerisms, but he was just a hippie who had been given a haircut by some rednecks in Florida.

"Remember the queers' table in the cafeteria in high school?" said Carol.

"Yeah, man," said Gordon. "They were always trying to recruit guys."

Gordon Breckenridge had never known military service and he wasn't the least bit frustrated. They were a lovely couple, Gordon and Astrid, and laughing they told Carol about how they met, each all alone, in the mountain wilderness in Norway and lived up there together in a cabin through the winter. They were married that summer in the village church in the valley and all the people had the same last name. They had a baby boy.

"Liten Jeppe," she said, her voice tinkling. "Liten Jeppe på fjeld."

They were married with fiddles and dancing. Carol asked them how they met.

"Somebody was knocking on my door," Gordon laughed, "and I had to find the door. Have you ever been married, man? Wow! You ought to get married."

"Tell me pretty maiden," Carol asked her, "are there any more at home like you?"

"Let me see. There's the intellectual one, the practical one, the one who's as strong as an ox . . ."

"And the one with the flat face," said Gordon, and Astrid slapped him across the side of the head.

"I had a girlfriend," said Carol, "who I'm still hung up on. She's a call girl. Ever since she got her hooks into me my head's been all squishy like a wet telephone book. Ol' shit for brains. That's me."

"That's okay," said Gordon. "John Lennon's head is a teapot that you can take the lid off of to put more hot water in."

"She's trying to make me piss ice cubes and shit soy sauce," Carol said, watching his finger rub back and forth on the table. "Hell, she told me about all the guys who committed suicide for her. The one who deflowered her had a motorcycle accident, and there was a Marine who blew his brains out on the fantail of his ship."

"Shit," said Gordon. "Those guys just want to play Spartacus and be crucified together. Look at the Civil War. Guys dying for their sisters."

"She operates out of a phony advertising agency called The Duckrabbit Effect. It's a CIA front."

"Man, this is a foreign country and it's a ripoff. Imagine what's going to happen when the dollar falls and all those frogs, limeys, krauts, wops, squareheads, guineas and gooks come over here. There'll be fucking in the streets of Littletown, U.S.A. There won't be any secrets left. It's the Revolution *malgré lui.*"

Carol wasn't sure immediately whether he liked the idea. He thought of Yvetot. She's what the sun has been practicing for. She's the hanged man's second wind. His heart filled with tenderness for her and he wanted to keep the foreigner at a stiff arm's length. But Yvetot was a prostitute. He formulated a description of her. She was like food that had been left in the skillet all night. She was like wearing a dirty shirt that had been ironed again. She was a fast buck.

"No more Jesus freaks," said Gordon. "They'll be doing the continental."

"What's a continental?" Astrid asked.

"It's a dance," said Carol.

"It's an obsolete currency," said Gordon.

Astrid got up and adjusted the logs in the fireplace. The flames danced and she watched them for a while, then she sat down again. The jukebox played "I'm a Truck," with Merle Haggard. Gordon appreciated the country and western music. He called the waitress and ordered more drinks. She was like an old folk song and she had a sweet bottom. She dropped a glass.

"What about Aquarius?"

"A what?" said Gordon.

"I met a man in McSorley's today who said he's Aquarius. You know, the Age of Aquarius?"

"You're sure it wasn't Norman Mailer?"

"Ha. But what if the guy actually is Aquarius? He's supposed to be around, you know."

"Then he's just a cult figure, like you or me," said Gordon, in a way which made Carol remember what had taken place in Sweden that time and what he had thought about it. They were getting around to talking about that.

"Look," said Gordon, "the hippies are all suffering, and I mean *suffering,* from lysergic acid poisoning. They're as superstitious as a bunch of ergotty mice. If you look at it that way then what happens is that you deprive their religion of its credibility."

"So we're cult figures, huh?" said Carol. "Then am I to understand that we are all Latter Day Saints?"

"Anything but." Gordon snuffed his cigarette. "What if some spade was to tell you his name is Holden Caulfield?"

"Dig it," said Carol, "and you ask him, you ask him if he's *the* Holden Caulfield."

The color TV over the bar was on with the sound screwed down and the jukebox was playing "Mathilda Mother" by the Pink Floyd. On the television screen three astronauts were being congratulated by President Troast and Mrs. Troast. Astrid thought the astronauts' wives looked like female impersonators and said so.

"Well," said Gordon, "at least they elected somebody who can keep a straight face."

Carol was pretty drunk when they left the Crewe's Head. He remembered the Japanese busboy finally sweeping up the broken glass and he remembered the waitress and that the wine tasted the way she looked. She wasn't wearing a brassiere and Yvetot's breasts were as sweet as two bats on a fungus. He felt pretty good and started shouting poetry in the dark street. It was a completely ravishing kind of toot in which you find yourself miles away and don't know how you got there. That is called Irish hyperspace.

They took a taxi across the Brooklyn Bridge, which Carol called the inside-out church, with the snow falling and arrived in the Bay Ridge section of Brooklyn where Gordon and Astrid were staying with a Norwegian family. Astrid was still nursing, which is why she had hardly drunk at all. She sat in the same upstairs room with the two men and let the baby suck while they talked. It was a sight to behold: Astrid and little Jeppe bright as a medieval allegory while Gordon and Carol tipsily alluded to filth and culpability.

"She's still in her car," said Carol, "sitting behind the wheel buried in the hillside. You say you cornholed her to death?"

"You must have X-ray vision," said Gordon. "I'm surprised those heapies didn't exhume her and do abominations. Didn't they even siphon the gas?"

"The hippies are very paranoid, you realize, and by not going to the police you allowed that commune to turn you into an idol. You're a hippie god, man. They have a can of cat food that you left there, unopened. People come there and put their cigarette packs on it."

"Bunch of Yorubas," said Astrid.

"She wanted a poop job, a brown," Gordon said, "and I was giving it to her."

He rose from his seat and the famous dimensions of his cock were apparent in the crotch of his moleskins, which were purchased at Troelstrup's in Copenhagen. Gordon the Okie Breckenridge. He was a cult figure all right.

"And she just died," he said, "right after I came. She had a D-cell vibrator going in her scrump and I guess it must have been too much for her heart. Maybe it was nirvana."

The Banks of the Sea 113

Carol and Gordon giggled the way little boys do who have gotten a little girl to piss into a pop bottle.

"She called herself Marie," said Gordon, "because she'd married a Frenchman and was hoity-toity. That was in Copenhagen. I liked the idea of crossing to Sweden with her afterwards. Rites of passage."

Poor Marie. Have you seen Marie talking to the soldiers in the square?

"Back in Fresno she was Mary Krudlick and had blackheads on her nose. One day Ma and Pa and us kids had a picnic in Roeding Park. I was ten or eleven years old. Anyway, I went off into the trees and was idly playing with myself when these three teenage girls came up to me and sniggered, like. Shit, man. American girls. Well one of them, Mary Krudlick, gave me a nickel and told me to call her up when I was fifteen."

Carol shut his eyes. He heard Astrid burp the baby, and she and Gordon exchanged a few words in Norwegian. Everything was whirling and he almost fell off the chair. He opened his eyes and there was little Jeppe smiling to him and laughing. Norway. Glaciers and fjords. The water in the mountain streams is green as absinthe.

"As much as anything," Carol said, "wars are fought for genetic resources."

He told them about the improvised target practice with Yvetot's BB gun and how it had corrected his opthalmic condition. He could shoot again.

"Sounds like somebody has plans for you," said Gordon. "I'm going to give you Arthur and Diane's address and telephone number. They live in Fort Lee, New Jersey, just across the George Washington Bridge. You can *walk* there."

He and Astrid set up an Army cot for Carol. They told him about the Swedish Seamen's Union on Hanson Place, right there in Brooklyn, and how he could get a berth on a Scandinavian ship.

Carol had a comfy bed with fresh sheets, a fluffy pillow, a couple of Navy blankets and a patchwork quilt. He was grateful from the bottom of his heart.

"Sufficient unto the dog are his dreams," he said. "Thanks a lot, and have a good night."

A clock ticked cozy as a locket and the house creaked and smelled lived in and good. There was a painting of an old Norwegian steamship in the room and in the darkness Carol pretended he was aboard it, ploughing through the South China Sea with his Kodak. He thought of Imogen and knew that she was worried about him. He should have phoned her. He would.

He woke up as grumpy as a menstruating hobbit and stumbled around the sleeping house with a hangover. It was still dark. He crept down the stairs and out into the streets. Was it the coverlet of snow on them that had lured him out of his warm cot among friends? He found a subway, and by the time he got to Manhattan the sun was rising like an east orange.

"Men are always standing in corners pissing."

He was on Delancey Street. The piers of the Williamsburg Bridge rose immense like part of the gray sky and hunkered.

"Shhh. The welfare recipients are sleeping."

It was so early, and what was he doing out on the street? It was cold and he should be home in bed where he belonged. He walked to East 3rd Street.

"He casts a wrong shadow."

He went inside a tenement and quietly climbed the stairs. The luncheonettes would be open soon, and the blood banks.

The trouble with Imogen was that in living with her he was becoming just another urban phenomenon, in his case one of those insincere young men who succeed because they accommodate themselves to the delusions of ambitious women. But what was he becoming in his fealty to Yvetot?

He sat on the top step and smoked a cigarette, then stepped out onto the roof. The sun was a little higher now, like the proof of the pudding, and the morning seemed so slow in its advance that it must be giving him time for something. He strolled in the thin snow and shivered, walked to the false cornice and looked down into the street. Far to the east a Department of Sanitation garbage truck was in operation. It was so quiet in the neighborhood that he could hear the garbage men's voices.

Across the street a dog started barking on the roof of the Good Humor barn. Carol thought of summer and wondered what the Good

Humor men did in the wintertime. Then he heard a noise behind him and turned around. In front of the stairhouse and brandishing a yard-long two-by-four was a big white man. He gnashed his teeth at Carol and hefted the piece of lumber but the dog—the man had a dog with him, a Doberman with savagely bandaged ears. The dog's jaws snapped and it let out a high-pitched snarl and lunged. Carol thought of himself as Orion at the horizon. He clambered over the rows of slated-shut chimneys, to the next building and the next, jumping onto the snow and tarpaper, trying the stairs. They were all locked. He had to find a way down. At the back of a roof he found a fire escape ladder that was painted green as go.

He descended quietly and with trepidation. One's steps are led where one's thoughts center, he observed. This was Yvetot country and he needed refuge. What if he went to her storefront and rapped on the window with a special code, and she let him in and let him appreciate her bed again? But if escape was as easy as a green fire escape then he was in that damned ESP school and they would have him dancing like a bear. He had to climb over two backyard fences before he found a cellar door that could be opened. It was really a cinch. It wasn't locked but only latched from inside, and it was a matter of removing a nut from a screw and pushing the screw in with a paper lollipop stick so that the latch fell apart. It was all fairly lubricated and easy to do without any tools and he was sure it had been set up for him.

He reassembled the latch like a good boy and found his way through the cellar with the aid of his Jap Ronson. He had that fear of stumbling over a corpse or falling into an open grave. The water was turned on somewhere in the house and the pipes gave a screech, such a sound as lizards made before they became acceptable as birds.

He was scared. Back on the street he started walking in the direction of Yvetot's place. He could ask her if there was any mail for him. But he had a perfectly good lockbox at the post office and his mail was being forwarded to it. He could put it to her straight, that he . . . But he mustn't be in love with her. The only thing wrong with him was that he was horny, hungry, and hung over.

He could throw himself at her feet, athlete's foot and crud that she got from her customers. What if she was doing an all-night and had a dude in her bed at this moment? She was a hooker and had all those hatracks at her disposal and didn't need Carol except for his love. That's what she wanted all right. That he should love her, from a distance. She needed the security of a man's love even though his physical presence was no more desired than the deceased Jesus's, and then when she decided to have his children he would—if she had set up the coincidences correctly—be waiting for her. Otherwise he would be dead and thinking of her. An enormous gulf of foreclosure opened before him.

He was about to turn the corner into her street when the front and rear doors of a parked Chrysler sedan opened and two heavies looked at him. Happiness is a warm gun momma. They were hit men, and the Chrysler's motor was running. One of them smiled and spread his legs a little, obscenely suggesting a parked car hustler, so Carol could see the pistol in his lap. He saw it and kept on walking. It might have occurred to him that he had enough money in his shoe for a week's rent at the Albert, but he was angry and felt put-upon. He gnashed his teeth and cried out "My God!" and Aquarius responded with the affirmation that all is fodder for his pen. He remembered that he had a brand new notebook and a new ballpoint in the pocket of his lumber jacket. He stood on Second Avenue with the bums watching him and wrote: *She awoke and opened her eyes and stretched. She was wild-eyed with dreams like the eyes of cattle that have just come in from their summer range...*

Imogen loved him. She was asleep in their bed dreaming furiously: Two astronauts fell into the sea and one of them released his helmet so that it would surface and signal their rescuers. The two men slowly rose to the surface and one of them, he without a helmet, was picked up by a boat. Meanwhile a nearby whale has approached. It gets right up close to the boat and sheds a great tear, which falls plop on the astronaut's head and drowns him.

He walked past the Men's Shelter at East 3rd and Bowery. The Toad Palace. The bums waiting for a kiss from the princess. A bum who looked like his father winked at him and smiled. He crossed the Bowery, and on Lafayette Street found a chalk inscription on the wall of the Women's Shelter. It read: I HAD A CUNT AND IT BLED. It was only a little way further downtown, in Lispenard's Meadows, that some three thousand women whom the British had shanghaied were stockaded for the use of the soldiers.

Carol felt that he had taken account of his contingencies and could therefore go ahead and get his nose dirty. He did not go to the Albert and ask Shem and Dora if he could sleep on their couch nor did he go home to Imogen's warm loins where there was love for him and concern for his well-being. He thought of Yvetot and hated and desired her, and resolutely set about finding out what the United States was cooking up. One of the first things he discovered on that beaming March morning was a smouldering heap of rubbish. Twenty-five cubic yards of it. There had been a fire in a private sanitation truck and it had disgorged its load right there on Seventh Avenue just south of Sheridan Square.

It was next to the curb directly in front of an off-Broadway theater which was running a play about heroin addicts. The private garbage truck was parked down the street, and although the fire department had already hosed and gone the rubbish was still steaming. Carol gave it a good going-over. It was commercial refuse, some from an upholsterer's loft, but the bulk of it was the broad red and black ribbons of paper backing for roll film used in such cameras as Hasselblads and Rolleis. There was so *much* of it. There were cascades of empty film spools and sheave upon sheave of ruined photographic paper. It smelled like a burned village.

There was quite a bit of traffic at this hour: people going to work, faggots walking their dogs, and long black Cadillacs sidled past the heap of rubbish, parking lights on, exhausts pooping. Some of them drove around the block and came back for a second look, for they were the limousines of witch generals who were scrutinizing the suddenly-resurrected garbage for auspices as though it were the entrails of a bird. It didn't look good for the empire. They saw Carol poking around in the mess, Carol Gamewell at the top of the heap, and they might have known what it was he found there among some soggy prints. He found a picture of a dead guy in a coffin.

It was obvious who Carol was, of course, to the morning people, the weirdos, the hardhats in their pickups and the coughing generals, for his anonymity was missing, it wasn't on him, he wasn't packing it. It is an affidavit far too valuable to walk around with in this town of rotten egg silverware and exposed children and the botch of Egypt.

He was a cockatrice laying his foul egg on the dungheap. He was a

Communist. A red. Communists, as everybody knows, are cuckoo birds which lay their eggs in the nests of other birds. In other words, he was crackers. Carol was "reading" the message in the casual script of the trash for it told him things like sermons in stones, the pictograph of accidental surfaces, the false language the ancient Greeks called *koinos spurios*. Like the afternoon he was mooning around in Central Park and he stooped over and picked up a piece of paper and read on it, handwritten and in plain English, *What are you doing in the park today and why did you pick up this piece of paper?* Cautiously nonchalant, he discarded the photograph of the corpse and made his way down off the trash pile. He looked like a chimney sweep. The Toad Prince cometh.

Here comes Carol, walking down Seventh Avenue with his hands in his pockets. He is hungry and thinks about breakfast. How would he like to eat some knuckles? Five guys come toward him and they too are horny, hungry and hung over. It's the same five guys from McSorley's the night before. They recognize Carol and close in on him.

"Say, buddy. You wouldn't know where we could get a piece of ass, would you?"

"I could tell you," said Carol, remembering them and truculent, "but I'm not a pimp."

"How'd you like to get kicked to death?" another one asked.

"Dark is stark," he replied, in a nasty South Bronx accent, "but sepia is creepier."

There was a fat guy wearing a sweatshirt under his lumber jacket and the sweatshirt had EAST VIRGINIA on it, Yvetot's home state. One of them would have been a cuckold except he'd never had a woman. And there was a coon, too. Carol dug the coon. It was the faithful companion of boy pranks, the bunch of them having been nursed by the same android mammy. One of them had a cleft palate.

Carol had replied correctly to their question.

"Just what the fuck are you?" asked the cleft palate.

"I'm Orion Man, you Jew's harp," said Carol, and spat.

"You maht jus' be breakfuss, too," said the coon.

"That's for you, cocksucker," said Carol, and gave cleft palate the finger.

"Chalfont," said the fat guy to the coon. He sounded like a panty waist. "Chalfont, your Mammy wants you to come suck on her black titty."

That black guy was really burnt up. He kicked at Carol's groin, but Carol caught it in his hands and with the strength born of intolerance twisted the android's foot off and tossed it over his shoulder to the rubbish pile.

"Violence is for fruits," said Carol.

"That's what you're getting," said East Virginia and they jumped him.

They pinned him up against a parked car and beat him with their fists until their arms got tired. Then they dumped him onto the pavement and kicked the wind out of him, and when he was writhing on the sidewalk in an effort to breathe they kicked him in the head until they thought he was unconscious. As they left him curled up next to the parked car he heard one of them say, "You can tell 'em you got the Schlitz kicked out of you in New York."

Carol opened his eyes and counted silica glints in the sidewalk. Perhaps he belonged to the Hess family, which has never been dedicated to public purposes. But he was an indecent exposure and there were gawkers. He didn't even have to move and soon there was a police car and the officers asked him questions. He didn't answer them and soon there was an ambulance. They picked him up and he saw the blood on the sidewalk. They asked him his name and he wouldn't tell them so they took him to Bellevue.

By the time they got there he was able to sit up, but he didn't like what he saw and made a break for it. Four cops ran after him and tackled him out on the ramp, pummeled him and dragged him to an old wooden wheelchair, sat him in it and viciously handcuffed his arms behind its back. They knew what they were doing and nearly broke his arms. Carol felt pretty good. He looked down at his feet. The policemen had taken his belt and shoes and now he could walk on water. The admitting nurse said something to him in Danish and he gave her his name. The most ineffable sweet warmth spread through his sore body and the only thing he felt was the singing of his poetic self, his whole spirit. The policemen levered his arms and tightened the handcuffs, but he didn't feel anything except the honey-fuck sweetness of religion.

"Bet that hurts, doesn't it?" said one of them. The nurse looked at

Carol and he felt her telling him that it had damned well better. Carol groaned as though he were in pain. Evil begins with the first lie.

"And the souldiers likewise demanded of him, saying, 'And what shall we do?'"

"I think you guys oughta go play with your yo-yos."

The padre was lying to the troops, inasmuch as he gave them only half the gospel verse, expecting they were either too cowed or too ignorant of Scripture to dispute his sermon. It was a sermon which satisfied the Crown and the colonial authorities, preached to an artillery company at Guilford, Connecticut, on May 25th, 1736, the day of their first choosing their officers:

"Among the many that came to hear John's ministry and enquire their duty, the souldiers came also to him and demanded of him, 'What shall we do?' The whole of the account is perfectly souldier-like; the enquiry is expressed with the very air and spirit of a souldier in it; they demanded; they speak as men of true greatness of mind, as persons who were not accustomed to be denied. 'Tis recorded of the other persons, that came before to John, that they asked, ——But the souldiers demanded, And what shall we Do? And by John's gentle and pious answer and directions to them, 'tis abundantly plain..."

There's money in cannon fodder. Ever wonder how German militarism got started? It was the Hessian mercenaries in the American Revolution. The Duke of Brunswick received eleven dollars and sixty cents for each soldier who was wounded, and three times that amount for each one who was killed. He expressed regret that the men were not killed fast enough to enable him to collect the larger amount for their deaths and to furnish others to take their places. During the eight years of the war the principality of Hesse Cassel received from Great Britain for the soldiers that it contributed £2,959,800.

"I am not come up into the pulpit to teach the arts of war. This is not the business of a minister of the Kingdom of Peace. But as souldiers may demand of such, And what shall we do: so as the Gospel descends to consider men in every condition and station they are placed in Providence. As it instructs them to be faithful in the calling in which they are, so it abundantly countenances and encourages persons being trained up in martial knowledge; and that those that have abilities

therefor, endeavor to furnish and accomplish themselves as good souldiers..."

Cornhole dryfuck American names American places popcorn fart shit from Shinola are on the lips of pimpled faces cluster fuck circle jerk turd in the punchbowl those who read these lines of wit fucking shitass cocksucker pogue roll their shit in public places shitheel brown nose motherfucker.

"This land of Christians has in a peculiar manner found the advantage thereof. Under God, our lives, our religion, our liberties are owing to the valiant & martial achievements of those of our forefathers, who were mighty in battle. Else to all human probability, they would have been swallowed up at once, as it were, by the vast numbers of their Indian enemies, whose tender mercies are cruelty. I can't look back upon the great Major Mason, in the Pequod War, without a peculiar regard and honor to his memory; nor are the succeeding worthies in later times of trouble to be neglected or forgotten, who signalized themselves in valor and success, against the Narragansset Indians and fort..."

Seriously. On the Great Seal of the City of New York there's an Indian with his bow 'n' arrow and a white guy playing with his yo-yo.

"I need, and shall say little under this head. The proposition being evident from those that are foregoing, and the end and design of souldiers. Let me just observe to you; almost every country have their differing ways of making war upon their neighbors. And almost every country, or age, makes some alterations in the instruments and methods of war. Besides, there are many strategems & methods of making war that are very useful and necessary to be known by souldiers. In a word, how to be and how to endure hardness as good souldiers..."

I was on leave in New York, and because I hadn't gotten laid and had to go back to the coast the next day I went to Greenwich Village and picked up a soldier in the San Remo. He gave me a blow job. It was my first blow job and that dogface darned near got lockjaw trying to make me come. You know what I mean? And I never did develop a taste for blow jobs.

"Victor Immature on a Greek Vaseline barge."

Our gunboat had gone aground under fire in the Mekong Delta and the Army sent an amphibious armored vehicle out to take us off. We all made it and it was a beautiful maneuver, Cong mortar shots exploding all around us and we could hear the shrapnel splat on the sides of the amphib. Well it was pretty crowded in there—feets, farts and assholes —and some of the guys were laughing their heads off and things were going pretty good. Now, the crew of the amphib had a few Vietnamese whores and they like started pulling a sleeve down off a shoulder and exposing a tit, and things like that, and one of them had her little daughter with her. I was lying on the deck just sort of relaxing and grooving on it and the whore—she was pretty good-looking too—and her little daughter didn't have any pants on underneath their skirts and I could see everything. The mother had some scars like old rash marks on her thighs and stomach, like from some kind of venereal disease. Not that she had it then, but from some earlier time, and I think there was something, she had some kind of sore on her lip, like a cold sore covered with a concealing cosmetic. But her little daughter stood on my hands while I was lying there and I held onto her feet and she balanced as I slowly lifted her up and down. She was laughing. Now that I think about it, that baby girl was circumcised. She probably, yeah, I guess she'd had all four lips taken away.

Each crater was twenty to forty feet across and five to twenty feet deep. The craters were very numerous and there were many generations of them from different air strikes. In the older craters a few sprigs of Imperata grass were sprouting in the center. The most recent ones were bare of vegetation but contained some rainwater. Moreover, the ubiquitous missile fragments in the ground cut the hooves of the water buffalo, causing infection and death of the animals. From an altitude of thirty thousand feet, where they were unheard and unseen from the ground, a typical B-52 mission comprising seven aircraft delivered 756 five-hundred-pound bombs in a swath saturating an area about half a mile wide and three miles long, that is, nearly a thousand acres. On a schedule of four or five missions per day of seven sorties each, the B-52s alone were creating about 100,000 new craters a month. In the seven year period from 1965 to 1971 Indochina was bombarded by a tonnage of munitions amounting to approximately twice the total used by the U.S. in all the theaters of World War II. This staggering weight of ordnance expended by the U.S. military forces in the seven years between 1965 and 1971 is equivalent to the energy of 450 Hiroshima nuclear bombs. Of the 26 billion pounds, 21 billion were exploded in South Vietnam, representing an overall average of 497 pounds per acre and 1,215 pounds per person. Over the seven years the displacement of soil by bombardment proceeded at a rate of nearly 1,000 cubic yards of soil per minute. But bombardment and defoliation were by no means the only methods used by the U.S. military in its struggle with vegetation in Indochina. The effectiveness of massed tractors organized into companies for extensive forest clearing was in some ways clearly superior to that of chemical herbicides. The tractor, called a Rome plow, was basically a twenty-ton Caterpillar tractor fitted with a massive eleven-foot-wide, 2.5-ton plow blade and with fourteen tons of armor plate. In a land-clearing operation in August, 1971, about thirty such plows scraped clean the remaining areas of the Boi Loi Woods northwest of Saigon. According to information released by the Army, at least three-quarters of a million acres were cleared in this manner through mid-1971.

> *And the soldiers likewise demanded of him, saying, And what shall we do? And he said unto them, Do violence to no man, neither accuse any falsely; and be content with your wages.*
> Luke 3:14

7 Pictures of Jerusalem

IMOGEN AWOKE TO A SUNRISE as red as the King of Arms. She thought Carol was beside her and flung an arm out to touch him, but alas . . . After an interval she got up and made tea, dressed, and carrying a deep mug took Hollister up to the roof. It was kinda cold and she shivered and slurped gulps of the steaming tea. She thought possessively of the almost organic roofscape of Manhattan which was spread before her in the smoke and brassy morning.

Maybe there was a lot of sunspot activity. The towers of Midtown and Downtown glinted with a synesthetic effect of Dadaist music. Kurt Schwitters. Odd. She thought of cake decorations of edible silver and gilt. The tea was good and strong, Assam and pekoe. The birds were up to something, the flush of sparrows at the other corner of the roof, busy in the pile of dog droppings which Imogen and the other tenants raked there to dry and be gathered in a bag "when there were enough." The English sparrows were brought to America, as everybody knows, to eat the oats in horse droppings, and now here they were foraging in the dog do. How perfectly appropriate, she mused. She took a picture of it, and another, entertained by the thought of enlarging them. Why some of those things were as big as three sparrows.

Birds are affected by sunspot activity. Are dogs? Imogen placed her mug of tea on a girder and watched what was happening. A few pigeons settled for a moment, then flew again and Hollister, refreshed, discovered the sparrows in the pile of trammels. Imogen took pictures of it. Hollister wagged his tail and nosed up on them and the birds hopped forth in a body, hopped along on the quilting cotton snow with the dog after them. It was so funny. They flew a short distance, their wings whirring like grasshoppers, and landed again and the Alsatian slithered after them on his belly like a cat. All at once the sparrows took off and Imogen yelled, but too late. Hollister yelped with eagerness and she saw him leap through the air after the birds and over the parapet.

Imogen and work-drunkenness. That's what really turned her on,

The Banks of the Sea

seeing somebody enraptured and oblivious in their work, working ignorant of time and mortality until the tool slips from their hand. There must be a better word. Work-drunkenness. *L'ivresse de travail.* Perhaps an Icelandic word. They have word-drunkenness. The Danish *at orke.* To be able to. The Swedish *at yrka.* To do or make. The Faroese: *Yrkinger.* Poems. She would walk about in the city and smile to dumb strangers as though to say See the city? See what we have built?

Such toil had gone into New York, the sudden metropolis, and it was so beautiful she could not understand how anybody could abuse or not enjoy it. The stupendous bridges and rapid transit interchanges, the spectacle of the New Yorkers at their daily affairs, the commerce—it astonished her and she wanted to rub her eyes. She rounded a corner and caught a look of intentness on a man's face. It was on 6th Avenue where a new office building was going up. He was watching another man busy unloading some equipment from a scaffold elevator. It was ticklish. Open-mouthed breathing. She breathed with them, and the recognition of their labor sent a thrill from where the air whistled into her mouth in a sudden, sweet cold piston down to her loins.

The day Imogen's dog died she had sweet-and-sour spareribs at a Chinese restaurant on 8th Street where her publisher took her for lunch. The reviewers were sniping at each other over *Men Working* and it was selling by the box like shirts. The Women's Liberation magazine hated the book, calling it "The Family of Men."

"You're famous," the publisher told her. "Are you happy?"

"Would that my love were in my bed," she replied, "and I in his arms again."

That afternoon she went alone to the Wildenstein Galleries and saw an exhibit of paintings called "An English Garden Idyll." The admission was two dollars, and when she was ready to go upstairs she used the elevator because it reminded her of a boudoir. The elevator reminded her of a play by Sartre, and of the large subway elevators in the station you use to go to The Cloisters. She was thinking of a folk song called "Devilish Mary" when who should step into the car right behind her but her old roommate Fredegonde.

"Why, isn't it . . ."

"Bryna," said Fredegonde. "Remember? Imogen, I'd like you to meet Danny."

So she was using her assumed name. Imogen thought she was much slimmer, and breezily dowdy in a dress that reached to her calves and made her look like an Orthodox Jewish woman. Her companion was a slicked-down brunette man in a pencil line moustache and an out-of-season blazer. They looked like three hoots.

When they had seen their fill of the paintings Imogen met them at the stairs, and smiling and chattering they went down to the lobby, got their coats and helped each other with them. As soon as they were on the sidewalk Danny said, ominously and with Sen Sen on his breath, "Okay. See you," and left the two women who then walked briskly west and crossed Central Park.

The marchpane street, the swanless park. A bunch of girls from Hunter College accompanied them a way, and it was as natural as sycamore balls that the two old friends should walk arm-in-arm surrounded by paranymphs. (Medieval Parisian custom: *Les jeux paranymphiques de la Sorbonne.* The student is courted on behalf of his intended by girls of her class or peer group. They keep him occupied while she's off earning her dowry.) It made Imogen feel comfortable and talkative. She told Fredegonde about her book *Men Working,* and Fredegonde said how wonderful. Now when Imogen asked her what she was doing, Fredegonde, or Bryna, looked at the ground ahead of her and said, "I help run a dating service."

"Oh."

"One of our girls was in Baltimore today on a date with an Iraqi diplomat. They walked around holding hands in the Walters Museum, then had amour in an industrial suburb called Dundalk. Danny has gone to La Guardia to fetch her."

They were about midway across Central Park. Imogen looked at the trees and at the buildings they were approaching and she wondered if this were like one of those restaurants where the second cup of coffee is free. She would document it. There was still enough light. They stood at West Drive and waited for the cars to pass. She took some pictures of Bryna.

"How do you know those things happened in Baltimore today?" she asked, watching Bryna posture. Bryna was nothing if not cooperative.

"She had an assignment. Our Washington affiliate had a control on it. You don't think we'd send a girl down there and . . ."

"That's not what I mean," said Imogen. "What I mean is, what if the girl decided to skip out on it?"

"There's an island called Kergeulen in the South Indian Ocean," Bryna purred. "She could go there. On a clear day you can see Antarctica."

"But that's like a nunnery!"

After the cars, came the bikes like a transmogrified exhaust emmission; and then the light changed, incongruously in the rural-seeming park, and the two women crossed. All things come home at eventide and in a few weeks bats would be coming out at this hour. How strange it was to be walking out of doors with only the trees and the sky for a roof. Imogen stopped and watched some small clouds move just to be certain that they did move. And as they looked into the pewter March dusk over the dorsal fin of the RCA Building, Imogen put her arm around her old roommate's shoulder.

"And what do you do for dates?" she asked.

"How are you fixed for blades?" Bryna rejoindered.

"This way! There's a little playground!"

Imogen Trellis. Not much meat on her for a Taurus, but what there is is sure good eatin. Sing, Taurus!

> "Goosey goosey gander
> Had her picture taken with a Voigtlander.
> Tee hee. That must be the funny part,"

Imogen warbled. "Don't you ever get any sailors? They treat you like a lady."

The kind of girls who don't wear panty hose, the strip of thigh squealing on the slide. Big girls horsing around on the seesaw.

"Sailors are chivalrous," said Bryna pettishly, "because whores is what they've got."

The sailors of Atlantis whose navy survived to fecundate aboriginal, say . . . Imogen was thinking. The bleeping orphan ships of a destroyed planet. One of them makes it to Earth and the crew, the exempt crew impregnate horny, stupid Amazons? But that's about where it's at, isn't it? One's conception of one's own intelligence. Such a burden to walk around with. No wonder men learned to fly.

"That's blasphemy," said Imogen.

"A stiff dick has no conscience," said Bryna, coarsely. "Chivalry implies a conscience. Treat her like a lady and you can treat her like a woman. The chivalry inspired by compromised women is the primum mobile of religion, and blasphemy is one of those words that went out with cuckold."

"You're a casuist," said Imogen.

"There are no female casuits, now, are there," Bryna said with a brogue, "except Gertrude Stein?"

The two girls strode chattering animatedly along the lake and exited at West 77th Street. In front of the marble and bronze of the New York Historical Society a young creep was bopping along under transistor earphones. Fredegonde had so many ideas. This time it was Pavlovian reflexes.

"... methodically reducing the subject's options by exploiting his most personal weaknesses, not for economic gain like common advertising but to obtain a tool for making a dent in the inertia of an atrocity-sated population."

"But do dogs understand poetry?" Imogen, perhaps flippantly, interjected.

"As much as any sparrow," Fredegonde gloated. "Incidentally, I know an ex-POW who has seen your book. He asked me if he could get a debriefing with you. Feel like a Manhattan?"

"Thanks, but I don't feel like blue mirrors today."

She hadn't told her about Hollister. Fredegonde's hand on the door of a cocktail lounge, prettily, pudgy wrist in a thin gold chain.

The location was windy, near Riverside Drive, and terribly cold in winter. Now, nearing April, the western breeze bore a dank odor from the river. At length they arrived at the place where Imogen would see what she would see, what Bryna called "the job site." More curious than apprehensive, she automatically made note of the address.

It was a pile of an apartment house in the West 80s. There was something oppressive about it, in spite of the view of the Hudson and the Palisades, and as they stepped into the porte cochere Imogen was pervaded by a feeling of hopelessness that made her want to take comfort in possible changes of the weather. The girl used a key and

The Banks of the Sea 129

opened the wrought-iron door.

"Once upon a time," she said, "there was a doorman. Over here. It's on the ground floor."

As they entered the apartment, suddenly music came from the next-door neighbor. Somebody started the "Spanish Galleons" track from a Doors album and it sounded as if there was going to be a party. Just as suddenly the music abated to a level in keeping with the lighting in the main room of the apartment. It was very large, and there was only one of those Jewish candles in a glass burning and a single photoflood turned close against the back wall where a few big enlargements were pinned. Incongruously, a double bed was placed in an alcove where there was a bay window. A dude in harlequin bell bottoms was sitting up on the bed eating maraschino cherries from the glass.

"Hi. I'm Ray," he said, proffering Imogen his hand. "Want some cherries?"

His body shirt looked like it was made of pajama flannel. She saw an old patchwork quilt lying wadded and crumpled beside him and she instinctively wanted to shake it out and fold it properly. She sat down on the edge of the bed and let her eyes get used to the dim light.

"No thank you," she said. "My, what a nice puppy!"

Yes, there was a puppy, an irresistably adorable little black Scotty for Imogen to cuddle. It nipped her wrists and licked her with that pink tongue and woofed gruffly like a little tough, and those *eyes*. For a moment she thought it was mechanical.

"Come, Laphroaig," Bryna said bossily, and the puppy gambolled over to her. The floor was lozenge parquetry.

She took the puppy with her to make coffee. Imogen was still sitting on the edge of Ray's bed, where he was propped up with pillows almost like a sick man.

It felt to Imogen that there was a focus of comfort here which could be dangerous if fallen into. Her parents were there and they love her dearly, or anyway she felt their presence as her eyes took in the room. And all the while she has blushed and turned her toes together and giggled when the King found her moist crease and brushed a nipple which became like a little rosebud. Her parents receive payment and leave the poor thing to him who, suddenly naked, tumbles her over and penetrates her. It hurts like a rope burn and if he comes quickly his gyssom is unguent to her, or if he enjoys her slowly she becomes all wet inside and likes it, biting her lip. Afterwards she will say something with a lilt to make him tarry or want to have her again, or else she is a whore and the King has sprung her caliper for every man jack and mother's son who has never gotten his rocks off in a woman. She can dance a step dance or she can skate on the ice, and she knows that no matter how she shakes it it's hole. She felt Ray's eyes on her, and blushing at her reveries rose from the bower just as Fredegonde looked in from the kitchen.

"We've been keeping this guy horny just for you," said Bryna. "Aren't you even going to lie down for him?"

"Veronicapussy," said Ray, and there came another blast of the Spanish music from next door.

"Mind if I have a look around?" Imogen asked. She deliberately strode up to a Louis Seize secretaire. A pair of bronze baby shoes.

"These are national treasures," said Bryna. "If you aren't on our side then you'll have to pay. Are you having coffee?"

"You invited me. Yes, I'd like some coffee."

"You may receive an invitation but you'd damned well better not come."

"It's that official, huh?"

Bryna's heels loud on the parquet. The room contained the trappings of a photographer's studio—some strobes and floods standing around, and a Speed Graphic on a tripod. Imogen touched the camera, admiring it, even covetously.

The room could have been an extension of the exhibit at Wildenstein's, with paintings of pastoral scenes and still lifes on the walls but in a Continental, predominantly French style from the rococo period. The furniture was expensive, either original or good copies, but so neglected. Shoved into haphazard positions along the wall, sometimes half covering a painting and with improbable things standing on it. Toys. A Playskool pegboard and hammer. A plastic didie doll. A maraca next to a marble clock covered with allegorical figures. Two twin-bed mattresses were arranged in the middle of the floor with a low platform table between them. On one of the mattresses was a young man, lying asleep bathed in sweat and twitching now and then with dreams of falling almost as though employed to do so. Imogen made a

The Banks of the Sea

foray into the dining room. She automatically picked up an artificial peach from a bowl in the middle of the table, went to the kitchen and asked Fredegonde if she could help with the coffee. There was a display card of children's sunglasses. "It's all ready," Bryna said. She picked up the tray and walked brisky to the living room with Imogen and Laphroaig following after her. "The fruit is Italian. Isn't it marvelous? From Florence. The Italians make by far the best artificial fruit. It's some kind of stone which they use. You want to take a bite out of it. Practically individual sculptures... coffee, Ray?"

"Isn't there any orange juice?"

A photoflood lamp was turned directly on a porcelain figurine on a modelling wheel standing close against the back wall of the living room. Imogen peered at the object. It was a Sevres shepherdess with rosy cheeks. A well-defined shadow was cast from the figurine onto an enlargement pinned to the wall, and it was a moment before she registered what the picture was. It was a close-up of Carol nigger-lipping a cigarette. She raised her head and looked into the shadows in the coffered ceiling.

"We don't have a darkroom," Bryna said, "but maybe you'd like to see one of the bedrooms. Not that anybody actually lives here."

I do not want to see one of the bedrooms. I have to take a leak but I do not want to see the bathroom. I am freezing in here. Won't you please open a window?

"May I use the bathroom, please?"

"By all means. I'll turn on the light for you."

A lot of things dawned on me just now. You must excuse me but I'm trying not to grab leather. The city is being held for ransom. Don't imagine that I am becoming incoherent. You put up with the blacks not for their entertainment value but as an insurance policy on the cities. You can afford to keep them, and you do so because you know you can depend on the humanitarian ideology of the other side. If you didn't keep them—why you could drop them one by one kicking down some radioactive hole in the Nevada desert. If you didn't keep them the other side would scrape you off the...

"Woolgathering, Imo?"

Realizing that she had seen the picture of Carol made Imogen feel as though a wound had been maliciously revealed to her so that she was ever after in vassalage to it, something which could not be forgiven away but had, rather, to be imitated. Bryna sat looking like a career girl on the Linzer settee, leafing through a copy of *Men Working*. "This is pretty good," she said. "In fact, it's dynamite. I suppose it's making you rich."

"I'm a national asset." Imogen sat down beside her and poured herself a cup of coffee. It was a Bavarian service, perhaps Nymphenburger, with violets.

"Too bad you don't have a picture of a man committing suicide. That's what really turns me on. And how they *toil* at it. Don't you think this would be a good caption for such a picture?"

She showed Imogen one of the pages with pictures of pimps. There were Carol's words: *They would rather be unforgivable than ineffectual.*

"The only thing a pimp works at is his macho," continued Bryna. "But a man committing suicide—that's another kind of mobilization. I once saw a picture of a naked man about to jump off a bridge. He's covering his dohickies and coyly, ah, averting his face. His clothes are lying folded neatly on a bench and his bike is parked, maybe even locked, and he's about to, ah, take the plunge. It's cheesecake!"

She snapped the book shut and cackled. Imogen knew the picture Bryna had referred to.

"Yes, 'The Stripper on the Brooklyn Bridge.' I know the photographer," she said. "Now what I want to know is, what do you do here? That looks like a light box."

Imogen pointed to an object on the Japanese table between the mattresses. The sleeping youth snored loudly a couple of times and turned over.

"That's what I was getting around to," said Bryna, getting up and going to the other mattress. "Arnold here's a photographer too. What do you think of this?"

She flipped a switch and the light box lighted up. "Did I ever tell you about the time I was a spy?" Ray asked, with warning in his voice. Bryna held up a magnifying glass and invited Imogen to inspect the big positive transparencies clipped to the glass top of the light box.

They were pictures of Carol, all right, in various situations in the streets of New York. Imogen and Bryna knelt together on the mattress.

Carol was craning his neck at something on what looked like a block in the 90s between Amsterdam and Columbus Avenues. In the background was a tinned-up brownstone and there were parked cars. What was he looking at? Imogen caught her breath. That was in the picture too. There was a teenage white girl helping her granny up the stoop, and Carol wasn't looking at the girl. He was looking at a piece of the old woman's thigh showing just above where her stocking was rolled and fastened with a thimble knot. Why should that have attracted Carol's attention and why should they be photographing him? It was revolting, and Imogen felt like she was about to wet her pants. Two sets of stereo headphones were lying beside the light box and Bryna picked one of them up and put it on Imogen, then rose and went over to the Sony. In a moment Imogen's head was filled with rock music.

> *Where are you walking?*
> *I've seen you walking.*
> *Have you been there before?*
> *Walk down your doorsteps.*
> *You'll take some more steps.*
> *What did you take them for?...*
>
> *At her requests she asks for nothing,*
> *You get nothing in return.*
> *If you want she brings you water,*
> *If you don't then you will burn...*
>
> *At my request I ask for nothing,*
> *You get nothing in return.*
> *If you're nice you'll bring me water,*
> *If you're not then I will burn...*

"We work with psionics here," Bryna said, putting the headphones back on the table. "The practical application of psychic phenomena."

"But that's Carol Gamewell," Imogen expostulated.

"Yes, the author of your captions and until this morning your bed partner. Just as we hoped, his aimless wanderings in the streets have finally gotten him where we want him. He is now in Bellevue."

Bryna removed the pictures from the light box and Imogen could see that they had been superimposed on a map of Greenwich Village.

"But Carol..." Imogen closed her eyes and pressed her fingertips against them. She saw patterns of light like exploding cattails. "What are you doing to Carol?"

She noticed that the two sets of stereo headphones were lying on top of a well-thumbed copy of Carol's book of poetry. Now Bryna removed the map of Greenwich Village from the light box and replaced it with a map of the East 30s including Bellevue and the East River. Then she took another sheet of film from a folder and held it out for Imogen to see. "What do you think this is?" she asked.

"Some kind of scientific gadget. Just what are you doing to Carol?"

"These are X-ray photographs in polarized light of a valve from a hydraulic computer in various functions of its operation," Bryna explained. "It's a component in a high-speed computer used in fighter planes, and it's powered off the jet exhaust like the reloading mechanism of an M-1 rifle."

She carefully placed the sheet of 35mm frames over the map on the light box, took another picture of Carol from the folder and held it up for a moment, then superimposed it on the series of the hydraulic computer valve.

"What are you doing that for?"

"To make him work. Make him think." Bryna shrugged. "You may wonder why we are practicing this, this 'methodical madness.' We are doing it for reasons of national security."

Imogen stood up and straightened her skirt. "You call it psionics," she said, "but there's an older word for it."

"Yes?"

"Witchcraft. You use modern paraphernalia is all."

"About the most vandalistic thing I'd consider doing again," called Ray from across the room, "would be to kiss the Blarney Stone."

"Call it what you may," said Bryna, "a rose is a rose. We have plans for your rustic swain. Gamewell is the next assassin."

"Carol is an artist. A poet."

"Right. Young poet making a name for himself. Vietnam vet. A splendid existentialist hero, don't you think? And when the shrinks get finished with his subversive notebooks... Besides, a guy like that. Ha! Some kind of red Pat Boone... His background is too plausible. We can't have a guy like that getting married and maybe *propagating* himself. Like the Greek said, he has solved all his problems save only death. Gamewell's going to be a rock-'em-sock-'em robot fairy."

"You've always been envious of me, haven't you?" Imogen said. "I'm creative and you're not, so you find something dirty to do like pimps making themselves indispensable."

"I told you, this is a national project."

"Carol and I are going to destroy you."

"We have plans for you too, honey," Bryna purred. "You don't know it but there's a waiting list for you. We already have your portfolio ready. Want to see it?"

"And so you're subletting a haunted apartment. Don't you people have any decency?"

"Ah. The ghost." Bryna strode over to the chiffonier, turned and faced Imogen. "We call her Melanie Honeydews. She used to be a poltergeist, but when we found her home movies she went in here and hasn't come out. Have you, Melanie?"

She picked up the maraca and gave it a couple of rhythmic shakes. Imogen watched her go to the coffee table and light herself an L & M. Now that's an adult cigarette.

"Shit," said Ray. "The dead must be good for something."

Imogen looked at him for a moment. "Is this what you call a safe house?" she said, addressing him for the second time.

"Good question," he said. "I never thought about it."

Laphroaig started barking at Imogen. Knowing that day follows night if one is true to oneself, she contained her emotions and sat down on one of the ballroom chairs and mussed the puppy's ears. They played tug-of-war with an old mule. Then she threw it across the room.

"May I use the phone?" she asked Fredegonde.

"By all means. You want to phone Bellevue, don't you?"

Imogen went to the wall phone and dialed 411 and asked the operator for the number for Bellevue Hospital Patient Information. While she was doing this Bryna twaddled, almost making her forget the number.

"... Stress extrudes the direction of a man," Bryna was saying.

"That sounds very poetic," said Imogen.

"He was a poet. Poor thing."

"Poor thing? What did you do to him?"

"He pooped out halfway through the program and wrote thousands of closely spaced lines on the fronts of abandoned piers along the Hudson. Gentleman songster off on a fugue . . ." Imogen was talking on the telephone and Bryna's voice rose to a shout. "Maybe you ought to go look for him. He might be in one of those piers, but I think he's probably a star by now. Don't you?"

Imogen hung up and sat down again. She wanted her old roommate and confidante to reveal herself with the old brilliance.

"Heavily nocturnal Pyrex hyrax," said Imogen.

"Lesson's motmot rhinocerocelot," replied Fredegonde. She was right in there.

"Well, he's there," said Imogen.

"And he can phone you. He's allowed a free phone call. That is, if he can remember your number."

The apartment door was heard to shut heavily. Then the hall door opened and two people came into the living room. It was a young girl with Danny, dapper and with five o'clock shadow. He glowered at Imogen. In spite of the quite different ensemble—she was dressed like a high-school girl in a sweater with hand-fashioned sleeves and a pleated skirt—Imogen immediately recognized the little commercial artist she saw at a loft party a few months ago. She rose, thinking of commonplace things.

"Imogen," said Bryna. "I'd like you to meet Yvetot Bouchardeau. She's just been down in Baltimore celebrating the Jewish holiday of *Tuchis am der Tisch.*"

The snoring Arnold was struggling into wakefulness. He sounded like a noisy garden, mechanical wind-go-rounds and weeping scarecrows. He had a healthy complexion.

8 The Hammer of Wednesday

> *The Unicorn Tapestry is in a mental hospital.*
>
> *New York graffito*

THERE WAS A FAT MAN at Bellevue and he was so fat there weren't pajamas big enough for him and he had to wear an arrangement of two surgical smocks. His flesh showed between the tie tapes and he sweated and couldn't shave himself. Sometimes, on hot days when there were no thunderstorms, the young Negroes would persecute him, pinch him and punch him. Poor Herman. The fat man of a thousand windows.

"You fat son-of-a-bitch. Turn you roun' and ream you out, you asshole-on-wheels."

Herman looked like a jukebox. Long ago, like a man whose back was broken, he had to choose between sitting and standing and chose the latter. He was too fat to sit and spent his days propped upright in a special wheelchair. What did they do with him at night? The nurses were resourceful. The Zeppelin in the broom closet.

The kitchen always had a few meals ready for night arrivals, loonies from the streets, emergencies snatched from the hoo-haws of extremity. Meanwhile the sleepers twitch in their fishy sleep. They dream in unison, all dreaming the same dream.

"The alien spaceship has landed," said a dream. "All radios must be turned off between twelve midnight and one A.M. Failure to do so will result in being able to understand the alien language only."

Among the new arrivals one night was another fat man. The fat man of the cement bedpan.

"Sounds like somebody's being raked over the harp."

"*Het* Bronx?"

"Turn off those damned radios!"

The man was so fat he couldn't get out of bed and lay there wheezing with simple metabolic effort. He was a "white" Puerto Rican and had been able to have himself tattooed in the manner of Europeans and Asiatics and was covered with serpents and roses. There were the usual sailors' favorites and some motifs peculiar to criminals, but tattooed over his left teat was a gigantic black widow spider whose bright red hourglass marking pulsed with the fellow's heartbeat and seemed as if it might burst.

The patients look like pajama'd Russians strolling at one of their resorts, and for some it is a spa to which they return again and again to unburden themselves and to tank up on the vibes. They may be a little strange, but that is their function.

"Withe her persimmon woodwinds she tried to make me into a fairy-tale war thrall wearing a cow's udder for a helmet. As the feudal army advanced the captured milch cattle were slaughtered. 'Milk them then eat them!' was the cry. There was meat for all and the milk was fermented with the blood to make a fortifying beverage. The thralls were given fresh udders each evening so that, if they had kept a cool head, they could cook and eat the old."

(**tulchan** *n.* Scottish. Calf-skin stuffed with straw or spread on mound beside cow to make her give milk.)

"The flowers of the hydrangea, whose name in Greek means 'water vessel,' would be white if it weren't for an ancient practice of gardeners. In order to make the flowers blue, a piece of iron, an old trowel or a broken rake, is buried with the roots. Now the point I am making is this; that women were the original human carnivore. It is the chronic iron deficiency in women of childbearing age which makes them literally bloodthirsty. If a mother spurns the afterbirth she will surely eat the infant. Women are the vulture perpetually devouring the liver of the chained Prometheus."

He spoke haltingly in single, unconnected words, his reedy voice like Jimmy Stewart's, shaking his head in expostulatory tics as though that would supply the missing syntax which would convey the gist.

"Feet," he said. "Shoe polish. Clean fingernails."

That's what the matter was, and not the problem of saying it. He didn't suffer like someone who stammers, but used his mannerism in much the way an old pipe smoker will—for emphasis—poke you with his pipe.

Certain South Sea islands have native populations who practice a

The Banks of the Sea 139

religious phenomenon called Cargo Cult. Ever since the white man wowed them they have been building dummy radios out of bamboo and vines, wharves where there is no harbor and airstrips where no plane can land, in the hope that the ship or the aircraft will arrive, or return, with the Messiah, the real thing, the cargo. When a bell was heard to ring in craggy lava all the cats were killed, and people threw all their money in the sea while killing all the pigs. Young boys played at putting lianas in crab holes and—speaking into tin cans—telephoning to Temar, the ancestor god of the volcano. Was the mission reporting anyone? Was a policeman coming? Did the administration want Luluai, Tultul or Doctor Boy? There was also the matter of the coconuts, and the Kopakaua evisceration dummy used in the sanitation ceremony. On the departure of the missionary in early 1949, the boys of the mission at Magam seriously debated whether it was right to have the women in common from now on. There was the flute-weapon concealed in a briefcase, and the ceremonial of degree-taking—*mage nemal*—which was introduced at Fanu and from there transmitted from Malekula by the people of Dip Point. The movement takes hold and its adherents proliferate. The followers of John Frum compared themselves to sweet potatoes: "At first there are only a few, then soon the island is covered with them."

Aquarius is in Bellevue. He went there because he wants help getting back home and the blue-eyed Italians, the ones with symmetrical veins in their arms, are helping him. The space ship has called for him, calls for him, waits around in the spires of the city. But Aquarius, like a ballet prince, believes in earthly love and so remains. The cold clouds call to him. His family are aboard and have revealed themselves to him. The Italians understand this and are helping him, for some of them have the electricity. Oh how he wants to go home. The levitating Chagall Jews are also helping him and he thrums like a funicular and almost turns to water. But he is in love. And the Spanish trumpets shall sound, a peasant war of individuals wielding sports equipment, cricket bats and aeroplane propellers made of willow timber weeping for a young girl's description of herself, her jot and tittle breast-secret hoardings.

"Would you like some of Yvetot's pineapple upside-down cake?"

Bryna asked. Ray and Arnold were in the kitchen making coffee and Imogen didn't want any of it. She got ready to go, thinking how unhappy Fredegonde must be.

"Fredegonde," she said, suddenly using her old friend's real name, "why don't you come to my studio tomorrow, by yourself? I'll make lunch for us."

"What a perfect place," Fredegonde said the next day, admiring Imogen's studio. "You're truly lucky, Imo, being an artist in New York."

During lunch Fredegonde got a little drunk on the wine and she asked Imogen if she could change into one of her dressing gowns.

"You want a bathrobe? Sure," said Imogen. "Make yourself comfortable."

She changed and perched on one of Imogen's kitchen stools, lit a cigarette and spread her legs whorishly as she watched Imogen clear the table. Imogen thought it might be some broad lesbian ploy, and as Fredegonde nattered with professional disparagement about men the bathrobe became loosened and Imogen saw the legs spread unconscionably until golly, there it was.

"... and what do you think of that?" Fredegonde asked, concluding what she had been saying.

It was genuinely impressive, what Fredegonde now revealed. It was like a trophy. She opened her legs utterly, up there on the stool, and it could be seen that her thighs were covered with a flamboyant pattern of lozenge-shaped scars, great welts and furrows of the kind acquired by black-skinned peoples from their method of tattooing.

"They really put a tread on you, Freddie," said Imogen, drying her hands. "You look like a woozy waffle. Did it hurt?"

She wished Fredegonde would cross her legs.

"It would have," said Fredegonde, "except that they rubbed heroin in the wounds. Would you believe it? I was kept prisoner for more than a year."

"Has your stretch seen that?"

"My stretch has seen it and he asked me for a complete rundown on it for his statistical records. He didn't comment on it, though. Hookers' gynecologists are a pretty close-mouthed bunch."

"I understand," said Imogen. She was rummaging in her equipment.

"You don't mind if I take some pictures of that, do you?"
"Of course not, but I'd better cover my face with something."
"Why? You planning on getting married?"
"Come on, Imogen."
"Okay. How about a Lone Ranger mask?"

Imogen spread her mother's best damask tablecloth. Fredegonde climbed up onto it, the table groaned, and she lay down without a word and spread her legs. Imogen looked closely, holding her breath. She didn't want to smell her old friend's pussy. There was something emanating from it, more of a plasma than an odor. It was as though Thurds she had been saving were coming out of it like a troupe of clowns out of a Volkswagon.

When Foote, Cone & Belding were handling the Contac® cold tablets account in the 1960s, they obtained the theme for a new advertising campaign by asking a random sample of the population what they thought of a summer cold. A lady in Chicago replied, "A summer cold? It's a different animal," and her response became the idea which resulted in the famous Contac® ads with a huge, amorphous alien being gloating over the city and panic in the streets.

The jukebox in the reception ward was playing "Today Is the First Day of the Rest of Your Life" (start it right with Total®). Like the lady said, summer cold is a different animal and it was cold in New York that summer. For weeks the icy clouds hovered and enveloped the tall buildings, and a wind blew through the streets like the tentacles of a monstrous jellyfish. The light at morning was the color of cherry yoghurt, halating to silver needing polishing by afternoon, and people went bundled-up. There was a photograph in the *Daily News* of this event clinging and streaming from the Manhattan skyline. The only exception to the commonplaceness of talking about the weather, it was the perpetual plume of snow streaking from the top of the highest mountain.

The weather is a metallic gray Citroen DS-19 convertible that arrived in New York aboard the SS *France*. The cargo, 22.4 million dollars worth of heroin weighing 246 pounds, was hidden in the remodeled gas tank and other parts of the body and chassis (from the

New York Times, Friday, June 28, 1968). An unusually damp and chilly June at the exodus of families for summer homes. As of yesterday, there have been 6.13 inches of rain. This will have been the rainiest June since 1938. However, Thursday's average temperature was 59 degrees, the lowest recorded for a June 27, and 15 degrees below the normal average of the day of 74 degrees. There are the catatonics and the shit-smearers and the violent ones and for them, sometimes, there are the cells whose only furniture is a washable mattress. Aquarius still feels like he is about to turn to water. Ever see somebody do that? In the middle of the sidewalk, a sudden puddle. And nobody screams. They have forgotten.

Aquarius was being admitted to Bellevue.

"Why do you ask?" said the doctor.

"There's your tie. It looks like a school tie. And your accent."

"You're very observant. I'm from Rhodesia, and I'm here on an exchange program with New York University. Now, let's test your reflexes."

The doctor took up his rubber tomahawk. The subject's knees responded to its thumps and his legs jerked.

"Hmm. Very good," said the doctor. "Now repeat after me: Mmm, tuba tuba. Mmm, tuba tuba."

"Kalamazoozamalak. Kalamazoozamalak."

"Farkas the carcass?" the doctor demanded testily.

"Mmm, duba duba. Mmm, duba duba."

"No, T U B A!" the doctor reprimanded. "Duba is Polish for, er, the place where you sit down."

"Oh, I know that place. It's on the corner of Spring and West Broadway. It doesn't have a name but they'll let you sit down there if you buy a drink."

"Fern's Smart Lick Beauty Parlor?" the doctor supplied through clenched teeth.

"Excuse me while I make a doob check."

"Certainly. Crazy, isn't it? I mean, this place."

"Why, yes. Frankly, it makes me, well, all hendershot."

"It is the crazy place."

"Doctor, this place is a fake and you're a fake and I'm going to take you apart."

The Banks of the Sea 143

"If you do, Doctor Barnard will have your heart."
"What do you mean?"
"When you get on the reception ward—incidentally, it's a real zoo—you'll find a copy of *Time* magazine with a portrait of the Vice-President on the cover. Well, the magazine has an address label and it's pasted across the Vice-President's mouth."
"Ansafone?"
"I beg your pardon."
"Ansafone."
"Oh, yes, heh, heh," replied the doctor. "By the way, I wonder if you could tell me today's date."
Aquarius told him.
"Amazing," said the doctor. "I'm surprised you can remember."
Just then the phone rang. There were four Department of Sanitation garbage trucks completely at their capacity with dead rats. Pieces of rat bodies could be seen smeared in the compactors and one of the sanitation men was rapt in extracting a section of tail that had lodged in the tread of his rubber boot.

"He has a lizard design applied to each side of his neck," explained Fredegonde, "in order to attract prostitutes. The translation of the name of the mark is 'sleeping with the one desired'—*Kwanche da Masoye.*"
"But you say he's from Los Angeles," said Imogen. "Surely they aren't all tattooed in that savage fashion. Why, they're Americans."
"Naturally. "You'd be surprised what some of them look like underneath their clothes."
"But I don't want to be surprised like that!"
"What about me, poor me?" Fredegonde snuffled. "Did you think I was working for *National Geographic?*"
Imogen adjusted the lights. "These are a little bit hard to photograph," she said, gingerly touching the rugae on the other girl's inner thighs. "You'd think they would have made them stand out by rubbing soot or lampblack into the sores."
"Why should they have?" Fredegonde blustered. "*They* don't use that. Here. Just rub them and they'll get red."

"But I don't *want* to rub them. *You* rub them."

Suddenly Imogen was tired of the whole thing. She wanted to call her old friend a damned whore and be rid of her. But then it occurred to her that rouge could be used to make the scar tissue corrugations contrast with the skin around them so that they could be photographed.

"Just like staining a microscope slide," she said aloud.

And it became interesting. And so it was with the boon of clinical detachment that she was able to look upon the obscene spectacle of Fredegonde, masked, frotting her thighs. It sounded like a skin washboard. She took pictures of it.

"He called me the whitest one," said Fredegonde, distantly.

"Who?"

"Biggs. The boogie who did this to me."

"That sounds lovely. Do you know what these remind me of?"

"What?"

"Fishnet stockings. What is his name?"

"He calls himself E. Power Biggs. Imogen?"

"Huh?"

"Can you imagine a world in which as a social prophylaxis all white baby boys are blinded at birth?"

"Why that's horrible!" exclaimed Imogen. "Who would do a thing like that?"

"The black doctor."

And all the cutlery went. Plate, napkin rings, sets of steak knives, cheese cutters, thermos bottles together with a lot of electronic equipment kept in the same space. Condition yellow hatch. The spade quartermaster's mate's Julie London records. Rasmus Trismegistus and the cats' light bill. Ol' Rasmus has three little nigger boys sittin' at his knee. He wants to know how black they daddies is.

Rastus: Mah daddy so black that when he jack off he use graphite. Tha's pretty black, an' *slipp'ry?!*

Custis: Mah daddy so black that when he fart, he fart *soot!*

Fustis: That ain't nothin'. Mah daddy so black that when he hide in de coal bin, you can't see him for *nuthin!*

Rasmus: Straight back, you hit de doa.

You should'a come in like you was befoa.

Fustis, now when you daddy in de coal bin he mus' be doin' sumpthin that make him smile, an if it's one thing you *can* see it's a nigger's teeth. Mah, mah, an Custis, if you daddy so black he fart soot, he prob'ly black 'nuf to fart crystal balls. You better check that out. Hmmm. Fo' a minit there, Rastus, I thought you gwine say you daddy so black he stroke it with coal oil. Is you gildin' de lily, Rastus?

One of the elderly Negro patients was lying on his bed. One of the Italian patients picked up a steel chair and cracked him over the head with it. Sudden red on black.

There was a fire alarm at a little old abandoned skyscraper and the fire company were there playing their searchlights up into the gaping windows and asking around. Soon the smoke was located and they attached one of their hoses to the building standpipe. A crowd of derelicts was standing watching. It turned out the elevator wasn't operating and the fire chief had to send men in on the ladder.

Bums know about Camp La Guardia, operated by the city, where they can go to get off the street; someplace out in the country, if they feel they know too much. Some of them prefer going to Bellevue, this academy of adulthood, this grammar of silence. The men are sloppy in their blue pajamas and they worship tobacco, the dragon sailors found when they sailed over the edge of the world. Not much is said in the Blue Jay Way of the wards. The little talk is hedgy and jittery, and often relates to the concurring dreams of religion and cataclysm. The men are afraid and watchful, and clamor in a crowd at the cubicles of the doctors who appear only fleetingly on weekday mornings, when the straw-hatted agents are ready with limmazeens and school buses to transport the obdurate cases to more permanent billets at the state hospitals; Manhattan State, Central Islip, dread Creedmore. There are many hospitals in those blocks of First Avenue along the East River. There is the Veterans Administration Hospital, Bellevue Hospital, the New York University Medical Center, the Sloan Kettering Cancer Research Institute, and they are interconnected by subterranean tunnels all of which wind up at the spiritual center of this complex of temples, which is an attractive green-glazed building on the corner of East 31st Street and First Avenue. It is the morgue. Yet, does anybody die of schizophrenia? They might die of paranoia, however. Directly across East

31st Street from the morgue is the Bellevue Psychiatric Hospital, whose other neighbor is one of the Department of Sanitation's garbage incinerators. Meanwhile, Aquarius has developed a case of Messiah's flinch. Now and then a Roman soldier shies into his awareness and Aquarius jumps like he was shot.

"What was it like, being a captive of the androids?"
"It was in a red-brick tenement on a corner in Harlem. The windows were all blocked over with sheet metal. I'm sure you've seen places like that from the street. And inside there was niggers' dirty laundry strewn all over the place. Ropes were strung up here and there in the apartments and dirty clothes slung over them. It was like some kind of swish set for *The Flying Dutchman,* those damned jigs thinking they were too good to do the laundry."
"So what happened?"
"So Biggs bought a washer and a dryer and a couple of drums of detergent and his nigger bitches made *me* wash their rancid stinking dirty clothes, threatening me with no heroin in my ongoing body decorations."
"But you allowed yourself to suffer for them. Don't you know any better than to become accustomed to unpleasant experiences? Why, it's the principle of addiction."
"They make me sick."
"Sure. Like a little boy's first cigar."
"What they want," said Fredegonde, tossing her ol' curls, "is to degrade a white woman."
"What kind of white woman are you? Why didn't you call the police?"
"What, and blow my cover?"
How she hates, thought Imogen, appraising her old friend as if for the first time. Such a rotten kitten. Look at Fredegonde long enough and she'll get a bashful look on her face and start to dance the hoochy koochy. Keep looking at her and out of sheer modesty Silky Valentine will take her clothes off. She's a sideshow attraction, the definition of a streetwalker. She's Little Egypt. She is peanuts, popcorn, and Crackerjacks.

"I'm the Messiah," said Aquarius. "Do you want me to sign your ouija board?"

"We have been meeting every weekday for the past month," said the Head Clinician, "for these talks together. It must be apparent to you by this time that we are giving you consideration far above the other patients."

"Do you want me to turn wine into water?"

Mrs. White was wearing a black dress that Friday and she had the deportment of a judge on the bench. A large woman with a commanding presence, the other day she was wearing love beads. They were, she explained, her daughter's. Her talk seemed almost nonsensical it was so disengaged. It was as though the daily conversations were a mere ritual of form, a snow job on the other patients, and Aquarius came out of the little room looking like he had just been serviced by the boss lady. They said she was in love with him. Today, however, she had the demeanor of an official administering an oath. There was another clinician in the room, and at an appropriate moment Mrs. White made the ominous introduction.

"This is my assistant Mr. Moncado," she said. "He will be working with you during the remainder of your stay in Bellevue."

Mr. Moncado was Cuban, and like the Cuban patients he smoked L & Ms. He wore a diamond ring.

"In Cuba," he smiled, "it is the custom for the young boys to dance with each other. I'm sure you will get used to doing it too."

"You still going to be President, Miss World?" Imogen asked.

She watched Fredegonde blow a column of menthol smoke into the air. Looking at her, you would think human beings were originally intended to walk on their hands. Or had she become an android? The girl was one of those flawlessly malleable products of the American way of life, children of comfort and advantage, pearls their parents cast before swine like thumbtacks in the path of a barefoot enemy.

"Do you suppose there is such a thing as inherited prostitution?" she asked, ignoring Imogen's question.

"In certain cultures, in the same sense that there can be hereditary assassins," Imogen replied. "Prostitution is a vocation like priest-craft, which arose in order that kings might be blackmailed. A king is a king, and he may also be a talented musician, for example. Priest-craft and prostitution exist to create conditions in which the king's inherited ability to rule can be questioned. Be that as it may, he remains a talented musician. Are you a talented whore?"

"Kings are tyrants and tyrants must fall," Bryna said, patly.

"Monarchies are endured," said Imogen, "so that people may remember their origins in the heterosexual family. There is only the tyranny of the truth, and that is love. People can dispense with monarchies only when they agree that they can love, for then we are all kings and queens, and we don't need priests and prostitutes and consumerism and war, and Jesus can come down off the Cross."

"Sure," Bryna chuckled wickedly, "now that the Jews have got their Messiah."

"Listen, Sister Freddie," said Imogen. "You just stop trying to obfuscate and obscure."

"For a shutterbug you sure have a vocabulary."

"You stink," said Imogen. "You smell like an old can of worms. You ought to read some Shakespeare and listen to some Bach."

"Shakespeare was gay."

"Well if you can't burn all the books at least you can slander the authors."

"Bach was a male chauvinist pig. His wife was an old woman in a shoe. She had so many children..."

"Yes, and don't you wish you were one of them? For the love of your parents, woman, to thine own self be true..."

"Unto thine hole be true, woman, for that's all you are."

"I'm not so sure about that," said Imogen. "I'm a pretty good photographer."

"You're a dyke, too, honey. That book of yours, *Men Working*. You think you're one of them."

"'I do not admit that a woman can draw like that,'" murmured Imogen.

"What are you talking about?" Fredegonde cackled. "A cowgirl? Annie Oakley?"

"Oh, I was just thinking of something Degas said about Mary Cassatt," said Imogen. "He saw some of her work and said, 'I do not admit that a woman can draw like that.'"

They walked as they talked, strode about in the studio, postured against the photographer's props and used the furniture according to its purpose and design. They were real persons, the two old friends, and they were indeed actors, playing in the long moment of difference between conviction and knowledge.

Fredegonde found some of the potted plants from the days when she and Imogen were roommates. They were well cared for and had grown much. She examined their older reaches for familiar details. It gave her a déjà vu.

"Very well, slim and successful," she pouted. "You may be a poet with a camera, but overweight girls are more orgasmic."

"If you're such a statistic then why can't you come? Because you *can't* come anymore, can you?"

"That's none of your business."

Fredegonde crossed her legs theatrically, held her head in her hands and wept.

"Is that why you use cocaine?"

Imogen brought her a dishtowel to cry into and spoke soothingly. Fredegonde let her hair down.

"Oh, Imo . . . I can't even get wet anymore."

After a while, with the sun gone down like red roses, Imogen got ready to fix the evening meal. She peeled a couple of extra servings of potatoes and put them on to boil and took the meat out of the freezer. When she came from the kitchen Fredegonde wasn't sitting where she had been, and for a moment Imogen thought she had gone away as through her ex-husband's and his lover's tesseract. But Fredegonde had found a dark place to curl up in and Imogen found her there, beside Hollister's sulking nook. She lighted a candle.

"Why don't you stay here tonight," she suggested. "You seem to have a lot on your mind. There's a comfortable bed for you and we can talk."

"Just like old times? Sounds like fun, boo hoo . . ."

Fredegonde, wistful, shabby valentine.

"Do you have any tequila?"

"We can go out and buy some. And tomorrow," Imogen said, "you might like to come along when I visit Carol in Bellevue."

"I really couldn't," said Fredegonde.
"Now look. You claim you and your friends put him there."
Imogen plumped a couple of pillows.
"So I think you ought to meet him, Freddie. He's entitled to it, isn't he? Why you can even keep the mask on."

9 Carrion Moon

> *It would be a grand sight, if it weren't for the pity.*
> Beatrix Potter on the bombing of Liverpool

"How'd you like to go back to Bellevue?" one of the policemen asked matter-of-factly.

Carol looked at them and managed to swallow the mouthful of food he had been chewing.

"You keep sitting there," the other policeman said, "and pretty soon you'll be jumpin' in the river."

"Cheese 'n crackers got all muddy," Carol mumbled, stuffing the food back in the bag.

"What did you say?"

"Are you a wise guy or are you just queer?"

"Jesus Christ and God Almighty," Carol repeated loudly.

"That's better. You just keep movin' for a while and you'll think of something to keep yourself out of trouble."

Carol got up from the tenement stoop where he had been sitting in the sunshine and took a walk up Second Avenue. Why had the cops been so gruff?

There had been another assassination. The victim lingered, and an old lady said to Carol, "If the coma persists they can put him in a glass oxygen tent and allow the public to pray at his bedside."

Carol was certain, from the photo in the newspapers, that he had seen the assassin in New York a few months before. It was that guy shivering on Astor Place beside the sculpture, *The Alamo*. He couldn't—or wasn't permitted to—use his hands or to speak and two Jewish girls were feeding him an apple, holding it out to him so he could eat it like a dog at its bowl, and they were laughing at him. Carol remembered quite clearly.

People knew that he remembered and for a while none of the merchants would sell him anything. He would go into a grocery store and pick something out—a jar of peanut butter and a box of Ritz crackers, say—and the grocer would turn his back on him or tell him to get out, conk hombres and huarache honchos emerging from the back room with little cans of Rheingold in their hands. It was like the time Aquarius tried to panhandle around St Mark's Place and the people, the only thing he got from them were silver coins minted before 1965. The counterman at Gem's Spa gave him a Franklin quarter and a look that said Somebody Wants To Crucify You.

The assassination victim eventually qualified for burial. Carol went hungry and slept in doorways and on park benches. Actually you could go a long way on a bellyfull of water. The best drinking fountain was in a corner of the little park next to the Beth Israel Hospital. It must have been the feeling of being hunted and punished, the memory being flogged out of him which obscured from him the obvious solution. But then one morning he sauntered wraithlike into a supermarket and bought some food—a pack of sliced salami, a pack of cheese, Saltine crackers, and a couple of cans of Newark beer. The checkout girl smiled like a neon sign saying Why Didn't You Think Of This Sooner?

He was eating those things sitting on a sunny doorstoop on East Third between Second and Bowery when the two cops stopped and favored him with their advice. He was dirty and hadn't slept much, but the sun was shining and pretty girls were picking their way through the bums and his breakfast was a banquet. He felt like a million dollars.

On Fifth Avenue, at the northwest corner of its intersection with West 14th Street, two buildings stand separated by a space about as wide as the radiator attachment of a vacuum cleaner is broad. Their adjacent walls are perfectly parallel and daylight fills the interstice too slender for a kitten to enter let alone be rescued from. One night some time back Carol taped his extra safe deposit box key to the north wall and now he wants to use it and move it to another snuggy. He wonders if it is still there. People wonder what that bummy character is doing. One of the buildings houses a branch of the Chase Manhattan Bank, and passersby wonder whether what he is doing has anything to do with that. Most certainly. Or he might be getting ready to relieve his bladder, up-against-the-wall motherfucker.

The Banks of the Sea 153

Now a monkey couldn't do this. Carol reached in and felt around. There it was. He was triumphant and remembered the place with affection and the look of the day. (It was summer smoggy forenoon, and the slit of luminescence was white without depth—he was reaching into a two-dimensional object—and resembled the long fluorescent tubes technology students like to demonstrate the Tesla coil with.) This was quite delicate. He flatted in with the back of his right hand and with his middle fingernail carefully scraped off the top leader of adhesive tape, then let the tape with the broad key stuck on it fold down with its own weight. Finally he alligator-clipped it between index and middle finger, and exhaling beatifically pulled it off the wall and put it in his pocket.

A springy saunter to the post office. Something in his box. A letter from his mother and a letter from Imogen, notification of a package at the window. Imogen's letter gave him a hard-on. The package contained six pairs of cotton socks, without comment except that in her letter his mother remarked that on the hottest days in New York people were said to kick pigeons and that it got in the news.

He rode the BMT to his bank in another borough. The guard grimaced when he presented himself at the vault. He signed in and the guard, turning the bank's key, commented, "Nothing like a walk on the wild side, eh Mister Gamewell?"

As the "tenant" of a safe deposit box he enjoyed the air-conditioned privacy of a little room with a writing surface and two armchairs. He sat down and opened the metal drawer and contemplated the stack of tens. They were his hoard-for-adventure. He counted them with satisfaction. Thirty-four ten dollar bills. He took the liberty of changing his socks there in the humidity-controlled atmosphere. He clipped his toenails, deposited the clippings in the ashtray; clipped them flat across so as to prevent ingrown toenails, a sign of somebody who takes care of himself, something only a detective or a coroner would observe. Forty dollars. Ten in his pocket, ten taped to his skin, and ten in the lining of each shoe. A fresh pocket notebook from the drawer and one filled with poetry in its place. Imogen's letter. He availed himself of the opportunity and masturbated into one of his dirty socks.

Back in Manhattan who should he run into but his old Nam buddy Bradley. Bradley was with a girl.

"Hey! Carol. Howrya doin? Lookin' pretty skinny. Hey, I'd like you meet Ponca. Ponca, Carol."

"Chow," said Ponca.

Carol tried to look not potentially dangerous nor as though he thought too much. He accentuated his war limp.

"You look kinda street beat," said Bradley. "Wanna come stay with us for a while? We got this little place in Newark."

Bradley had shucked the soutane and now he and his old lady were high-grade shoddy establishment blanket heads. Bradley talked rapidly and effusively the way people did in Nam when they were on speed. Not very cool, either. The two of them were carrying kilo bricks of grass in their blanket bags. Ponca was crazy, was without sense of either proportion or value, cooked stupendous rations of ectoplasm for ghost armies and gathered child hordes under the epidemic wings of her aegis. They looked like Sonny and Cher and Carol asked her if she sewed Bradley's shirts and generally flattered her outrageously, the three of them making their way somewhat rudely through the crowds of kitchen shoppers on Ninth Avenue. They got to Pennsylvania Station and somehow made it aboard the Silver Meteor. Bradley and Ponca had *tickets*. It pulled out at 2:50 on the dot and the three found an unoccupied compartment in one of the Boston to Miami sleeping cars. The train picked up speed in the tunnel. They would arrive in Newark at 3:05.

The Hudson is a deep river. Its lower course is a submarine canyon called a drowned valley, which terminates at sea with the escarpment of the continental shelf. The tunnels under the Hudson—the Holland, the Lincoln, the Hudson Tubes and the Pennsylvania Railroad—are pigs in blankets, metal sausages nestled in a batter of abysmal muck. In the middle of this railroad tunnel as black as a volcanic "pipe" full of soot, Carol, in the everyday light of the Pullman bedroom, thought he detected an odor of brimstone about Bradley's person. It was when he noticed a patch of fur stitched to the flap of Ponca's bag. He was sitting across from them, like a Sybil on the upholstered lid of the commode. He reached over and stroked the fur.

"That's very soft," he chuckled. "Soft as a dog's 'tain't. Upon my word..."

"It is a dog's 'tain't, Carol," Ponca said smiling saintly as a mother. "You're pretty smart, you know? And for that you get what's-his-name here's sister."

The train left the tunnel in a flood of afternoon and they traversed the Meadows.

Bradley's sister Jae Ann lived in an apartment over an abandoned art supplies store on the corner of William and Arlington in Newark, New Jersey. She had lived there since the riots, and was satisfied with the place on account of the view it gave of the downtown area, which had remained standing in a blocky jumble as the streets all around it burned. She was a contented schizophrenic and had a child born with a suntan. It was because of the child that the blacks let her live there. She received welfare and turned tricks. Carol was to stay with her as long as he liked.

They got along well together, Carol and Jae Ann, but when the time came for him to ball her he didn't want to.

"I'm not going to put it in there."

"Why not?"

"I want that kid to see you give me a blow job."

"All right. But what for, when you can get in here?" She showed him by putting his hand on her pussy. He gave it a squeeze.

"I don't want that kid calling me a motherfucker."

In the days that followed they walked romantically in the weeds and rubble, and she would always draw him aside and whispering like a child ask him to ball her. She led him between parked cars and into gutted storefronts, beside copses of tall new sumac in the vacant lots full of bricks and wildflowers. The streets were still paved, still named. There were idyllic, almost rural vistas of Newark with a brick or masonry building here, the clump of downtown there, and always the Negroes, slow, uncurious. It was a city brought to the lowest denominator of its citizenry.

"There will be a girl you love," said Jae Ann, "but if you ever get drunk you'll forget her name."

"What is her name?" Carol asked.

"She'll tell you."

"How will I know it's her?"

"Because there won't be any others."

She walked up to a garage standing beside the foundations of a house and opened the doors. The roof had burned and was gone, but the floor was swept clean as though somebody had thought of putting a new roof on and parking their car in there. The place was full of spiders. It was crammed with their webs in all sizes, arrayed one behind the other like combs in a hive. They billowed a little from the doors being opened, shimmering in the noonday sun. A few dried leaves were on the floor. Carol immediately felt a theatrical atmosphere and sensed a backstage kind of attractiveness. But then there was a dead baby bird wrapped up in silk and the big spider busy over it. All at once he thought Jae Ann was going to push him in there and lock the doors. He turned to her.

"Do you mean to say," he said, "that all of the others will be, er, ineligible?"

"Am I ineligible?" she asked wistfully?

Carol's hair was half-long and lank. If he shaved his beard he would look like an actor in an old B-movie about a military academy whose long-haired cadets were played by boy extras saving their locks for A-movies. But what he had been experiencing and the things he had seen people doing had the quality of perfect authenticity of action being played out on a Hollywood soundstage. He thought of his wanderings in the catalog of humanity that was New York. What he had been living was simply the best of all possible takes, and the rest were on the cutting room floor. He let his mind observe the two of them—himself and this girl—and he came to the conclusion that it was a crazy thing that to live in one's native land should require a willing suspension of disbelief.

"You are your brother's sister," he said, "but I don't think you're what either he or I went to Vietnam for."

Jae Ann grinned oafishly in her popular insanity. "Wait'll Bonnalynn comes over," she said. "You'll like her twat. It's a real zinger."

"That remains to be seen," he said, pissing into the spider webs. "I'm not about to let myself get screwed blued and tattooed. And anyway there aren't any tattoo parlors in New York City. They're against the law." He buttoned his fly. "If a white man wants a tattoo he goes to Spider Jack's in Mount Vernon."

"Are there astrologers in New York?" she sniffed.

Carol laughed outright. "All of her friends had had acne, and then she met this spade chick who was wearing a dirndl..."

Jae Ann pouted with her voice. "You're making fun of me, just because I'm a woman."

"Nonsense. The Majorska was drunk and the soldiers..."

"Now *you're* taking advantage of me."

The Banks of the Sea

That night she tried to get him to put his extra finger in her extra eye.

"C'mon," he said, making her hunker up so her titties brushed his crotch, "I want to make you skip your breakfast again."

American girls give good blow jobs. They rub their breasts up and down their guy's body and nuzzle his dong and, inspired, lick it. Then they take it between their fingers like eating stuffed celery and put it in their mouths and suck it. There is something sweetly submissive about this common American act of cannibalism. The girls are like mandrake roots sprung from the final gyssom spurt of hanged men. They are willow trees whose trunk is his hard-on and whose leaves, tickling his thighs, are her weeping hair. As Carol was coming he heard a distant but familiar voice whisper in his mind.

"American girl," said the lil Injun, *"suck unicorn."*

Bonnalynn showed up in her Chevvy the next morning with a bottle of Scotch which she set on the table for them to think about all day. Carol looked at her, liked her, and found himself saying:

> "I see your children are ridin' a bay,
> But underneath they're nursin' a Gray.
> I'm sure that when he's ready for the street
> He'll turn 'em all whiter than a sheet."

"Where did that come from?" asked Bonnalynn.

"I dunno," said Carol. "I just thought of it. Must be from the Civil War."

They had brunch and then went downtown in Bonnalynn's car. The girls wanted to see something at the cultural center so they parked the car near Lincoln Park and walked around, two white girls, a white guy, and Jae Ann's mulatto child. The girls apparently wanted to look at the posters around the entrance of the Newark Cultural Center, which is the old Mosque Theater by another name. They stood cooing and chattering over the glossy photos of operatic and concert performers. What they dwelt longest over, however, was the poster advertising a Bach recital to be given by a young Negro harpsichordist a week hence. Carol, meanwhile, wasn't much interested in these announcements of cultural events. What he was thinking about, in full view of the crowds on the street, was his discomfort at being in company with the mulatto.

What he felt was a biological revulsion at the notion that the child might be mistaken for his or that he might be taken for the consort of its mother. Or whether or not he was any of these things, and even if he wasn't, the assumption among the visible population was that he, as a viable white man, ought to consecrate his life to the care and rearing of this child and, ideally, litigate protractedly in the courts to become its legal guardian. It seemed to him that this was a moment in time in which the alternatives were unsatisfactory. And then he saw, walking along together there on Broad Street, two albinos.

After a drive through Weequahic Park they went to Mulberry Street and did the shopping. The girls were interested in exotic food and bought ingredients for a Greek dish made with several kinds of fish. The market street was lively and it reminded Carol of Ninth Avenue in New York with the kind of butcher stores that have calves' brains in the windows. It was a hot day and the runoff from store air conditioners streaked glistening at intervals across the sidewalk, evaporating before it reached the curb.

It was cool back at the house. What is a whorehouse without an air conditioner? After an early supper they turned it off and opened the windows to the evening. In a while some Negroes built a bonfire in a vacant lot and made music around it far into the night. A guitar, harmonica, spoons. The girls got kind of stinkarooed.

Carol snuggling with Bonnalynn.

"Jae Ann has been telling me about this," he said, sliding his hand inside Bonnalynn's underpants. She let him remove them. These girls wore skirts in the summer and had tanned legs.

Bonnalynn rubbed the front of his pants and after a while opened them. She fished his cock out and stroked it with her fingertips. She wanted him to play with her breasts.

Jae Ann was horny and lay on the other bed smoking grass and masturbating. She would be a lot of fun tomorrow when the phone company employees got paid and the installation crews came over for a coffee break. The phone company was just half a block away. Think of all the telephones in those burned houses. Jae Ann got up and came over to Carol and Bonnalynn and knelt beside the bed.

"Carol, I know you don't think much of me," she said, "but I know you'll always do the right thing."

The Banks of the Sea 159

Carol, in his delirium of pleasure with Bonnalynn, smiled at Jae Ann and wordlessly stroked her yellow hair. She started to cry and became spiteful and said, "Tomorrow is the mulatto's birthday."

Oh Bonnalynn, the smell of fresh cut wood on this new continent, the western breeze warm in the night with the smell of distant rivers. Consider Pennsylvania with her two watersheds. Some flows into the Delaware and some into the Ohio. Big sweet girl. He got inside Bonnalynn and soon they were unfolding like a galaxy. The Scythians used to saddle a horse with a packsaddle that had a metal brazier fitted to it, and in this they laid a bed of coals and covered it with a punched screen, at night. Then the animal was let loose to run—sparks streaming from the brazier—in a straight line across the steppe until it fell down dead. This was done before important military undertakings and was a ceremonial to "bring back the comet" because a comet, in remembered belief, had caused the destruction of a walled city. This practice they called "saddle lights."

They were up early and had bacon and eggs and biscuits with Sioux Bee alfalfa honey. Bonnalynn and Carol took a shower together. The girls cleaned the place up, and when Carol tried to wash the dishes Bonnalynn shooed him away. "You don't have to do that," she said.

In the living room there were suddenly condom boxes and a roll of kitchen towels on the end table beside the Castro Convertible. Jae Ann put her arms around his neck and pecked him on the cheek. "You know where to go and how to get there, don't you?" she said.

He thanked her, kissed Bonnalynn and was on his way.

Grasshoppers fluttertongued across the weedy sidewalks.

Twice a month, in order to supplement their meager incomes so they could have a little fun out of life, Jae Ann and Bonnalynn were "Telephone Pioneers." They can't be blamed for that, can they? And anyway, even though it isn't in the schoolbooks, America was won by women as well as men, women creating causes and heroes for them, inspiring armies and refreshing laborers. It is they, this silent service, these mute mere women who effect social change. So, Hi! for the life of the helping hole. There was also a tube of K-Y, the water-miscible emollient, on the end table. What did they use in the old days? Bear grease? Bonnalynn didn't make him wear a condom and she was wet so it must have been for love. He felt diddled. Suddenly, perhaps like a fad,

Carol was angry. He found a phone booth on South Orange Avenue and called Jae Ann's number. The mulatto answered. The mulatto had a surname which derived from the French *Le Beau*. He wished the mulatto a happy birthday.

"Happy birthday, LeeBoo," he said. "Bet you didn't know that the pinto is the sports model of the horse world."

There were men's voices in the background, Jae Ann screeching and one of her Joe Cocker records. He heard Bonnalynn tell the mulatto to tell whoever was on the phone to call back in half an hour and the mulatto repeated this, quite articulately, to Carol, who said, "Thanks, LeeBoo. Now you better get back to the door," and hung up.

"So how do you like Darkadelphia?" Bradley asked.

"Interesting," said Carol. "Historic city."

Ponca rose to leave the room for something. She was a tall, good-looking though rather sallow brunette and she was wearing an India Print dress from Tantra Imports.

"You'd better phone Baltimore," she said to Bradley, then smiled warmly to Carol, understanding the good time he had been having at Jae Ann's. She left the room thinking of the name of her dress, which was "Stephanie Mini." Bradley picked up the receiver.

"I'm phoning a phone booth on a street in Baltimore," he said. "A man is waiting in a car and he will hear it ring a certain number of times."

Almost disbelieving, Carol watched Bradley dial (301) 727-9073. The connection was established and Bradley held the receiver so Carol could hear it ringing. It rang five times, then he hung up with his finger and replaced the receiver.

"That means you've arrived," he explained. "Now the man will go to a bar across a vacant lot from the phone booth, buy a bottle of National and ask if he can use the phone. Then he'll phone a Navy Department office in Rosslyn, Virginia. That office, however, is unoccupied. It's got furniture in it, and the portrait of the President, and the telephone is operational. A man in an adjoining office will hear it ring five times. He will look at his watch and in half an hour he'll phone here. If it rings five times, that will mean: Acknowledged. Proceed as planned."

Bradley was obviously pleased with this cloak-and-suiter arrangement. He gave the telephone a fanny pat.

"Pretty neat, huh?"

"The Navy Department?" Carol burst out. He thought of his discharge papers in the safe deposit box. "What in Fuck's name is going on?"

"You're a national treasure, buddy," said Bradley heartily, "and you're one of the principals in the cargo cult."

"Large charge," said Carol. "Big deal. What do I need with a cargo cult? All I want to do is get married, settle down and raise a family."

"But the Myth of America..." said Bradley from his swivel chair, fingers together. "You wouldn't want to be responsible for the Last World War, would you?"

All at once Carol was transformed into your stereotype irate motorist, leaning out the window of his car shaking his fist.

"Fucking cocksucker!"

"Shush shush," said Bradley. "You sound like a Puerto Rican. All those percussive expletives..."

Just then Ponca tiptoed in and beckoned for the two men to follow her. Her face wore a look of glee and she wanted them to enjoy something with her. They silently made their way down the hall to a room next to the kitchen, over whose door was a hand-lettered sign. *HUSKIES.*

It was the only air-conditioned room in the house and it was the abode of a mated pair of Alaskan Malamute husky dogs. A porch storm door permitted a view of these animals who were now—Ponca motioned for the two men to watch—playing tug-of-war with a severed human arm. Such huge dogs being cute, asses in the air and tails wagging, emitting ferocious sounds through their viselike jaws. Grrr!

"That's not Newark *Schvartze*," Bradley explained of the arm. "That's Brooklyn *Schvartze.*"

Ponca gave the aghast Carol a poke in the ribs. " 'Stephen won't give his arm,' " she chortled, " 'to the Gold Star Mothers' Farm.' "

Bradley and Carol exchanged a look of understanding having to do with their war experiences in Vietnam. They knew that the dead bodies of white people turn black and that the corpses of black people most certainly do not turn white.

"Look at the tongues of those dogs," Ponca said. "They're as mottled as an orchid. Huskies must be part chow."

The dogs had left off the arm and came grinning and waggling to the door. Their tongues, all alollyslobber, were indeed mottled and everybody knows that the chow breed have a black tongue. Could the chow, then, have been the companion of the first gook nomads to cross the Bering Straits to Alaska?

"Stands to reason, don't it?" Ponca cackled.

Bradley looked at his watch and he and Carol went back to the office. Bradley lighted a Tiparillo little cigar and put his feet on the desk. Carol thought Bradley had acquired an air of the mercenary soldier. He stroked his Ken Nolan moustache.

"You must have heard of the death plazas of Uganda," he said.

"You mean like Forest Lawn?" Carol said.

"Naw, the President of Uganda, he calls his own people niggers and has had these death plazas built in every town and village. It's these cement hardstands, see, with neck shackles and tie rings for the feet. The victim is stretched out with his hands tied behind his back and is, er, despatched by the Racker, who wears white vinyl high-heel hip boots and uses a sledgehammer, ker-*thock!*"

"Why that's revolting."

"It is a pity," agreed Bradley. "Rather like destroying a work of art."

The ashtray on the desk was made of hammered copper and was fastened with copper straps to the back of a tortoise which Bradley was on the verge of deciding to call Aldo. As the two men thought their thoughts and eyeballed the room the tortoise suddenly revved up and started moving across the desk, plowing through papers and shouldering aside piles of books. Bradley watched it approach him.

"Beautiful dreamer," he said. "Crowninshield."

Or he would call it Waldo. The last time he called it anything it was Rocky Mount, in commemoration of his discovery that the Puerto Ricans had discovered country music. He thought about that. Next time he would call it The Barracuda, even though such tortoises can't swim but sink like stones when placed in water. That was how he and Ponca got the damned thing to shit in one place, by putting it in a sinkful of water every evening. Or he would have Carol call it The Barracuda, or have him call the reptile Federal Way.

The tortoise strolled right up in front of Bradley who availed himself of this felicitous circumstance by knocking the ash off his cigarillo. The phone rang.

"Thanks, Waldo," he said. He refrained from looking at his watch. The phone rang five times. "Okay," he said.

After a festive supper in honor of Carol's arrival at the commune, all of its members gathered in the backyard for a little ceremony. Grass was smoked and the tortoise—incense burning now in the copper cymbal on its back—was placed on the lawn, where it hustled across to the dandelions and ate one. Then the communards chanted a Rag and Bradley, as Guru, intoned a creed.

"This is the Other Newark. Newark is Something Else. Built over deep labyrinths of Eerie and Lackanookie. This Newark is Love! Riots of Love! Enormous Strobes-In-The-Sky kind of Love! Dancing People in the streets! Let's hear the Gospel from the New Arrival."

"Yay!"

Carol was fatigued and undernourished after week of marginal living on the street. He had sores from constantly walking, swollen feet, and had begun to develop boils on his legs. He was wearing a pair of clean trousers and a shirt which Ponca furnished him from the commune's slop chest while his own clothes were being laundered by the girls of the house. The humidness of large-breasted women in the heat of summer. The girls whispered admiring, catty exchanges about him as though he were a foredoomed rock star, and now there he stood in the gathering dusk and was expected to pontificate the doctrine of Aquarius. The assembly were as critical as a furled umbrella.

"Have you heard the one about the very shy monocle?" he began. "It didn't want to make a spectacle of itself."

Carol thought that was pretty funny.

"Seriously now," he said earnestly, "I'd like to tell you the Parable of the Oarsman and the Wastrels. There was this lifeboat, dig? And it was full of castaways adrift on the ocean. They were torpedoed, dig? And the only thing they managed to take with them were bottles of booze snatched from the severely listing ship's bar. When that was gone they had nothing but the lifeboat's case of emergency rations and its cask of water. Well, after a few days the supplies gave out and the people began to piss and moan, saying, 'What shall we do? Surely we are goners.' All except for one man, who instead of guzzling all of his daily ration of water had saved some and now had a good supply for himself."

He paused for effect. They were hanging on his every word, albeit frowning. He continued.

"Well, the others grew weak and despaired and were unable to row the boat, but the man who had been thrifty with his water ration said, 'I will row the boat. In three days we should reach Bermuda.' And so he did row the boat, slowly but surely, resting now and then, and swigging a little water when the others weren't looking. They were so weakened from thirst and hunger that it amazed them when the oarsman kept rowing hour after hour, day and night. Then one of them, pretending to be asleep or unconscious, saw him drink of the water which he had saved for himself and cried out, 'Look! He has saved water for himself!' They all ganged up on the oarsman and with their last strength beat him and drowned him in the briny sea. Then all of them died horribly without ever sighting land."

They were silent, and then a wee voice piped, "What's that s'posed to mean?"

"Easy on the birdseed, Perkins," said another, and they all laughed at this reference to the substance of their macrobiotic meals.

"The moral of the story is," said Carol, "that to somebody who says I've got mine, you should say I love you."

"Fascist!" shouted a wire-rimmed female voice. "Fascist male chauvinist elitist racist pig!" and after a moment, "Capitalist!"

They tossed it around for a while and one of them suggested that the moral ought to be "When you're out of Schlitz you're out of beer." Carol laughed with them and brought the proceeding to a conclusion with the Testimony of Bunky Tauber:

> " 'I am both product and critique,
> A system within a system,
> A partial outsider to my creator intent.
> I am humble to that intent.
> I am!' "

The communards cheered and made animal noises. Ponca went up to Carol and hugged him. She kissed him in front of everybody and whispered in his ear, "You're a hit, honey. For that you get me."

Teenage macrobiosis and spliturition. Marvin's Floating Crash Pads

The Banks of the Sea

Directory and Demian Bunions Digest. The commune was called Red Skeleton and there was a medical school skeleton hanging in the front porch. It was painted red and it clattered.

The house was a slum within a slum, an enclave of intentional poor white on a street named Cabinet in what had become one of the most intensely black areas of the city. Once upon a time these were stable neighborhoods of Irish, Ukranian, Italian and Jewish families who lived in the frame houses which they were proud of and kept up, painting them, putting up storm windows, tending gardens. They were quiet shady streets with well-behaved children and neighborly concern. And then in the late nineteen-fifties, when it seemed that these parts of Newark were in the flower of their maturity—with thick green lawns and shrubs, the scent of burning leaves in the autumn along the pleasant streets whose slate slab sidewalks were quaintly buckled here and there from the roots of healthy trees—in the space of a political term of office the good people all moved to the flimsy suburbs and drove to the shopping center in their flimsy cars. It is never easy to move, especially from a place you like. There must have been a good reason. Maybe it was the asbestos siding.

The only light in the living room came from the color TV. They were watching an eyewitness report of a demonstration outside the Public Theater on Lafayette Street in Manhattan. Bunch of people chanting with clenched fists raised. Placards and banners. BLACK BELONGS, and LEONTYNE PRICE *IS* AIDA. A New York Shakespeare Festival production of *Othello* had an Arab and not a Negro playing the title role. A car was set on fire in the parking lot on Astor Place. The windows of the Cooper Union Library were smashed and the books dumped out and burned. Carol watched this bemusedly like Andy Boy seeing Scotty grow. Something made him glance away from the screen just in time to see a cockroach shimmy across his hand. He roused himself and got up, nearly spraining his wrist in the slimy couch, and stood for a minute trying once again to make out the contours of the other person in the living room. Then he turned and something standing on the TV set caught his eye. It was a can of Figaro cat food with an unopened pack of Pall Malls on it.

Along about bedtime Ponca found Carol, took him aside and told him, "I'm afraid of Duane, see. He has that machete over the bed and if he thinks I . . ."

Carol refrained from breathing a sigh of relief. For a bed that first night Bradley curled his lip and flung him a moldy sleeping bag which he, Bradley, had just shagged Ponca on.

Slept on the living-room couch. Dreams interspersed with cockroach scintillations, rubber bullets and hollow switchblades full of V-8 juice. Somebody trying to commit suicide with an electric hotplate. Got up once to "feed the monster." Went upstairs to the bathroom and as he was groping for the light switch a cat scratched him. He turned the light on. He turned it off again.

Souls are a resource. The energy of pent souls moves both the windmills of the witches and the galleys—as well as the galleons—of the churches. Individual souls, indistinguishable in the diffuse plasma, nonetheless are singular and tabs are kept on them. They may be interceded for or their value influenced in other ways, letting one become a mascot, say, and another a voice in a choir. In life a bit of soul always rubs off onto intimate objects and haunts; consubstantiation is a stock-in-trade of antique dealers, and it is the principle manifested when fans tear the clothes off their idols at rock concerts or in front of their hotels. There are too many people. Just look at some of the cities. Their inhabitants are so feebly souled it is surprising they have anything to say to one another. It is as though Smith stuff were being spread kind of thin in our day and age. Yet mankind is unlikely to achieve the statistical delusion that there are more living than dead. At most there may be a convivial feeling of triumph in the overwhelming numbers, followed by the suspicion that either the dead have been holding out or that they have been far too generous. Be that as it may, the thin-souled are not always weak-spirited. Indeed the souls of some seem to consist in a mixture with another substance and some individuals must be inhabited by the other substance entirely, their little souls having long since been drained out of them like blood into a common barrel and replaced by the different fluid. There are cities in America where strangers may lose their souls simply by registering a combination of certain sensory impressions. The common stuff of souls can be jellied for specific purposes or atomized for others, and it can be compressed and put in a bottle. The essential nature of the individual soul—its "germ"—is not a replica of the living person. Souls can be likened to stones picked up on a beach. Some radiate information eternally without repeating themselves. Others conjugate their impartings into branching successions of variants. Still others are a single statement, explicit and immutable.

The next day Bradley took Carol on a tour of downtown Newark. They took the Number 9 bus and got off at Klein's. Bradley was wearing smooth shiny black boots and wanted them polished, so they went to the shoe-shine stand in the lobby of the Raymond Commerce Building and mounted the chairs. Bradley tossed the shoe-shine boy a small, unlabelled can of black polish.

"Try this," he said.

The boy slapped and patted Bradley's boots, buffed and popped at them, even blacked the welts for him West-Coast style. When he was finished he asked Bradley what kind of shoe polish that was.

"Next time it'll have a name on it," Bradley said.

The old shoe-shine boy looked first at Carol's unshineable boots and then at Bradley's shiny, shiny black boots—he could see his reflection in them—and the blank white can of polish, smudged now with his fingerprints. He looked up at Carol and started to tremble. He looked at Bradley.

"Yas, *suh!*" he said.

"What did you do that for?" Carol asked when they were back on the street.

"So he'd think you're the hit man," said Bradley. "We're going to waste the nigger harpsichord player."

Carol saw another albino. He wanted to ask Bradley why there were so many albinos in Newark.

"Why are there so many albinos in Newark?" he asked.

Bradley guffawed. "Must be because they like each other." He slapped Carol on the back. "C'mon, buddy. I'll buy us some grub."

Hobby's Delicatessen on Branford Place, in cozy proximity to Minsky's and the Branford and a hangout of newspapermen. Obviously Bradley preferred its lunch to the commune's peanut-butter-and-jelly, though it wasn't certain which was more likely to make his tongue cleave to the roof of his mouth. Not so much a hedonist as a thrill opportunist, he had always seemed to Carol a man exempt from having to consider whether he was guarding his honor. He won crap games.

Lent money at immodest interest—Sunday school interest, he called it—to guys in the division who habitually spent all of their pay their first couple of nights on liberty. The profits from this shipboard usury he sunk into an on-limits skin joint in Bangkok. Beachcomber Brad's. The first drink was free.

"Sink your teeth into one of these," he said.

There was at least an inch of thin-sliced pastrami—steaming and fragrant—between the rye. Carol was one of those people who eat their sandwiches from left to right. He watched Bradley, looking like a Hungry Charlie's sign, open his mandibles and with one bite leave a crust like the crescent moon. He tended his moustache as he chewed and swallowed. They drank beer. On each table was a bowl of pickled cherry peppers. Carol tried one. It opened his sinuses. The peppers were a Newark tradition, Bradley explained.

"Still got that place in Bangkok?" Carol asked.

"Naw, I unloaded it to Trader Kelly's. Remember a number called Chinese Mule Train?"

"Leaky High?"

"Forget it."

"Come on, man. You're like a puppy dog that ate a box of Crayolas. You shit in colors."

"I'm not shitting you."

"The Navy Department, man. Since when has the eagle stopped shitting?"

"You been walkin' around New York. Is that some kinda bonus march or is it just your fornookies?"

"There are a lot of people living on the street."

"Ponca's got a place in her heart."

"And you've got a hole in your head."

Bradley appeared to be hit someplace. He quaffed sanctimoniously. Carol went on.

"What you're into. It's like the C-side of a record."

"The jewel is in the lotus."

"Yeah and the Lotus is in the *Andrea Doria*."

Bradley. Gestures of cooling it. Spread palms over the tablecloth.

"What I was talking about in the office. You know Janis Joplin? You're out on the street lookin' good . . ."

"Goddam disc jockey."

"Everybody's eyes are on you, buddy, so just be your sweet self."

Carol was humming a tune. Bradley's exaggerated gesture of recognizing it. Exasperated.

" 'John Brown's Baby?' If it isn't 'John Brown's Baby' then I know a guy who got ten days in the brig for singing it."

Carol was tapping his glass with the saltshaker on the off-beat like the Anvil Chorus. He and Bradley gave each other the high sign and started singing.

"Mine eyes have seen the gory second coming of the Lord;
He has wallowed in the paddies where the blood of life has poured,
And men with mangled bodies have the pangs of dying roared,
We've never lost a war.

Gory, Gory Hallelujah,
Gory, Gory Hallelujah,
Gory, Gory Hallelujah,
We've never lost a war.

His sweet participation in the slaughter of the hosts
Doth reduce to insignificance our puny earthly boasts;
He'll always shine his light o' love where human tissue roasts,
We've never lost a war.

Gory, Gory Hallelujah,
Gory, Gory Hallelujah,
Gory, Gory Hallelujah,
We've never lost a war.

Professors and psychiatrists have heard the sacred call
And instructed us with symbols that the enemy must fall . . ."

"Commie bastards! What's da big idea?"

"It's the Ballad of the Historical Jesus . . ."

"Peacenik cocksuckers!"

"It's a free country."

"Mind your own God damned business!"

"Hippie bastards spoiled my appetite."

"Somebody oughta call a cop."

Carol and Bradley jaywalked hotfootedly and ducked into an alley. Between Branford and Market ran a picturesque declivity called Nutria Alley, part of quaint old Newark, second-oldest incorporated city in the United States. Nutria Alley, Nutria Street, Schoolhouse Alley, tiny thoroughfares intersecting and forming a nuclear village of backs of buildings. There was even the rear entrance, or "family entrance," of a burlesque theater. Old fluted enamel streetlamp shades on telephone poles, wires and cobwebs flat against the sunny bricks and mortar. It was like the East Coast locus of Middlewest America, Greyhound towns in Iowa or Illinois . . . Abruptly Bradley turned around and put his finger to his lips. Carol thought they were being pursued from the delicatessen and started to scramble but Bradley caught him by the tail of his Levi's jacket and pulled him into the shadows. He jerked his thumb at something and all at once Carol realized they were witnessing a strange tableau. There, among piles of rubbish in a shaft of summer sunlight, was a young cat from the Red Skeleton. He was doing something to a bum lying in the alley. The bum was giggling.

"He's started saving bums," Bradley nodded with the mien of a parson.

"What's he doing?"

"He's crazy, or anyway he'd better be."

"Why?"

"Because he's the hit man."

He called himself Serge Mottzytrottz, a hand-me-down surname of old Detroit queers. Newly queer, Serge had picked it out of an old Detroit phone book.

"Why Detroit?" Carol asked.

"Because," explained Serge. "Haven't you heard of the P-Stone International?"

"You got a pee stone?"

"Detroit is where the P-Stone is. It's in Palmer Park. It's, like, Mecca. For queers."

"Why are you queer?"

"Because. These people made me so," said Serge. "They can make you do anything, even have your corneas removed by electrolysis. Now, won't you let me relieve you of that wad you're walking around

The Banks of the Sea

with in your prostate? I know you have it."

"Nope."

"Why not? The other fellows here helped me get started."

"I'm saving it for a girl, that's why," said Carol. "For my beloved."

"Where did you learn that crap?"

"Well, nothing else has ever occurred to me," said Carol. "I guess it's because my mother and father were in love."

"Honey," Serge purred, "your mother and father are an illusion."

Serge had a key to the basement. He showed Carol.

"Honey, I'm serious," he said. "The more you find out about this the harder it will be for you not to be involved in it. Do you remember the steam pipe that exploded in one of the new high-rise office buildings down near Wall Street in New York?"

"Yes. It killed seven people. They were parboiled to death almost instantly. Why? Are you trying to tell me that these people made you do it?"

"That I know who did it and how."

"Ugh."

"It was one of the construction workers. He embedded a wax bottle of hydroflouric acid in the insulation around that pipe. Hydroflouric acid eats through anything except wax."

"And when the heat came on the wax melted?"

"Yeah, sweetie. There was just enough acid to weaken the pipe. High-pressure steam. One cold workday morning it blew the wall out."

BLAU! went the rifle. POP POP POPPITY POP! went the little pistol in Serge's hand. He fired in a suitably frenzied manner the .25 Browning Charter Undercover Special he said he was going to shoot the nigger harpsichordist with. BLAU! BLAU! Carol was privileged to be firing a .300 Savage hunting rifle. Expensive ammunition.

"When I hear an *appoggiatura*," Serge shrieked, "that's when I draw my pistol..." POP! POP!

He was practicing to acquire accuracy along with the hysteria. He and Carol firing down there sounded like a duet from a Bach cantata: the fluttery soprano Soul and the reassuring bass Jesus. There had once been a home bowling alley in the basement and it had been made over into a firing range. The basement was sandbagged and soundproofed; and it was poorly ventilated, which is why there was a smell of brimstone perceptible about Bradley's person. Carol thought Bradley might have a little heater like Serge's in his boot and for a minute he was really afraid, afraid these people might kill him and bury him down there. But weren't Bradley and Ponca afraid of him? Why weren't they afraid of Serge? Thrall goes amok.

"I don't know why you like to milk guys off," he said. "That's greasy kid stuff. Why don't you let a woman do it for you? One of the girls here..."

Serge pouted. "I'm not tough enough to be a pimp," he said.

"Nonsense. You can be a sweet pimp."

They compared their target cards and cleaned the guns. Then they went upstairs. The instruments of Serge's passion were laid out on the chintz tablecloth on the table in his room. There were the tubes of K-Y and the stack of Kleenex pocket packs, and one of those white enamel piss pots for male hospital patients. He put on some Scarlatti and they sat for a minute bathed in the crisp stereo. Suddenly he got up and turned it off.

He was constantly masturbating to augment his collections, he explained. He showed Carol. They went down to the kitchen and Serge weakly opened the door of one of the refrigerators. It was filthy, crammed with furry leftovers containers and flat soft drinks, and it couldn't have been defrosted since Hector was a pup. It stank coldly of rancid bean curd and shrimp nobody had wanted to peel.

"It's that jar there," he said.

It was a white plastic quart jar. Carol took it down. Pasted up the side was a seven-inch length of measuring tape with pencil marks at various places—probably one of Ponca's arrangements. It was nearly full.

"They gave me a plastic jar," Serge said, leaning the refrigerator door shut, "so that I couldn't smash it."

Carol drop-kicked it across the kitchen and out into the hall.

"Don't! It might cause a plane full of marines to crash."

"Why it's an analog of the moon. You're sure it isn't egg whites?"

"I suppose you could make meringue out of it."

Carol wrinkled his nose. "You say they want you to either drink it..."

"Or shoot the nigger harpsichordist."

"Aw come on. Let's give it to the huskies. They get dry dog food don't they? Dogs love jizz. We'll pour it over their trough of Gravy Train."

"I wouldn't go in there," Serge whined. "Those animals are Ponca's pet project."

"*I* would," said Carol. "I'd damned sure as hell would!"

He put his hand on the chill aluminum latch of the door to the husky room. The dogs saw him and started frisking. There were chewed-up objects all over the floor, among them the upper socket of the arm bone. It gave him an inspiration.

"Better yet," he said, " 'Let Your Fingers Do the Walking.' I believe I remember seeing a Brooklyn Yellow Pages in the office."

"I wouldn't go in there either," Serge moaned.

"Look," Carol said firmly. "You find some stuff to wrap this jug of jive up with. I'm going to get an address from that phone book."

In a few minutes they were in Serge's room again. Serge had collected a cardboard box, newspapers, supermarket bags to cut into wrapping paper and a handful of string.

"This," Carol exulted, "is the unnatural solution to an unnatural problem. I remember this place from my, er," he affected a pitch of insanity, "street somnambulations."

He showed Serge a piece of paper with the address of a cosmetics factory in the Williamsburg section of Brooklyn.

"But that's Duane's paper!"

"Duane's *love*... His pasty-faced sister can be the return address."

"You mean you want me to mail it to that place in Brooklyn?" Serge wailed. "But what about the postage? I don't have any money. All I have is the concert ticket."

"I have money," said Carol. "Here's ten dollars. You can put some gas in your Yamaha."

Meanwhile Bradley and Ponca were in New York for a couple of days doing a drug thing. They got back on the morning of the day of the concert and Carol told Bradley, "I'm going to do something practical today. I'm going to the dentist and have a tooth filled."

"I didn't know you had money," said Bradley.

One of the first things Ponca did when she and Bradley got back to the commune was to look in the refrigerator. Then she went up to Serge's room and softly demanded, "Where's your jar, Serge?"

Serge was lying on the bed listening to Ralph Kirkpatrick on the stereo headphones. He didn't even take them off to hear what she said. Some time back, when he first came to the commune, she sweetly gave him a big wax rose which she wired to the foot of his hospital bed. Now, when he saw Ponca enter the room and saw her lips move, he took his Browning Undercover Special and with one shot blasted the rose to bits and pieces.

Carol walked downtown. The dentist's office was on the Bleecker Street of that city and near the Newark campus of Rutgers University. Carol was suspicious of the university. It was being enormously expanded with the kind of lumpentoybox architecture popular with institutions of higher learning. He suspected it—because it needed lebensraum—of having caused the riots that burned the city. He encountered another albino.

"Why are there so many albinos in Newark?" Carol asked the dentist. "Seems like every time I go downtown I see albinos."

"They're Symbionese," the old man explained. "Bunch of people come down from the Ramapo Mountains now that they can get on welfare. There used to be whole families of albinos in there, and families of people with too many fingers and toes and webbed fingers and toes. You had some of these teeth filled while you were in the service, didn't you son?"

The most disturbing memory Carol had of Navy life had nothing to do with Vietnam. It was something he saw in the earliest days of his enlistment. Many of the recruits at boot camp were country boys no more than seventeen or eighteen years old, and because their teeth were so decayed the Navy dentists, instead of trying to save them, pulled them all out in order to avoid dental crises later on at sea or in combat situations. The kids abruptly had their choppers yanked, their gums closed with stitches, and then manfully subsisted on soup and ice cream until dentures could be made for them. And it often happened that a guy hemorrhaged from the mouth and suddenly there would be a splash of red, almost orange blood on the coarse asphalt of The Grinder, which is what they called the parade ground.

The high-speed water-cooled drill. The dentist was garrulous. Dentists know a lot. He told about the Symbionese and their history as Carol lay back in the chair with his eyes closed, rapt in the TV-series

The Banks of the Sea 175

adventure of the old man's narrative. Early Dutch settlers. The Hovenkopf. Tuscarora Indians from North Carolina in 1714. During the War of Independence Hessian deserters. General Clinton's thousands of rough redcoats and the delicacy of New York's loyalty. The British War Office. Colonel Jackson was to obtain thirty-five hundred women and would be paid two pounds each in gold for them. The brothels of London, Liverpool, Southampton. Housewives with shopping baskets abducted in the streets by Jackson's press gangs. The convoy, carrying a thousand Englishwomen, set sail for America. One of the ships foundered in a storm and fifty women were drowned. Jackson, considerably short of his quota, scrounged Negresses in the British West Indies (Donovan: "West Indian Woman"). Lispenard operated a distillery near what is now Greenwich Village. Collect Pond. The stream running to the Hudson along the path of what is today Canal Street. The soldiers enclosed Lispenard's Meadows in a high, strong, wooden palisade fence with a single gate. Inside rude shelters were built for the inmates and a quantity of firewood was brought in and distributed—"pushing colleges," where the girls pray with their knees upwards. George Washington and his army about to enter New York. On what the British know as Evacuation Day—November 27th, 1783—the women were liberated from the stockade. Some three thousand of them—driven out of New York with their sickness and brats—made it to the Jersey side and disappeared into the Ramapos. Tory fugitives. Renegades and outlaws. Runaway Negro slaves. At the time of the Civil War there were between five thousand and ten thousand Symbionese. Irish. Italian immigrants in 1870. On December 10th, 1912, three Ramapos men were arrested for making threats against the life of President Woodrow Wilson. It was a good filling. Comfortable.

"What do they do with their extra fingers and toes?" Carol asked.

"They have them amputated. Otherwise they couldn't get into their shoes, now could they?"

(See: Snedecor, Spencer T., M.D., and Harryman, William K., M.D. "Surgical Problems in Hereditary Polydactylism and Syndactylism." In *Journal of the Medical Society of New Jersey,* Vol. 37 [Hackensack, 1940], pp. 443-449. Illustrated.)

"All God's chilluns got shoes," Carol smiled.

"Yes, and Be kind to your web-footed friends," the dentist responded.

"That folklore has been with us a long time now, hasn't it? Don't eat before two hours have elapsed."

He strolled from the dentist's office to the nearby Newark Museum and enjoyed its renowned collections of Tibetan art and Americana. Cross-legged angels and patchwork quilts with mandalas.

"Don't forget, though, in Tibet rich women always have men servants to arrange their hair and paint their faces with clay. It is also the men who till the soil and do the fighting."

There was a delightful garden in back of the museum building. Carol sat on a bench there in the sun and grew drowsy writing poetry in his notebook. He was thinking about a girl he would love. How would he meet her? It would be soon and it would have taken some fortitude of spirit. He was tired of people trying to recruit him, of being regarded not for what he was or desired to be but as something they could use in their nefarious designs. He was tired of feeling bound to the falling cinder of the star shell of America. There must be a girl who people were trying to destroy so that they could justify their excesses, and he would find her by dint of poetry. He fell asleep angry and woke up with knowledge. If thoughts are events, then what is a state of mind? He was up against a system contrived by society's professional symbol manipulators. He was a poet. He would smash the system with images of his own.

Three hours had elapsed. Ravenous for solid food. In a place on Broad Street near Market, a minute steak with a baked potato. Afterwards walked around and enjoyed the weather, the first cool and breezy day in weeks. White men smiled to each other. Something interesting about a building at the corner of Washington and Raymond Boulevard; an airy arcade of stucco columns supporting part of Bamberger's discount store, maybe it had been an early gas station. But the pumps and lanes were gone long ago and now it comprised part of a parking lot. He looked up at the tops of the columns and busted out laughing. Their capitols were stucco sculptures of grotesque human faces. Some medieval German town. The figures on the *Rathaus* in Goslar. The faces grimaced at him impishly. They were picking their noses.

Directly across Raymond Boulevard was the Police Emergency Station. He waited for the traffic to thin and walked over to it. A wire ran from a little window to a doorbell button. There was a hand-lettered sign: PUSH BUTTON FOR EMERGENCY. He looked around to

The Banks of the Sea 177

see that nobody was watching him, then cooly stood a round of rifle ammunition on the windowsill and pushed the button. Then he casually descended into the cool and clean City Subway station there, the car came immediately and he rode it to the Penn Station terminus. But it was a gas; old Public Service trolley cars. He got on the next outbound and joyrode the meandering swaying line—laid in the bed of the old Morris Canal—to the last stop. Walked through Branch Brook Park. A guy waved his weenie at him. Left the park and crossed some tracks, found himself examining the architectural details of a medieval fortress of some kind. He walked around to the front. It was not the U.S. Army Corps of Engineers. It was Tiffany's jewelry factory.

By the time he got back downtown it was late afternoon. He sat for a while with the old-timers in Washington Park, then went across the street to the Public Library. In the New Jersey Reference Room he read just about everything there was available about the Ramapo Mountains people. The Interstate Park Commission's scheme of flooding them out by making an artificial lake. It did not surprise him that—in this independent delving in American history—the sign of Aquarius, the water carrier, was disclosed to him. The "Symbionese" had had cottage industries. They used to make boat-bailing scoops out of bent maple, and these became standard equipment on the lifeboats of trans-Atlantic liners.

The concert was at eight.

Crickets and the scent of jasmine in the southwest corner of Washington Park. People being easy in the windless evening. He stood watching an out-of-state bus unload its passengers in front of the Adventist church on James Street. All of them were deaf-mutes.

He walked back to the library and poked around in some of the other rooms. The building was in an opulent neo-classical style and he dawdled like a kid on the marble staircase. In the Periodicals Section he happened upon a *Newark Star-Ledger* lying on one of the tables. He glanced at it and his eyes riveted on the headline: MAYOR TO ATTEND CULTURAL CENTER GALA.

"Nuts to the harpsichord player," he said. "What they want is the black mayor of Newark."

He went to the phone booths and called police headquarters. It was five minutes to eight. He drawled into the microphone like a bumpkin smoking a Between The Acts.

"The Old Mosque is playing a hit tonight."

"Who the hell are you?" demanded the policeman on the other end. And then, "How do we know this is for real?"

"Pick up the brass," he said, and hung up.

He was certain he had just done something crazy. He walked around the block to a black joint called Dove's Tavern directly behind the museum garden, went inside and ordered a ginger ale. He paid for the drink using a Franklin quarter. The other patrons and the bartender—all black—were watching a baseball game on the TV and he felt a little uncomfortable and wondered why he was there. He longed for the green smell of open country beyond the graveyards of the cities. He made the ginger ale last about twenty minutes. Then the ball game was interrupted by a special announcement.

"The Mayor of Newark was shot to death twenty-five minutes ago as he was being escorted from the Newark Cultural Center in the old Mosque Theater. The assailant, a black man, fired six shots from a pistol at point-blank range on Orchard Street near the stage entrance of the theater, which was being evacuated on an anonymous telephone threat. The Mayor was rushed in his official car to Essex County Hospital, where he was pronounced dead on arrival. Newark police have not said where they are detaining the suspected assassin."

He got off his stool and added a dime to the tip.

"Peace," he said, and left.

Early mornings Avenue B is locked up tight, steel shutters on all the storefronts. Or almost all. Even the Gladiators' Gym is shuttered up. Maybe the boys are afraid their weights will be stolen by the Trojan Health Club over on Delancey. The lawyer's office, the realtor's office; they don't have shutters over their windows. And the truss store has a shiny, inviting expanse of plate glass. Who would break into a truss store anyway? Trusses, artificial limbs, crutches, elastic stockings, bedpans—who would steal one of those? The unemployed wake up with time on their hands, time they don't know what to do with. Did it ever occur to them to fall in love? After all, at any moment somebody might put them to work building pyramids. Then let them try to get romantic. Like *West Side Story*. Maybe it's because of a difference in language. It takes thirty percent longer to say something in Spanish.

So here I sit in a Greenwich Village bar, cooly ratiocinating in Danish while my companions in the locale are wrestling with it in English. All of them understand one another and read each other effortlessly, and it isn't helping them any. The lady sitting next to me has just ordered a Borneo Cruiser and the bartender is hunting around for the ingredients. She helps him, nodding or shaking her head at the labels he touches. Surely there is a message for him in it. She looks like what I imagine Yvetot would look like if I imagined an Yvetot who uses a wig. Then she reaches over the bar and points to the bottle of arrack and I get a good look at her escort.

The last time Carol saw Yvetot was on a sunny early afternoon in late summer. The dentist in Newark had recommended an exhibit of Olmec art (pre-Columbian thalidomide babies) at the Metropolitan Museum and that is where Carol was headed as he strode jauntily under the marquee of the Plaza Hotel. The Pulitzer Fountain was spraying water and overhead flags were snapping. There was an American flag and a flag that said "New York Is A Summer Festival," while flying from the flagpoles up on the face of the hotel were the Stars and Stripes, the flag of the United Nations, and the flag of the Republic of Morocco. A limousine was standing at the curb and the doorman saluted Carol. Who should Carol bump into but the President of Morocco, whose companion was Yvetot Bouchardeau, nineteen, wearing a Christine Gorby frock. When she saw Carol she turned white as old snow and ran around the corner of the hotel and vanished. Carol was thinking, What's happened to her uchi? She doesn't have any uchi anymore. Must be from rocking back and forth on it so much.

The horse-drawn carriages on Grand Army Plaza. One of the Moroccan gent's bodyguards followed Carol into Central Park, far into the park, all the way to the band shell where Carol stopped to listen to the Vanilla Fudge concert. The dude even took off his jacket and rolled up his sleeves and glowered at Carol like he wanted to fight. Or was it only the heat? Then the crowd, like a gene pool, separated them.

One Saturday afternoon Carol was at a gallery opening on West Broadway. There were familiar faces among the gallery afficionados and he felt a cozy gladness at the thought of the approaching autumn and winter, for Imogen would soon be home from her summer teaching job at Cranbrook, Michigan, and he wanted to see her. Oftentimes there would be wine served free at the openings. Wine and cheese and bread. And it was possible, on alternate Saturdays, to go from one gallery to another and meet your friends, get a nice buzz, go to a party afterwards and get laid. Carol was feeling pretty good. He had just been talking with a friend of Imogen's and was looking at some more of his paintings when he saw a guy he met at Bellevue. It was Lacey, with his paper bag full of crusty old milk cartons and cans of beans. They looked at each other. Lacey took a gulp of milk, wiped, and asked, "How do you hitchhike to Boston?"

10   The Blind Clarinettist of St Mark's Place

POPPET VALVE GEARS basically have two forms, those in which the cams oscillate and those in which the cams rotate. The cams are sometimes in contact with the valve stems and on other occasions the movement is imparted to the valves through levers. The stuffing box is a form of steam-tight seal in which hemp rings saturated with paraffin, or asbestos gaskets, are housed in a recess around a piston rod or valve stem and tightened as necessary by screwing down nuts on the stud securing the gland to the cylinder cover or valve chest. Higher pressures have rendered this method of obtaining steam-tightness obsolete, so that it has been replaced by metallic gaskets. The Southern gear is virtually the Strong gear reintroduced on the Southern Railroad. A fixed horizontal link is incorporated in connection with a vertical radius bar. Movement to the valve stem is imparted by a bell crank, being initially obtained from a return crank in the Southern form. Stroke is the distance traveled by the piston in the cylinder. Reference to the tractive effort formula will show that the force developed by the locomotive is directly proportional to the stroke. Piston speed, which may be plotted in relation to mean effective pressure or indicated horsepower, is equal to rpm x twice the length of the stroke in feet per minute. It is unusual in orthodox locomotives for the piston to average more than a thousand feet per minute. Conjugated valve gears are based on the principle enunciated by H. Holcroft, that if the harmonics of two valve gears of different phases are combined, a third harmonic of a different phase is produced. The savings in weight resulting from the use of such a gear are considerable. The blast nozzle is the orifice on the end of the blast pipe through which exhaust steam is discharged prior to entering the stack. Its function is to impart velocity to the steam in order that the resulting jet may create a partial vacuum in the smokebox and entrain the gasses from the tubes. The blast nozzle is the one feature which, in a coal-burning boiler, co-relates the boiler output with demand, as the greater the weight of steam passed through the nozzle the more intense the blast and the resulting draft through the firebed and tubes. Must have been piecework. The spectacular Pasadena Bridge. Concrete at the collapse site appeared damp and crumbly. Sagging slabs, sinking foundations, defective piles, corroded reinforcement and cracking plaster, and there were no haunches. Ponding. Chips, leaves, sawdust, and blocks of wood in the columns. The design had been changed from time to time to protect "secret" manufacturing processes of the company. The almost entirely unshored second floor, accidental shaking or disturbance of these posts might easily have knocked some of the beams off their supports when, with considerable noise, almost the entire building collapsed in one minute on the evening of November 22, 1910. Most of the floor reinforcement had pulled out of the standing columns. Two men were killed by the roof collapse which followed form removal. It had been raining, and the form removal was a "make work" operation to keep the men busy. An example was these two guys finding the burned-out lightbulb in the subway station. A line of ceramic light sockets was in the ceiling at trackside above each of the four platforms and they were dark, and these two Puerto Ricans—Transit Authority employees—were going along changing the bulbs one-by-one using poles with rubber fingers on the ends. Each man had a pole, a canvas bag to contain the expended bulbs which he found, and a cardboard box full of good bulbs. They would quickly unscrew a bulb and replace it, quickly another one, a middle-aged man and a young guy working rapidly and without conversation as trains entered and left the station. Then suddenly, in the silence between trains, one of them changed a bulb and the whole line of bulbs lighted up, to the astonishment of the people waiting on the platform who all oohed and aahed. But there was more to it than that. In a little while all four lines of bulbs were lighted, and what the two employees did with the burntouts is they whopped the canvas bags of nogoods against pillars and the floor again and again, whop whap, until they were all broken, then emptied the fragments tinkling into trashcans. What surprises me is that the lights were wired in series.

—*OK–AM Porter you won this one. How can you possibly work with this worn-out broom? I'm sure you can get one OK? It takes quite a while to scrap the station.*

—Take your beer cans out of this room. Also the other side of station. AM Porter.

—AM Porter I do not drink beer. Asshole, find out who is doing it OK? I drink Scotch on my time off. PM Porter.

The motorman threw the catastrophe brake. He thought it was a suicide.

Shopkeepers, sempstresses, officers, soldiers, lords, ladies, Duke d'Naz, children, nursemaids, cossaks, police officers, a dancing bear, etc.

He had a thing about inguinal thigmokinesis.

"It's like a mattress burning on Hester Street," he explained, "or a puppy dog tied to a leaky fire hydrant. Yes, the moon is the white horse in the ad."

Inguinal thigmokinesis was his personal homing device. The old-timers arched an eyebrow at each other.

"What kind of puppy dog?"

There was a music that evoked the poignancy of instilled emotions. Bread singing "Baby I'm a Want You." He identified it as what whales know as their longing for the continent; they try to get up the Sewanee River. There was many a cat who would give a nut to have had what he had with Yvetot. Her body was just like her face, which is ideal, of course. The same strawberries and cream. An undeveloped Libra, she was a perfect vessel of passion. Marilee Rush singing "Angel of the Morning." The fragrance of her flesh when he was awakened at night by a siren. It was almost too good to be true the way he fell into things. Like his chicks. The way he gets himself set up, man? Inguinal thigmokinesis.

"A Group Image puppy dog, man."

Men's power games melt, their arguments vanish before the hot fact of her flesh. Words were only good for one thing and this was it.

Flower Power. John was a street hippie and a born rhymer. He brushed his hair back from his face and effortlessly improvised:

> "The sheep in the thickets
> Are tearing their hair,
> I'm searching for you
> And I've looked everywhere.
> I've looked on the mountain

And searched in the plain,
I've even poked through
All the cans in the rain."

"Oh God," he concluded as was his wont, and put his recorder to his lips and played a melancholy bar.

"Excrescence upon efflorescence of uncontrolled wheeler-dealer in terminal metastatis," Robespierre muttered.

Carol looked around. It was a hot September night just after Labor Day and St Mark's Place was plastered with nyctotodes. Tattered home front battalion. Thick-tongued scab-lipped labor horde, mother-loved limbs acrack with scurvy. A pellagra-lassid pietà. Snot-clogged diarrheics, diphtheric finger-webs, casein eyes. Packs full of shuffles on a string of time come. Nyctotodes. Multifarious many-colored pointillistic gaudy camouflaged nearly two-dimensional entities, nyctotodes are visually perceptible travelers on more complex creatures including man. Using them more for vehicles than as hosts, the nyctotodes were all over everything and everybody and each other. They existed in a mental habitat of immense ocean depths. He saw a deep sea toad, and an escaping sea robin. "Hang on tight!" said Big Ladybug. They took a ride on a dog's ear. Its name was Thin Dollop. All at once the exit doors of the Electric Circus opened and people started pouring out onto the fire escapes. John was heard to mutter, "Lady Will Power."

"Hey man, who's playing in there?"

"The Chambers Brothers," said Robés cautiously.

"What a total groove," said Chauncey. "Must be a bomb scare."

Chauncey de Pew was another of the more flamboyant East Village dealers. His little Swiss commuter's rucksack contained scales, a roll of Alligator Baggies and a pound of Acapulco gold. He carried a cane with a steel spike on the end, like the kind used by North German tourists in the Bavarian Alps. It was hollow and enclosed a column of horse-doctor's capsules full of organic mescalin. He was strictly macrobiotic, used The Paradox as his base of operations and had been knifed once in the environs of Slugs. He polished his monocle.

"What a total groove," he repeated. "If it's the Chambers Brothers then Sydney must be in there. It's a total freakout."

"I thought Sydney was with you," Robés said. "I thought you invited her to go to the zoo with you today."

Robespierre was a tall ruddy blonde cat, kind of rawboned and introspective. He wore a Confederate officer's jacket and was into Russian authors.

"Come on, man. I thought she was with you."

"What a stoned drag."

"What do you mean?"

"There was this baby orangutan, see, and a mother orangutan. And the mother orangutan broke the baby's arm..."

"What do you mean, man? Were you and she on acid?"

Everybody knew that Chauncey was hung up on one of the girls from Sylvja's Pottery Shoppe. Polly, her name was. Every now and then he would smile cheerfully and tell you he had seen Polly. What he meant was that he had seen her on the street. Well, Yvetot knew her too, but by another name. She had bought a sewing machine from her and she and Carol went to her apartment on East 5th Street to pick it up. They were in the same Gurdjieff group and Yvetot introduced her as Susan Constantine.

Carol laughed. "See you guys around," he said.

"What a total groove. Where are you going?"

As he turned and walked away he heard John shout triumphantly, "Do your thing, man!"

The Fire Department. The Number 11 pumper and the Number 9 ladder from the station on Great Jones Street. A girl had immolated herself with lighter fluid in the Electric Circus. A dog was standing waiting for the light to change. Carol crossed Second Avenue.

The city was all around him and everything was for sale, strangers proffering useless items at incomprehensible terms. "I can buy this city," he said aloud, "with a joke."

On the other side of Tompkins Square Park the police found a body in the trunk of an abandoned car. Carol knew what it was, and when they got the lid opened just as he walked past what was so amazing was the cloud of flies which suddenly disseminated into the neon and mercury. There were two patrol cars; one of them was double-parked alongside the Camaro.

"Hey fella. Wait just a minute."

He was already making his way through the onlookers. The cop grabbed his shoulder.

"The river's right that way."

An Avenue B bus passed, a couple of kids hanging on to the rear end. Carol looked at the policeman.

"Gotta make a train," he said. They looked him up and down.

"Let me take a guess. Songwriter."

"He must be an anthropologist."

"Right. We got a case for you, anthropologist. Come on. Maybe you can make heads or tails out of this thing."

They were harassing him. He scanned the bystanders, looked at the policemen again and said loudly, nodding toward the Camaro, "See if he's wearing his dogtags."

He found a street where kids were playing in an open fire hydrant, squealing and slithering in the great trunk of precious water from the Kensico and Groton reservoirs. They shrieked with glee when he knelt down with his face in it and it tumbled him on his butt. He picked himself up and thought he heard a girl say something to him.

"I am Little Faith," the voice said.

He wanted to go home, but wasn't exactly sure where that was. He thought of good times and favorite places. Some kids were playing basketball on the sidewalk. The ball was fumbled, skidded his way and he picked it up, jumped and lofted it through the rungs of a fire escape ladder.

"I am the oil-immersion ear and the sweet cranny you remember," said the voice. *"I am your poetry."*

The stone breaker came around one day and talked with the farmer. A couple of afternoons later he showed up again on his bicycle, carrying his hammers on one shoulder, and went directly to the lee side of the barn where there was a pile of field boulders. Then he set about splitting them. He enjoyed his work and the grin on his face was as much from the pleasure he got out of it as the effort. His veins stood out. He was very strong and it was intelligent work. The sledge arc'd with mathematical grace through the air and struck the rock, which broke. It was the traditional labor of convicts, but this man was free. He knew those rocks, where to knock on each one so that it would open for him. He sized them up and clove them. Inside they were brilliant, crystal and tracery, the perfection of revelation. Oh to be an athlete, a lover! To be

The Banks of the Sea

perfect! He rested in the middle of it, perspiring, and the woman brought him beer. The sun was going down and the autumn sky huge over the flat country. When it was done, the rocks broken, he would eat a meal in the kitchen and be paid in money. He rose on the balls of his feet, the hammer vertical, and hauled down on it like a pole vaulter and the steel struck the stone with a splash of sparks. Dogs barked far away.

He was walking on stilts through a field of wheat. His father allowed him to do this. "Yes, you learned stilts so you can walk to the water without trampling the grain." At the bottom of the field was a water hole about the size of a troll's floor plan. When the field was in crop the water was only accessible to creatures who could walk on stilts. This was the stork's advantage.

"The man on stilts is treading water!"

Carol was tramping around the Lower East Side thinking about how to find his beloved. The voice called to him, helped him navigate. How do lovers meet? It has to be your own symbol system, he knew. You have to follow your poet's ear.

"I am the sweetness of heat lightning," it said.

Tenement fronts like soap carvings. Stick around and watch it all wash away. He had reached the water hole at the bottom of the field. He walked up the front steps of an abandoned tenement and went inside.

The water cures warts.

Carol's unshineable shoes nosed through the garbage and debris in the hall of the tenement. He felt his way up the stairs. Light seemed to be coming from one of the rooms. Even though it might have been heroin addicts cooking up over a candle he made for it. His heart thumped in his throat. They might have killed him with straight razors. There was no door in the jamb. He inched cautiously until he could see inside the room. A candle. A mattress on the floor. There was a young white girl. After a moment he stepped inside and introduced himself.

"I'm glad you came," she said. "I was hoping this candle wouldn't attract hobos."

She told him her name. Her voice was from before he was born. They knew they were intended for each other.

"I am the American girl with her dowry of nails," she said. "They wanted me to be raped."

"You're the sick wife," he said.

"I am the unburdening of my mothers. I am perfect."
"I am a glacier and will unload my boulders on your plain."
"They are from far away and I am the place. Melt."
"I am magnesium from hitchhiking and this is a lie."
"Love me."
"A story told by a substitute teacher."
"I am the rediscovery of Greenland."

She was Little Faith, a glass fruit knife hollow ground and blue as the edge of a mirror. Her hair was long even if it was short. Her legs were slightly heavy and her mouth was so sweet it wouldn't matter if she had bad breath. She was the nakedness of horses.

She drew him down beside her on the mattress, pulled her T-shirt up and opened her bellbottoms and showed Carol the cross on her tummy. He peered closely in the candlelight.

"Look at this," she said, running a finger over the intersection of fine hairs and shadows. Carol thought, A cross is something you pitch a tent with in the snow.

"It means that I'll bear children easily. Do you want babies?"

They were like old lovers who happen upon each other, kiss and caress until time drowns them in all that water under the bridge. Carol was one of your strong-smelling patriots, George Washington taking his shirt off the better to throw a coin across the river. Ellen was as whaley as an Eskimo and her kisses were as sweet as a glass of water. She was hiding from the breweries. He kissed her breasts. She was a virgin.

A snare drummer began to play. The sound came from a window up in one of the buildings across the canyon of backyards that now, most of the tenements abandoned and fences broken for firewood, was a thoroughfare of tumbledown and ruin. Flams and paradiddles, rollickingly on-course catamaran. The moon was over the slum, and light glowed from the windows of kitchens where there was no water. The drum tune was like a suburban train clacketing along. The drummer played "The Downfall of Paris," and as imperceptibly as changing from third rail to pantograph he swung into "The Crippled Shad."

"Hello purring good-smelling tuckered-out kitten."

He grasped her legs behind the knees and tenderly stroked her wet hole with the tulip of his cock until it found its way in and he could feel it podded on her maidenhead. They remained that way, kissing, until she put her arms around his waist and hugged him, and all at once he got into her. Ellen Evangeline Clergl.

Startling as the sunrise, sweet Broadway brass. She roared with laughter. My beloved. My water bell.

"My love came to me, blankets of childhood sleep and sweat of dreams. My darling. My boonkeeper. We are dandles on the hillside."

"You are the sweet ouch knee, the grassy sprain, and I am the mechanic at valley. We are the gong of earthquakes and the eeled Hudson."

And so they whispered and touched each other, hardly believing.

It was some of that strange Hudson Valley weather where it rains on one side of the street and not the other. One little cloud, a relative of New England line storms, passed overhead and it rained down hard on the Lower East Side, the first drops obliging the leaves of the ailanthus, the Tree of Heaven, bouncing in the dust on the sidewalks and the tops of cars. The smell of wet fire escapes.

"What's a nice girl like you doing in a dump like this?"

"They had me on a fugue. They gave me a pair of mirror sunglasses and wanted me to forget. But I memorized the city, wanting you."

They lay side-by-side buffeted by the storm of colors in their heads, as the rainwater streamered from broken gutters and splatted on gaping kitchen sills. They were a pool of light the sea rose up and left in the grassy palm of the land. Milkweed girls and apple girls, the sweet-finger thighs of her. Oh girl, to have docked where you keep your tides.

They blew the candle out and played unafraid in the wrack and mildew, saw the moon come out again. Enjoyed some cake and wine that she had hoarded. She gave him a present.

"This summer on the streets I was so poor, and people were constantly tempting me with their wretchedness. But I had a toy and I was happy because of it. Do you want to know what it is? I've never told it to anybody. It's a poem. A soldier's bawdy ditty. My mother and father taught it to me when I was little and it's the best thing I know. Want to hear it?"

Carol nestled in Ellen's thighs, she stroking him and hugging him to her and speaking to him. He wanted to come in her again.

"Who wrote it?" he asked.
"An ancestor of mine. At Valley Forge."
"You're putting me on," he laughed.
"I'm putting you in," she sighed.

"The swans were awake on the lake by the ben
Where we tarried and dallied. I loved her and then
In the broth of the stars on the beam of the morn
The shadows were shorn when I loved her again.

Like rainbows on ham, like come on the lam
The night I got into her freshwater clam,
By waters' dark creaming and flowery gleanings
And bullrushes brushing on wherry and pram.

From the house on the lawn to the cow on the hill
Birds whisper and settle, fish weep from their gills,
For our love was so strong in the break of the breeze
In the boughs of the trees that the nations are ill.

There's the cries of the wounded, the beating of drums
And herons and dragonflies doing their sums
And we couldn't care less, on carpet of cress
In your pretty new dress, where the money comes from.

There's the rose by the roadside, wild iris besides,
And clouds in the blue like swans on the tide
And we're still together, my love in the heather,
Though war wears a feather and death chooses sides."

11 Silky Valentine

IT WAS 7:10 IN THE EVENING and already dusk in the first week of October. The train had just left Galesburg, Illinois, and in a little while would cross the Mississippi at Burlington, Iowa. Fortunately Amtrack had not damaged the art deco interior of the club car, an old streamliner fishtail named The City of Chicago. There were the venetian blinds on the windows, and the bar was on the starboard side in the middle of the car like the island on an aircraft carrier. The chairs had been recovered and new carpet laid on the deck; but the stainless-steel ashtray-drinkholders were original, and it was possible to imagine the time when this gleaming splendor first hit the rails. Fredegonde sighed and stretched her legs and took another sip of ginger ale. She was on her way to Salt Lake City.

Fredegonde was a handsome girl, modestly attired and clear of eye and complexion, and she had that sweetness of mouth peculiar to young unmarried women. Her hair was parted in the middle and she wore glasses. She looked like a hometown girl who probably did well in school. The man sitting beside her had just remarked on a card game at one of the tables and they both sat nonchalantly amused, looking at the people in the club car. Some of them had just come from the diner and there was joviality and animated exchanges.

The trucks shuddered over switchbeds and drinks rattled. They watched the bartender for a while.

"Shouldn't we go feed our faces?" he suggested.

His name was Lawrence and he wasn't bad-looking. He lighted one more cigarette before finishing his bourbon and soda.

She smiled and sipped her ginger ale, watching him rest his cigarette in the ashtray and look at her expectantly. With a gesture of response, she took a book of matches from her handbag and lighted one of them, extinguished it by shaking it in the air, then placed it in the ashtray directly under the man's cigarette. The match smoked for a minute, imparting to the tip of the cigarette the resinous precipitate of a drug developed by the Bardo Society. The drug was called "Strawberry Fields," and it produced a sudden and profound nostalgia.

What Fredegonde had done to Lawrence's cigarette she did openly and smiling, so that how he reacted to it would be according to the astuteness of his paranoia. Would he be a he-man? Or would he be chicken shit and put the cigarette out and light another one like a chain-smoker? Or did he anachronistically not have a clue?

"Hungry?" he asked, grinning, and took a puff. The effect was astounding.

Fredegonde stood over the man suddenly crouched in the flexed burial position on his chair. People were staring.

"Go fuck a duck," she said in his ear, and walked out of the club car.

Dear Diary. We have often wondered what use the Pygmies have for the scythes they have so eagerly been accepting from us. Today we found out. They have already used several wagonloads, which is remarkable in a primitive people small in stature and of decidedly limited agriculture, and it appears that they indeed use them for a kind of grim harvest. The local Pygmie cacique, naked as a jaybird, today allowed us to witness an elephant hunt. The Pygmies goaded a cow elephant into a prescribed clearing by driving her calf away from her, whereupon the maddened creature, pelted by Pygmie arrows and spears, snatched at the many scythes which had been firmly anchored in the ground. The elephant was thus made to slice off her own trunk, and was afterwards easily followed and encircled while she bled to death. The Pygmies feasted wildly, inviting neighboring villages and gorging themselves on elephant meat. Apparently the introduction of these simple metal implements has brought about a Pygmie millenium.

Quogue, said the locomotive through the fog and night. Quuooaague . . . The mournful sound roused Fredegonde from a reverie of marriage. What would life have been like for her had she fulfilled her fond parents' hopes? Marriage. Money into more money. A potent husband. An announcement with her photograph in the *New York Times*. Fredegonde Trebbidge and Hasbrouck Braunfels. Nuptials announced. Noopiddy noop. Married Maidens' Dilatory Domiciles.

She yawned, scratched her left armpit and switched on the light. She pulled the shade and glanced again through the *Chicago Tribune.* There was an article on racial disturbances in the United States Navy. She thought with satisfaction of the nuclear-powered aircraft carriers of the United States Navy and of their five-thousand-man crews. She thought with satisfaction of the brothels of Yokosuka. Fredegonde put the paper down and wrote in her journal: *We're going to kill all the white father-image motherfuckers and sterilize the rest. We don't need white men—the arrogant pigs—except as slaves for the hard labor of the Transition, and when it's accomplished we're going to kill them too. We don't need men except as slaves, and a few groovy black studs for reproduction purposes.*

She chewed on her ballpoint for a minute, then wrote: *The average New York street hustler, if she's white, grosses between 20 and 25 dollars per trick. If she's black she grosses between 10 and 15 dollars per trick.*

To which Fredegonde—suddenly jocose—appended: *It hurts my Scotch heart.*

She switched the light off and raised the shade again. The train was rocketing further and further into the American heartland, leaving the river fog behind in the hollows and hoggy farm spreads of Iowa. If water flowed as the crow flies then Fredegonde would be Aquarius with a chip on his shoulder, an oar, a sailor walking inland until somebody asks him, What's that thing on your shoulder? Iowa, Nebraska, Colorado, the stars over the prairie now companioned by the non-returnable fling shrines of a contrite humanity: burnt-out rockets, pieces of spacecraft, lost tools, dead dogs, iron-lung daredevils. Beeping robots like bottles with messages. Davey Jones's other locker. By the light of the Crisco moon Fredegonde finished writing in her journal. What was it Brian had called her that time, tickling her to make her laugh? He made her laugh, and she laughed so hard she cried. He called her Housemover's Dolly.

What I wanted to escape from, she wrote, the train jarring her hand, *is the tyranny of the truth.*

She sat there in the darkened Pullman bedroom looking out the window, growing hungry. Neighboring compartments, lighted, shades up, projected rectangles of silvery light that bobbed and slid, sometimes vanished in the contours along the right-of-way; reappeared glissanding like the gongs of grade crossings. And gradually the train sounds became like old folk melodies; the spang of the wheels, the car rocking in its trucks. She heard an old white man pick a song on a five-string banjo.

> *"Your cheeks they are too rosy*
> *Your fingers are too small,*
> *Your face a cannonball.*
> *You know it would not change my mind*
> *If I saw ten-thousand fall..."*

The locomotive moaned. She abstracted her head by repeating over and over the names of the sleeping cars. "Hickory Creek." "Port of Buffalo." "La Porte County." "Ashtabula County." In a few moments —like a lady from the age of swoon—she roused herself and went to the dining car. It was long past the last call for dinner, but the colored waiter was solicitous and a little jivey and he brought her a snack of a turkey sandwich on white toast and a glass of milk with ice cubes.

Fredegonde ate her snack and further abstracted her head, while it chewed and swallowed, by making herself think of something factual. She thought of Saint Brendan the Navigator, the Irishman who discovered America in A.D. 525. He was looking for the Land of the Saints.

She abstracted her head in order to keep it from alarming people. Everybody did it: the semi-unconscious, semi-involuntary repetition of obsessive-compulsive lists and formulae. The reassuring "jamming" of the mind. They did it for mental privacy, and Fredegonde had something to hide.

After finishing her meal she decorously returned to her bedroom in Ashtabula County, which meanwhile had been made ready for the night by the sleeping-car porter. She put her Etienne Aigners in the shoe-shine box, hung her Saint Laurie suit in the closet, put on her Bonwit's nightie, brushed her teeth and her hair and crawled into her berth. She read from the Book of Mormon for a while, and then put her glasses in the little hammock and switched off the light. The shade was up and the moon precessed across the sky.

The Banks of the Sea

The walls shelter, the temple shadows, the autumn clouds gather overhead. They wait patiently, for the Saints who will assemble in the morning. For this is the harvest season, and they witness the harvest of souls. The semiannual General Conference of the Church of Jesus Christ of Latter Day Saints was convening tomorrow. A new President of the Church was going to be elected and Fredegonde was on her way to Salt Lake City to assassinate him. All the way beyond Chicago in the afternoon across the windless hours and the harvested farmland, the smoke of stubble fires had risen high into the sky at intervals from the grainfields of southern Illinois. Those columns of smoke—incense of the immense bounty of this land—had seemed for a moment reminders of the finality of America to all generations in their dreams and drivenness.

Hotel Ocean Crest. Yes, that was it. You are cordially invited... to enjoy a Cool, Carefree Summer at H— O— C— on the Boardwalk at Beach 62nd Street, ROCKAWAY. Now you can enjoy the luxury of a Hotel Ocean Crest vacation... Three delicious, mouth-watering meals served in our Dining Room overlooking the ocean. Dietary Laws Strictly Observed, under Rabbinical supervision. All outside rooms that invite your complete relaxation. Convenient Bathing Facilities. Free weekly entertainment—free Bingo games. Convenient to New York—only 2 blocks to the new subway station at Beach 60th Street. Free parking for our guests. Our staff is dedicated to your complete comfort, relaxation and enjoyment. We are looking forward to having you with us this summer, but—Please! Make your reservations early. HOTEL OCEAN CREST. For complete information and reservations call GRanite 4-4389 if no answer, please call evenings or Write Hotel Ocean Crest 102 Beach 62nd Street, Rockaway, N.Y. Under personal direction of Mr. and Mrs. Eugene Roth, Proprietors. Yes, it was that abandoned Jewish hotel in which she found shelter from the lightning storm. What in the world was she doing here? The weather-blasted rooms. The grand piano that spoke once when she pressed a key, and that was all, the works of it salt-and-verdigris crusted in the sea wind which blew unhindered through the paneless windows front to rear through all the rooms and made the exhaust fan in the shambled kitchen spin in its bearings. Old bed frames. Burst suitcases. Laundry. Smashed bathrooms. Some Jewish boy's asthma medicine. She wanted to wake up from the dream but she found herself in a room with the wind whooshing tattered curtains like vapor off an airplane wing, and saw through the empty window as in a motel room with color television the Atlantic surf under a blue sky crash and slither up the beach. She had had trouble eating her breakfast. When she sat down and glanced at her place it seemed as though the silverware had been set upside down with the tines of the fork, the blade of the knife and the shovel of the spoon all pointing toward her like that surf booming and running at her. Some two-hundred-and-fifty Mormons—men, women and children, with livestock and twenty-six wagons—started from Panguitch. The expedition took nearly four months. After traversing seventy miles of desert they came to the edge of the canyon. Two thousand feet below, the Colorado River rolled. To get across they blasted a notch—the Hole in the Rock—down through the rim into a side canyon, and from there carved a crude road to the riverbank. In some places the wagons had to be lowered on ropes. After fording the river, these undaunted people climbed the other side and continued on through the unreal sandstone wilderness . . .

She got up early and went to the diner. On the way she found Lawrence's suit jacket lying on the floor of a car vestibule. The Dutch door was open and swaying on its hinges and there was a terrible roar of the train. He must have jumped. Disgusted, she shut the door with her foot. It slammed metallically.

She had breakfast at a table together with a couple in their early thirties. Ham and eggs and hash browns. For some reason she wished she had ordered waffles. Their names were Marge and Davey, and they looked like they had been on the train the better part of their lives. They had already finished eating and the woman was stirring her coffee when she asked Fredegonde if she minded if she smoked. In response Fredegonde handed her a glossy white matchbook. Margie thanked her, lighted her cigarette, inhaled, flinched, and then disintegrated on the shoulder of her companion. "Oh love me, David," she whimpered. And they were Scientologists, Fredegonde thought.

Fredegonde was upstairs in the dome car when the train pulled into Denver at 9:30 in the morning. The police came aboard. She watched as Lawrence's jacket, his topcoat and what must have been his luggage were handed by a trainman and a porter to a couple of policemen on the platform. Jesus Onderdonk! she thought. Heads turned and looked at her. It was like a customs inspection. In the meantime Margie was being helped from the train. She saw them disembark in the company of what must have been a physician, Dave supportive, Margie streaked and inconsolable in the downdraft from the Rockies.

They were processing all the passengers. They came to Fredegonde. "There was an apparent suicide," the police detective said. "Did you see this man on the train or speak with him at all?"

She looked at the photograph. Cute. Quite a bit younger. She wondered where they got it and whether the whole thing wasn't a put-on.

"He gave me his card," she said, pawing through her Lancel. "Here it is. We were in the tavern car together for a short while yesterday, that's all. He seemed a little sad. I'm awfully sorry."

"This was in his wallet," said the conductor. He showed it to her, and people were looking at her. It was an undeposited check for five hundred dollars, drawn on The Oystermen's Bank and Trust Company of Sayville, New York, 11782, Organized 1899. She dwelt on the logo: an eagle, spread, facing right, on a fasces. She could tell they were thinking: So. You iced one of your own. You little snotgut.

At 10:20, after a twenty-minute delay, the train left Denver and headed north for Cheyenne. Right after she got in with the Mormons they invited her along on a Saturday canoe trip on the Delaware River and she had to make up an excuse because she couldn't wear a bathing suit. And almost immediately afterwards she started dating a young Latter Day Saint named Nephi, who had just returned from a mission in Guatamala. She thought he looked like a cowboy in a business suit.

Fredegonde always used her real name with the Mormons, for, in a phrase she coined, You don't lie to a people who have a monopoly on the dead. They were into genealogy, and had a probe on just about every white family in the United States. As Nephi told her, the two of them walking romantically under the leafy summer trees beside the Hayden Planetarium, there was a cave in Utah where the Church had computerized genealogical files. The cave was in a hidden valley. Did he say there were eighty million entries?

They got to the apartment where he was staying and he showed her his own genealogical charts. Why it was even more addictive than astrology. Afterwards they went out on the balcony and necked. She was seeing the lights of the Queensborough Bridge when they were blotted out by the head of Nephi, who kissed her tenderly and lengthily and she experienced something she hadn't enjoyed for a long time. She saw head flowers. She kept her eyes closed. Fredegonde had not anticipated that the Mormons were so, well, heterosexual, nor that Nephi would feel her up. He was so cool about it, too; kissing her like that, then laughing an apology when she suddenly, chastely clamped her thighs shut. They watched television the rest of the evening and necked some more. In a few days Nephi went back home to Utah, mission accomplished. . . . *and those who are not pure, and have said they were pure, shall be destroyed, saith the Lord God.* (Doctrine and Covenants, 132:52)

They were making up time and it seemed like another day somewhere else, the sun already on the afternoon side of the Rocky Mountains, the wind in the sage. The British family in the Vista Dome, seeing America. Their children were reading Rupert Comics, whose characters speak in rhyme. Someplace between Laramie and Rawlins the train crossed the Continental Divide, and Fredegonde went to her compartment and masturbated for the last time.

For as long as there has been an antiquity people have wondered about what might be going on in der ground. Spelunker death, hearing meadowlarks. There is a great sloth down, back in that cave and it has been there for a long, long time. Are there two giant sloths? How many of them can there be and what do they eat? A family of mossbacks, eh? Arboreal creatures who crept into the cave, crapped, and couldn't creep out again. They eat bats. The wine is in the cave, and the penicillin.

Down in the cave the worshippers were drinking the saliva of the corpse and had fingernails that were shiny with the tracks of snails. The sealed titanium casket of the dead spelunker is already completely sheathed in a transparent coating of marble. Soon, very soon in geological fact, the film of stone will no longer be transparent, like a cataract on an eye, and it will assume the appearance of that fountain on Copely Square in Boston in winter. The casket is growing, and someday it and the walls of the cave will meet at the accomplishment of accretion —drip by melodious drip—of the soluble mineral. It will be an altar

The Banks of the Sea

without worshipers except in the hypothesis that something will be remembered, for there is not enough time in all geology. As the train approached Utah Fredegonde opened the writ of the only chthonic religion available to civilized man and read, . . . *having traveled in a land among many waters, having discovered a land which was covered with the bones of men, and of beasts, and was also covered with ruins of buildings of every kind, having discovered a land which had been peopled with a people as numerous as the hosts of Israel . . .* (Mosiah, 8:8, The Book of Mormon)

Amtrack didn't serve Salt Lake City. It was around 10:30 at night when the train stopped in Ogden before going on to San Francisco, and passengers for Salt Lake got off. With their baggage they made their way to the bus stations, and in the Greyhound depot Fredegonde was approached by a smiling Beehive Girl who proffered her a Church tract entitled "Purity, Not Parity."

From their conversation it was apparent that many of the passengers on the bus were on their way to the General Conference. Fredegonde blended in, and when a loquacious Mormon asked her what she was going to do in Salt Lake she said she was going to the Tabernacle tomorrow. It sounded all right, and that's what she was going to do, too.

She had a strange head. The bus arrived at the Greyhound station in Salt Lake and she walked around in a fugue. The family she was supposed to stay with had not shown up and she lugged her suitcase to different parts of the building. She found herself at the notions and souvenirs counter and looked at the postcards. Some of them had tiny bags of salt from the Great Salt Lake sewn on. Bags of salt for the boxcars of electric trains. O gauge. She twirled the paperback book rack and found a new edition of Dylan Thomas's *Adventures in the Skin Trade,* and it was a minute before she understood that its cover consisted primarily of a color photograph of one of her own inner thighs. Conceited as the acquitted Jesus, she bought it. The salesgirl blushed. Fredegonde smugly put the book in her Lancel, alongside her Colt .45. All at once a roaring such as the kind of natural catastrophe the gum mint pays for filled her head, and she heard rock music that shouted at her YOU'VE MADE YOUR FIRST MISTAKE. The fugue dispossessed her of objective and she traipsed about, following wisps of smiles and scraps of memory. She stood for a few minutes in the middle of the waiting room rocking back and forth on the balls of her feet, not knowing where to go or whether to the left or to the right or straight ahead or backwards, nor even knowing enough to stand still and wait. Thus oscillating, she was frozen for a moment in a phenomenon known in synchro-servo parlance as "hunting." And so she stood while buses were announced and people in transit there got a last look at her. Then the Boyces came in smiling and out of breath and waved to her.

"Something was wrong with the car," said Mrs. Boyce. "Hope you haven't had to wait too long."

Their eldest daughter Vonnadean was pert and athletic and she carried Fredegonde's suitcase for her. Fredegonde first met this family at a Fireside Evening in the basement of the Manhattan Ward the Sunday before she was baptized. Mr. Boyce inquired after Bishop Woodruff in New York and Fredegonde said, "Oh, we're all prospering. I expect he'll be here for the Conference, don't you?"

She tried not to sound like a young battle-ax, Fredegonde, coy as a roach and irrevocable as a dower nigger.

They drove through sparkling Salt Lake City and out into the sprawling residential districts. It was a clear desert night and the winter stars shimmered above the silhouette of the mountains. They drove along a road that seemed to lead right into the big chuckwagon in the sky.

"Do you like Halloween?" she asked Vonnadean that night. They were in bed in Vonnadean's room and Vonnadean, who was almost nubile, made sleepy affirmative noises. "We had wonderful Halloweens," Fredegonde mused. "Pumpkins and Indian corn. Do you have Indian corn out here? Our school was named the Whippoorwill School. Have you ever heard a whippoorwill?"

For breakfast Mrs. Boyce served up waffles with strawberries and sour cream. Mr. Boyce and she thought Fredegonde might like to visit the Temple with them during her stay in Salt Lake. Fredegonde thanked them for their invitation.

The family went to Temple Square that morning: two adults, two boys, two girls, and Fredegonde. There were families everywhere, clean, unaffected and wholesome. The little girls had on pretty dresses. Neatly-dressed young boys moved about in talkative groups, deliberate and responsible, for they were already Deacons of the Church. When a little older they became Elders, just as Beehive Girls became MIA

Maids and the young marrieds are Junior Gleaners. New Zion, in the state of Deseret. The Boyces showed Fredegonde the Seagull Monument, and the Handcart Monument.

New Zion lies beyond the aspen wall, is watered by the high Wasatch and is founded near a lake full of old taxes. In the center of this amazing city is a tract of ground notable for a collection of remarkable buildings, and like a park with water, trees and flowerbeds, shrubbery and pleasant paths. Temple Square is like something a couple of girls at the awkward age would make while alone together off in the trees, or two little girls who have found an island and go there now and then in a rowboat which they have hidden. They build a bower on the island of love and friendship as they talk together of the most beautiful and secret things they know, and as they talk, whispering even in the seclusion of their island, they make garlands of wildflowers and ivy, lianas of forsythia, gather handfuls of moss and twigs and arrange these things on the floor of the innermost clearing in a pattern which is only a quipu of the runs and pauses of their dialogue. Such a place is sacrosanct. And the buildings were beautiful and strange, of design and workmanship beyond the Masonic. What a glorious day! It was like a love-in, with all the beautiful people on the lawns. They were slowly strolling in the direction of the Tabernacle when two obscene thoughts concurred in Fredegonde's mind: Brick shithouse Americana; and, Every faggot wants to menstruate.

Mrs. Boyce looked at her with curiosity, and half-smiling suggested, "I suppose we had better get in line."

They stood in the line of people trickling into the Tabernacle and Fredegonde was wondering when the control contact would turn up. She scanned the crowd for signals, signals which would confirm her in her purpose. The line was inching along and Heber, the Boyce's youngest boy, had to be reprimanded for something. Then a smiling and well-dressed young couple came up to Fredegonde and the man said, "Hi. I'm __ ___. Aren't you Bryna DeVoto?"

"*What's* your name?" she asked, startled out of her skin and immediately aware that she should not have asked him to repeat his name, for now the Boyces would remember it.

"Of course it's been a long time," the man said. "I'm from Detroit. Larry Considine? We went to Redford High together."

"I'm sorry," said Fredegonde. "I'm from New York."

"Oh. Well, excuse me." The young man and young woman laughed the same laugh. "We're going to get on line too."

The great organ was tootling away in its upper registers. Then, when the people were inside and the doors were closed, it roared out and the Tabernacle Choir and the congregation sang "Come, Come, Ye Saints." It all went very swiftly for Fredegonde. The new President of the Church was introduced by one of the Council of the Twelve. There were prayers. There were television cameras. The President stepped up to the Rameumptom and began to speak. He spoke on the theme of "Purity, Not Parity," directed to the young people, exhorting them to keep the ways of the Church and not be "tempted to imitate in corruptness the habits of our neighbors on the outside, but instead convince them by your example of the truth of Gospel and the wisdom of the Church." He denounced beatniks and hippies, calling them unmanly and their practices frivolous and ungodly. He quoted from The Doctrine and Covenants (49:22): " '... and again, verily I say unto you, that the Son of Man cometh not in the form of a woman, neither of a man traveling on the earth...' "

The old man could be eloquent and he was homespun. He told them the story of "The Fish with the Deep-Sea Smile." "And that was the fish with the deep-sea smile because that fish never swallowed a hook. So don't ever swallow temptation because there's probably a hook in it and then you're caught." He paused for effect. "And if it isn't a baited hook it's most likely a carrot on a stick."

The congregation chuckled. Mormons were so easygoing. The President went on.

"I am reminded of an old legend from Iceland. It's one of the Legends of the Cross, and there's a story in it about Solomon and the Queen of Sheba. Well, Solomon married the Queen of Sheba but she never let him see her feet. She always kept them out of sight. Or out of reach. Well, one day when he was sitting on his throne he had the servants sprinkle flour on the floor of the throne room and then bid them summon the queen to him. Well when the queen came into the throne room, King Solomon looked at her footprints and saw that she had cloven hooves. So..." The President paused again. "So Solomon bought a pig in a poke."

This was the turn of the key which sparked Fredegonde's countdown. She turned pale and rose from the seat she was sitting on and said, "That old man'd make a cute bum."

You could have heard a pin drop. She excused herself to the stunned Boyces and squeezed past their knees and toes. As soon as she got to the aisle she reached into her bag and drew the pistol with a flourish. Somebody—it might have been Nephi, or Bishop Woodruff—called out, "Sister Trebbidge!"

Meanwhile the President was going on with his speech.

"It's like the old German folk tale of the peasant who had a witch for a wife. The Devil invited them to supper, but all the dishes tasted flat. The peasant—in spite of his wife's nudging him to keep quiet—kept calling out for salt. When it was finally brought he said, 'Thank God! Salt at last,' and the whole hideous scene vanished. People undoubtedly wonder why Brigham Young picked a salt lake and a salt desert when he said 'This is the place.' It so happens that the Devil can't stand salt. It freezes him out. He's cold as ice to begin with, and salt makes him colder than freezing. It's like what happens when you put salt on the ice in your ice-cream freezer. It turns him into a hot fudge sundae..."

Fredegonde stood at the foot of the Rameumptom. They were laughing at her. She raised the pistol in both hands and took aim at the President's head. She cooly noted the fine red and blue capillaries in his cheeks.

"You old dollar bill," she said. "This is for Joe Hill."

She fired just as the old man tossed his glass of water at her. He was unharmed, but Fredegonde fell apart. She was overcome with shame. Silky Valentine. She could have been a nice fat wife. She hiked up her dress and her slip, then hunkered down in the tropical obstetric position for "shitting a watermelon." Then she stuck the clumsy revolver between her legs and shot herself through the cunt.

12 *The Wind in the Elevator Shaft*

IT GOT IN THE PAPERS, about the heroin in the post office, and for a while there weren't so many crap games in the toilets and there was less boozing in the locker rooms. You didn't see so many inebriated stiffs flaked out on the skids or in the plain pipe racks. Nonetheless, in spite of the peepholes, one-way mirrors and Inspectors "A" in the toad galleries overhead, one night a case of Polaroid-Land cameras addressed to an Army PX in Germany was stolen off a skid in the PAL bagging room. Skidda marinka rigga jig jig do.

Chopped down boogie gitchie caibaul. Joel was throwing off on the culling belt in room ten when he happened to pick up an empty piece of mail, a small parcel sent by a jewelry store. One end of it had been opened and the contents removed—probably a watch which had been repaired and was being returned to a soldier. He automatically glanced at the mail handlers who were emptying bags onto the belt. He thought the mail handlers were stupid and loutish, and now they were suspiciously quiet. Instead of simply tossing the rifled package into its APO tub, he dutifully went up and handed it to the foreman. Joel was a president buff.

He could recite anecdotes about all the chief executives of the United States, and knew odd events of historical interest which had taken place during their terms of office. He knew, for example, the name of the yacht aboard which Grover Cleveland was operated on for cancer of the mouth on July 1st, 1893. She was the *Oneida*.

Later in the evening he was transferred to room eleven, Navy letter mail, Fleet Post Office, New York. He always liked working FPO First Class mail because it was interesting. The addresses were fascinating and the names of the ships stirring. There were the great aircraft carriers and the guided missile submarines. He knew that the nuclear-driven submarines had two crews, the Red and the Blue, who manned the submersible alternately.

Suddenly he felt gloriously patriotic, and the work took on a happy rhythm which he identified with an Early-American husking bee. The feeling was contagious and soon the whole aisle was ajabber with postal clerks sorting letters into distribution cases accurately and at a profitable clip. Joel liked to gab with the black chicks. There was a little spade number in Manhattan named Shirley he went and visited when he was flush. After four years she was still charging him the same price. What the hell. She was the first woman he ever had and he was faithful to her. All at once there was brass in the aisle and the chattering ceased. The General Foreman and the Assistant Tour Superintendent of the postal station were escorting visitors. There were two well-dressed young engineer types wearing outside contractor's ID badges, a Navy lieutenant commander, a lieutenant JG, and a chief yeoman.

Joel was polishing his glasses when the GF walked right up to him, cleared the mail off his ledge and personally replaced it with a fresh tray chosen at random from the pie wagon. He was instructed to box up. He sorted mail, perspiring under the gaze of these heavies. He wondered what was going on. Whatever else, it was a show of power and a promise of goodies future. The GF and the Navy gold striper smiled in a friendly, encouraging way and let him get into the swing of sorting the letters. Then the GF asked him for a letter.

"Go on boxing up," the GF said.

It was hot in the aisle and the spade chicks were quietly flibberty gibbet. He mustn't turn his head to see what was happening for that would be gold-bricking.

"Another letter, please," said the General Foreman.

He requested letters at about twenty-letter intervals, Joel determined, his wits about him. Maybe what happened was a sham, an experiment in crowd responses. In any case it was WOW! like a new dashboard or a field test of an effective new ritual, a mockup gizmo ray gun or simply a weapon against the proliferation of counterfeit postage stamps. Somebody said it was subversives who started a rumor.

After a while the GF stopped asking for letters and Joel, going to the pie wagon for another tray of mail, saw that one of the outside contractor's representatives had a piece of electronic equipment slung on a strap over his shoulder and chest. From the equipment ran a short cable with a scanning device on the end which the lieutenant JG was passing over the letters. A sailor copied the information on the envelopes—

sender and addressee—onto a sheet of paper on a clipboard. Joel saw a blue light flash on the electronics and heard a loud beep, then all hell broke loose.

"White motherfuckers!" said a black man, and picked up his transistor radio and smashed it on the floor.

> *Tie dyed sky canoes and timpani-tuned tambourines,*
> *Yipping bitches under the moon and jungle fun gyreens.*

The riot started in room thirteen and spread to all parts of the huge building. Without warning the black mail-handlers overturned a culling belt and started attacking the white postal workers. As this was happening the black women began yipping like coyotes and she-wolves, like the chicks in their cells in the Women's House of Detention when they got riled. There was a preponderance of black postal workers. The men took up the wild cry and howled like wolves the way the inmates at Attica did. Maybe some of them had friends there. Howling "jeep" drivers drove their electric tractors into lines of parked skids piled high with mailbags full of Christmas parcels. In one of the swing rooms a bunch of stiffs ganged up on a black and beat him until they could see blood. Windows were smashed, post-office furniture overturned and broken up and foremen molested. "The Monster," the sack-sorting machine, continued its operation, but because there was nobody to empty the separations it shut down when the end chute jammed with sacks full of bales of *U.S. News & World Report* for Long Island. In the Customs room the mail was set on fire. The two groups went at each other with fire hoses as the guards tried to restore order by firing shots into the air, cases of Florida citrus exploding.

So how do you hitchhike to Boston? Though it might be going from the frying pan into the Coprabanana, where is the best place to hitch out from? It's a trade knack. Like you can spot an American in Paris, you know a good place to get a ride, where the traffic is unlikely to be local and slow enough to let you size each other up. A place to stop safely. It is to know how to read shapes, the woodsmanship of the streets, being able to follow for a day an incidence of smiles and at the end find your beloved, the way an old man raking leaves might uncover a lost tool or a piece of sawed wood like an old eave end, and he remembers dreaming

The Banks of the Sea

years ago about finding it. If you had a toy you would want a child to give it to.

"It's a good thing you got us press cards," Carol said, pouring some rosé wine which was warm from standing on the table.

"Press cards are fun," said Imogen.

She closed her eyes and hugged herself and curled her toes with glee, for she liked her work and Carol, and the wine tasted good and it was cozy and outside the city was going to pieces.

"Be that as it may," he said, "I don't like to risk my neck. I like to neck with it."

He and Imogen were snug in her loft. The potbellied stove was orange in one quadrant from the oak parquet planks burning in it. He had obtained them with a crowbar and a knapsack—load after load of them—from a townhouse on Lispenard Street which was going to be demolished for a parking lot. It was Christmas Eve and there was a fuel shortage. They had opened their presents and were playful under the quilt. An untraditional Christmas dinner and lots of long-distance calls. Afterwards they took a brisk walk to buy the *Times,* boldly swinging their held hands in the dark and deserted streets. Only a single Chinese newsstand was open on Canal Street.

Carol liked Imogen's little pussy. They kissed and he played with it and pretty soon she just let him make love to her, and all the while the kitten he had given her for Christmas pounced in the gift wrap. Then it was all of a sudden purring on the bed with them and there was just the Christmas-tree lights and the wind howling around the loft.

"Do you remember the party where we first met? Some friends of Yvetot's invited us along."

"I wonder who they were," Imogen murmured.

"There were Dumpster combers, lint trovers, stick-man stylists, label warners, somebody from WBAI..."

"It must have been the Warners."

"... a shirt egg, a spackle grounger, a ball-of-stringer. There was Choosy Queasecake and Staggered Binks, Yush Flonker and his sharpaper tingle..."

"But they're my *friends!*"

"The guys were all round-assed and skittish as girls. They smoked stogies and played squirrel and the girls didn't have any uchisus. None of the girls had any decent ass at all and if you spoke to them they thought you were making a pass . . ."

"Yes and you *did* make passes." She punched and pummelled him in the quilts until he was wheezing with laughter. "You made a pass at me, all right, and there's nothing wrong with my ass. And I don't look like a guy."

"Boy, was Yvetot jealous."

"Well whores shouldn't be jealous. Oh Carol . . ." and she covered him with kisses for she thought she was going to lose him.

Do you remember when we went to The Cloisters one November day? We were up early and ate breakfast at my place, and you wore a dress and I had on a tie, and weren't we magnificent? Artists, and proud of it. It was the first time I was with a girl at The Cloisters and how I loved you. We saw things we never knew were there and you said, Look. There's Mister Tambourine Man. And there he was, small but wound up tight, shouting and thundering. French, fourteenth century. I think it's in the same tapestry there's the figure of King David seated with a harp on his shield. Something about that harp—the shape of it and that the strings slanted like tree-bent Broadway—made me think of Manhattan Island. Or the idea of a lute-shaped boat. In any case there it hung, mute as the harp that once through Tara's halls the soul of music shed. The smiling figures. The harp said something. I swear to God I heard music. Maybe it was only an echo in the voices of tourists of the lost Frenchman shouting Halloo! to the ruins of Angkor Wat. There was that great jewel over Hector's shield clasping his tunic. The jewel of the hero. The sword and the harp kling klang klong. Do you remember the ship? Leaves blowing in the whiley November wind and the Hudson was dark, dark under a blue sky, dark from the Palisades and the wind on the water and there was that heavy great ship slowly o slowly upstream. A light flashed once from the bridge. I told you about the old sea captain in Cobh Harbour who used to signal every passing ship and they signalled back to him. We stood on the western parapet of Fort Tryon watching the ship until it got too cold to stand there or until we realized that the light the ship flashed was a signal to us.

"Carol?"

"Huh?"

"What will you remember about New York?"

The Banks of the Sea

"You mean if they succeed in putting out my eyes?"

"Come on. I mean when you're a rich and famous old poet and living somewhere else."

"Oh, I'll remember the brilliant glamour of the Empire State Building piercing the twilight over the myriad colored lights of the city."

"Come on."

"Well, the sight on a clear summer night of the stars like bottlecaps flattened into the asphalt."

"Come on. Really."

"Stiff-arming the turnstile."

They were awakened Christmas morning by the phone ringing. Imogen answered and it was a brief and agitated conversation.

"My God!" she said, hanging up. "The blacks have brought down flamethrowers and are setting fire to Little Italy!"

The sun's clangorous rising over the city filled the loft with yolky light. Third Avenue elevated potbellied stations kerchunk turnstiles thick-pitted illuminated magnifying glass many times buffalo nickel. Carol stoked the stove, chocking it full of short oak planks. Many board feet of them were stashed high in the kitchen hall. Enough for a Civil War locomotive.

Quick shower. Hearty breakfast. Warm clothing. Imogen gave the kitten a triple helping of Figaro. She selected equipment.

"Do you want a camera? Here," she said. "You might get some good shots. We can work from different angles."

"I'm not going to risk my neck," Carol said. "I don't want you to risk yours either."

"*I'm* going to work," said Imogen. "Now then. What are you going to do?"

"I might go to church."

"Well say a little prayer for me," she chirped, kissing him. "Let's go. Rome is burning."

Down the old elevator on icky tracks, the upward lunge of the counterweight like something from an amusement park. The political sticker was covered over with a public service reminder: THINK SAFELY.

"Merry Christmas, dear," she chirped. "Phone me later."

He looked up the street. The Puerto Rican Mormon bodyguards

were waiting.

"I will," he promised. He kissed her on the mouth. "Merry Christmas."

Off in the region of Mulberry Street a column of smoke from burning houses rose into a sky busy with police and National Guard helicopters. There was gunfire and sirens. As they walked up Broadway Imogen took pictures of the old cast-iron buildings.

"What those buildings need," she said, squinting and clicking, "is a paint scraper and a wire brush, a coat of red lead and two coats of outside white."

"And a de-gaussing job."

The streets were full of special vehicles. A policeman and a national guardsman checked their press cards. Carol asked the cop if the subways were running.

"Everything is functioning perfectly," the cop smiled ruddily. There was an air of concern and jubilation. Especially jubilation.

Carol and Imogen parted with conspiratorial waves of the hand. Half the bodyguard peeled off with her and he watched them make their way into Grand Street.

Imogen walked lithely into the beseiged neighborhood. She could shoot thirty-six exposures and reload faster'n cherry pie. In front of her was a street barricade the police had erected out of a couple of layers of abandoned cars. The cars were gutted and smoking but the barricade was fairly bulletproof. Beyond it a battle was taking place between the blacks' flamethrowers and one of the fire department's super pumpers. Fredegonde would say she was looking for a Terry Riley wedding gown.

Carol loped to Houston Street and down into the Broadway-Lafayette subway station. He took the F train one stop to West 4th Street and bounded up from the lower level. The police were using the mezzanine. He stood looking at it in the hazy silence. There must have been at least a hundred people decorating the pillars, standing handcuffed in pairs back-to-back or crumpled in puddles of urine. A woman was wailing. A mezzanine soprano. Ethel Merman belting The Star Spangled Banner from Wanamaker's mezzanine in Philadelphia. A train rumbled in overhead and he dashed up the stairs.

He took the A train. He thought of a poem. A New York poem. "Waiting for the Express." Would there still be such things? He sat

The Banks of the Sea 211

down across from the only other passenger in the car, a pretty girl. Her coat lay neatly folded on the seat beside her together with her ol' tote bag which had trumpets and wrong notes and the names of pop stars inked on it. She had nice big tits and the front of her sweatshirt said HOME PLANET. Almost inadvertently he noticed the book she was reading. Why it was his own volume of poems. Feeling like Everygirl's orgasm familiar, he refrained from disturbing her and got up and walked the length of the train and stood at the front-end window. The express torrented through the hole in the ground. The black motorman opened the cab door once and looked at him.

He got off at Dyckman. Blinked a little in the sunshine, crossed the street and sat down in a phone booth in the wall. He fished out his notebook and opened it. For a bookmark all that summer he used an old postcard from The Cloisters. An altarpiece. Flemish, Late Middle Ages. He had thumbtacked it to the monk's cloth alongside the love beads over his and Yvetot's bed. It was a painting of the Annunciation; and meanwhile in another panel Mary's husband Joseph working with brace and bit in his carpenter shop. Carol sat in the phone booth looking at the postcard. He always felt there was a message for him in the painting. Two open windows, one open more than the other. Archaic tools lying on the workbench. The plane could have been an early prototype of your new Polaroid camera. The saw looked like a machete. An old saw. He thought, You're never too old for a caboose. And out the machete saw handle a string of tools. A nail-puller, a hammer, and a chisel. A nail-puller for the Christ child.

Through the park gate. The woods on Inwood Hill were primeval again. Deer thickets. Bear. Limbs and whole fallen trees in crowds up and down the dales. He jogged like an Indian. Lenses of granite. The summer berm and the winter berm and the drowned valley. Spuyten Duyvil and the Harlem River, estuaries in a trough of Inwood marble. The Manhattan formation is a well-foliated mica schist. He found himself standing over the toll plaza of the Henry Hudson Bridge. Directly across that bridge was the hitchhiking place to Boston. He stood for a moment watching the sparse traffic.

He turned and walked down the dirt path and around the pier of the bridge; looked at the turbidly swirling current of the Harlem River, then up at the vaulting girderwork of the bridge and his heart swelled with admiration for the great works of man.

There were two bridges, like the two narrow windows in the painting on the postcard, out the machete handle of Manhattan Island. The string of tools. Man things. Something you pitch a tent with in the snow. Ellen. You're never too old for a caboose. So Carol took the other bridge, a railroad bridge out where the Harlem joined the Hudson. Just because there was poetry in it.

He walked lightly and quickly across the deep-leafed forest floor to the tracks and jogged to the bridge. There was no footpath and he had to walk on the ties, the water flashing close and green. It was colder than a witch's tit. A gust of wind almost made him put his foot between the ties.

Summer things like the smell of creosote and a fishing line. He wanted to untangle it and put it in his pocket. And there was so much equipment. Pipes and electrical conduits. Iron things. Fishplates and spikes, bars, rods, rails. Brake shoes. He glanced to the right and saw a sailing yacht and she was Bermuda rigged, and he understood that it behooved him to cross that bridge in a hurry because if he didn't it would open on him and then he could wave to the rich people. He ran, coat flapping, like an outside calipers. The yacht lay hove to. She blew her air horn. He heard a bell ring overhead and all at once things started creaking under him. The ends of the rails lifted out of their nockets and the bridge began to rotate on its turntable just as he stepped across onto solid ground.

Panting and trembling, he traversed a terrain of weedy riverbanks and tumbledown shacks. There was a boxcar on a siding. It was country and he thought of home. He could build a bonfire in this idyll and catch his breath and get warm. Or should he avail himself of the hitchhiking place up there? He walked slowly through the winter grasses, burrs clinging to his legs. Ahead of him, below the bluff of the Bronx, was a commuter stop on the Hudson Division of the New York Central.

He crossed the third rail, stepped up onto the platform and sat down in the little metal shelter out of the wind. He was certain he had just accomplished something but he wasn't sure what. Was he waiting for a train? Just then a horn blew loudly and a commuter train pulled up and stopped. He had money. Should he get aboard? An elderly couple got off and it immediately pulled away. Carol looked at his watch, then

The Banks of the Sea 213

looked at the train as it picked up speed and disappeared around a bend up the river. Then he noticed the station sign. SPUYTEN DUYVIL. Old Peter Stuyvesant would be happy.

It was 10:50. He watched the old couple make their determined way up a long and steep flight of steps cut into the Fordham gneiss of the Bronx. Something about them made him want to follow and so he went where they went, up over the lip of the cliff. He found himself in a quiet neighborhood of recently-built apartment houses. A bell was ringing lustily. It belonged to a pretty anomaly of a little old Congregational church there on Independence Avenue. He picked the burrs off his trouser legs and went inside.

He hung his overcoat in the vestibule and combed his hair in the mirror, then stepped inside the church. A woman wished him a Merry Christmas. He saw the old couple and vaguely the rest of the small assembly, and took a seat.

He sat transported in the magnificence of the winter sun streaming through the church's Louis Tiffany windows. In those minutes waiting for the service to begin—the minister standing at the lectern, the organist ready at her console—as his eyes became used to the light and were gratified in the simplicity of the art nouveau interior, it occurred to him that this was the jewel of the hero.

The idea toyed with him. He thought of The Peaceable Kingdom. He thought of the act of love and it delighted him that he could imagine such a thing. He thought of his mother and father and was all laughter and well-being and the giving that is the desire for one's beloved. The organ started playing. The congregation rose. As he was finding the hymn Carol became aware of the girl who was standing beside him. They both turned and looked at each other. It was Ellen. She was four months pregnant. They blushed and touched hands. The herons of her veins.

Carol and Ellen sang with the congregation, and as they sang Carol closed the book, for they both knew the words.

Possum in the stump,
Rabbit in the hollow,
Pretty girl at our house,
As fat as she can swallow.